THE NIGHT GOVERNOR BRATVA

Brutal SECRETS

RAVEN CARLYLE

BRUTAL SECRETS

RAVEN CARLYLE

Content editing and formatting: Sugar Free Editing

Cover design: Deranged Doctor

(www.derangeddoctor.com)

To every kid whose heart was ever shattered into pieces
Your broken parts are what make you beautiful

PROCEED WITH CAUTION

Brutal Secrets is a dark mafia romance. The hero is in the mafia, so he breaks the law and does other things your grandmother would not approve of (or maybe she would and your grandma is cooler than mine). Certain readers may find some of the book's themes upsetting. For a full list of trigger warnings, please go to www.RavenCarlyle.com.

PLAYLIST

Lonely – Justin Bieber (with benny blanco)
Mad World – Gary Jules, Michael Andrews
Criminal – Britney Spears
TiK ToK – Kesha
Russian Roulette – Rihanna
Ochi Chernye – Sophie Milman
Walk On the Wild Side – Lou Reed
Daylight – David Kushner
Let Me Down Slowly – Alec Benjamin
You're On Your Own, Kid – Taylor Swift
Demons – Imagine Dragons
Coming Back For You – Maroon 5
Chandelier – Sia
I'll Be Your Mirror – The Velvet Underground, Nico
a thousand years – Cristina Perri

CHAPTER ONE

Kesera

Billionaires are cheapskates. No one ever tells you this when you're sitting in a trailer, dreaming of fountains of champagne and walls of diamonds and glitter, not a grimy room with a sticky carpet.

The paint is yellowed with nicotine, the air is dusty and stale, and unidentifiable marks and smeared fingerprints smudge the walls. It looks like someone was clawing to get out of here. I shake away images of the many famous singers who've flown to Moscow to play for a million dollars an hour only to find themselves desperate to get back home.

Topped the Billboard 100 last year? Get backstage and don't bother the important people at the party. Can't walk down the street in Nashville without getting mobbed for selfies? Go and wait in the broom cupboard until we need you.

At least Jimmy leaves me alone here and I don't have to cringe away from his disgusting touch.

Jimmy thinks I should watch my figure, but if I could choose, I'd ask for a basket of fried chicken and a few bags of

1

Skittles at every stop. I run my hands down my waist, smoothing the spandex and letting my nails catch against the gold sequins. As I roll my shoulders in a circle, they make a clicking noise.

Every muscle in my body is bunched into tight knots after the flight from Nashville. Jimmy drank bourbon after bourbon at the start of the flight, knocking them back and talking about the careers he'd made and the singers he'd dropped when they didn't do what he said. As his words started to slur, the threats became less thinly veiled. Thankfully he fell asleep and drooled onto his Ralph Lauren jacket before getting too close. Only then had my muscles relaxed, but the damage was done.

I'd love a massage, but Jimmy would just see that as another reason to put his hands all over me, and I'm already shrinking away from him—quite literally, as I think I've never weighed less.

All I wanted was freedom, but I've never been less free in my life since hitting the charts.

I flop onto the worn sofa and rest my boots against the wall. Add some footprints to the grime and make the next pop star wonder if someone was actually attempting an escape. I pull the crumpled blue envelope out of my old leather backpack and run my fingertips over the faded pictures as if they're talismans.

Tracing the image of me on my dad's shoulders at a Rolling Stones concert, I feel a sharp stab at how much I miss him. He looks so alive and vibrant as he effortlessly holds me up, his dark-skinned hands wrapped around my little legs as I reach toward the sky.

The second image is from a few years later. My father and I sit at a table with my grandma, her wild blond curls haloed round her head. She and I are pressing pie crust into a pan, and my father is laughing at us.

The last image is of my mother on the beach in Okinawa. Her black hair hangs in a straight curtain as she shades her eyes from the sun and smiles at my father, but I can see myself in her narrow frame and wide, high cheekbones, even if I don't look Japanese.

I don't look like I come from anywhere, but I grip the photos tightly in my hands to remind myself that I do. I come from these people who are no longer here, and I'll protect myself now that they're not around to do it for me.

The sound of heavy footsteps thumps down the corridor outside, and I slide the photos back into the blue paper and shove them away before pulling down on my sequined dress. It's gold, my favorite color, but it barely covers anything. When I'm moving, all you can see is shimmer and glistening activity, but when I'm sitting like this, I feel exposed. My panties are so small that when the strings of beads slip down around my waist, there's not much left to the imagination.

The door cracks open, my spine stiffens, and my shoulders climb toward my ears.

"You ready, honey?" Jimmy rasps.

Not that you expect monsters to have fangs and claws, but Jimmy Jimboi Ullrich is ordinary to look at. He's almost unassuming, with his soft blue eyes, a jaw dusted with a bit of gray stubble to hide his softening chin, and a warm smile. He looks like someone's handsome uncle or older brother. He looks like a nice guy.

The Jimmy I know is anything but.

Jimboi Ullrich might be famous as a producer and manager, but the man who manages me is nothing but a vampire who sucks the life force from teenage girls and uses their youth and talent to fuel his desire for money and fame. I want to wrestle control of my life and music out of his hands, but I have no idea how.

"It's showtime. They're waiting for you."

I stand and pull the strings of gold beads and sequins lower to cover my underwear before walking past him to reach the door. As I do, Jimmy steps behind me, kicking the insides of my ankles and making me stumble against the door frame. He crowds me from behind and uses his knees to widen my stance as he pushes me against the door.

The glass beads attached to my dress press against my thighs, and his erection strains against his jeans as he crushes it between us. I squeeze my eyes tight and tip my forehead against the door. Four breaths in, four breaths out.

You're a star. You're not really here. One day you'll be free.

It's my mantra. I repeat it to myself again and again as he grips my hips, rocking his hardness against me. As he nuzzles my neck, his fetid breath wafts toward my nose, drowning me in a cloud of stale coffee and sour milk.

"You're not going to give me any trouble, are you, honey? You're going to go on and be a good girl."

I go completely still. I don't speak. I don't move. I don't dignify his creepy request with a response. Freeze. Escape in your head. Take yourself away. No one can touch the part of you that burns on the inside.

"Go on then, darling. Get out there and show them how it's done." Jimmy eases away, and I step into the darkness.

I walk down the corridor and wait for the stage to embrace me. Under the lights, I become someone else— someone I should have always been, someone who I will one day fully become. On stage, I am free and I am a star. It's just me, my voice, and the lights. I can't even see the audience when I'm beneath the spotlight, floating in a space beyond time.

Nearing the dark stage, I lower my head and run my eyes along the pointed outline of my boot tips as I send my energy into the earth and pull everyone who ever loved me into my core. I can feel my mother. I can see my father picking me up

4

and whirling me around. I can hear my grandmother laughing. Everyone is gone, but everyone is here inside me as I pull their love into my lungs with the next breath and pour it into the audience.

Break up, break down, break out.

This is what I'll say when I step into the spotlight. My voice will soar over the heads in the crowd. It's my anthem. My call for help. My battle cry. I'll throw my arms wide, reaching into the darkness as I let the sound pour out of me. Though I don't know who's out there, I'll sing to the one person who might need to hear those words as they sit in the shadows beyond the reach of the spotlight's glare. I'll sing to tell them they aren't trapped. I'll sing to tell them I understand. That we can do this together.

CHAPTER TWO

Vadim

Antonov's money is on display tonight. He's a nickel baron, pulling ore out of the Siberian ice that should have gone into people's pensions and using it to spray around Moscow on pointless evenings like this. This party is to celebrate the opening of his vodka business.

So far tonight, we've had a comedian from Channel One making jokes about foreigners, a dance show featuring twelve teenagers wearing nothing but G-strings, and now we'll be treated to the latest one-hit wonder from the US. I don't know why Antonov does it. He spends a lot of time ragging on America. According to him, it's the great Satan. They've wounded our pride, and we need to arm ourselves against them. But then he can't wait to see who's topping the charts so he can pick them up in his private jet and cart them onto the stage of BoHo Rooms.

He wears a cravat. What kind of fool wears a cravat?

The kind of fool who gets into bed with my boss, Yevgeny Guelman, the man they call the Night Governor. Right now, he stands behind Antonov like a waiter, balancing a tray of shot glasses and an icy bottle of vodka from the Antonov distillery as if there's nothing he'd rather do than pour you a drink and hang on your every word until he knows all your secrets. And then?

Well, then, once you've let him get that close, he either owns you or he kills you. Or he gets one of us to kill you. I hate that part of the job, but Sasha gets a perverse thrill out of it.

Antonov spins a bottle of vodka around as two girls in sequined G-strings hang off his shoulders. He grins at them stupidly and doesn't spare a glance for the bald man balancing a tray behind him.

It always amazes me how people see what they want to see when they look at the man who governs Moscow's darkness: the clubs, the girls, the smuggling rackets. I suppose that's how he got to where he is—the ability to fade into the shadows. He's never more dangerous than when some rich man thinks they've got him under control. He's good at playing the role of a dog brought to heel and happy to be ordered around.

Antonov grins like the rich fool he is and pulls one of the giggling dancers against his side as my boss stands behind him with a face of stone, not reacting to the grinning billionaire or the half-naked girls. I've learned a lot about stillness and reading a room from him, but I'm not half as powerful.

I don't think Antonov will survive to the end of the month. This is one Russian billionaire who might be of more use dead than alive as far as the Night Governor is concerned.

One of the dancers sidles up to me on the bench and tries to stroke my leg with her sparkling heel. "Move over, honey," she says. "My friend wants to get close to you too."

The blond pulls her long hair over her shoulder, giving me a good look at her breasts as she peeks at me from under her lashes. Does she think this is attractive? She's drunk and I can smell the fumes as she teeters against me, putting her hand on my shoulder and stroking it down my arm.

"Did I say you could touch me?" I ask, prompting her to inch away from me, but not far enough.

I swat at her like a mosquito and focus on the rich man waving his personal brand of vodka at a crowd of strippers, as well as the shadow who looms at his back. For such a large man, Guelman is remarkably able to fade into the background. It's a kind of power, but one I don't have with my face. It irritates me how women always want to fuck me. Like I don't have anything better to do.

One of the girls moves away, but her friend starts simpering and leaning down so that her nipples poke toward my face, obscuring my view of the stage and the guests moving through the dark tables. Most importantly, she's blocking my view of the exits. I can't bear sitting anywhere if I can't see how to get out. Do these fools think I haven't seen breasts before?

I bend down and pull out the knife that I tucked under the red bench seating. The curved blade and black handle embossed with mother-of-pearl stars is of much less use than the flick knife in my boot, but it was a present from my best friend Sasha and it looks threatening. He and I pull these out for show because they're only good for teenage girls and other irritants. Both knives are too blunt to kill anyone, which is why we like them. You wouldn't want to slip and accidentally hit a passing artery.

The knife goes with the scar that slashes down the side of my left cheek—a souvenir from my time at the orphanage. Sasha got to the guy before he could do more than draw a line from my eye to my mouth. At times like this, I'm grateful for it, especially when the scar and my thunderous expression finally have the desired effect on the two teenagers. But to make sure they've gotten the hint, I point the tip of the blade at the tall blond.

"Take your little friend and give a man some space." I gesture with the knife, watching it catch the stage lights as they start to flicker.

The blond pouts.

"Move it," I say, speaking louder as the room darkens. I need to see my way out and let my eyes adjust before the act starts. That's what I'm here to do. To be the Night Governor's eyes and ears and make sure everything goes to plan. Not that I know what his plans are. He doesn't share his ideas with the hired muscle.

As the girls shuffle away, I view the straight shot to two exits and find nothing unfamiliar. I search the darkness for Sasha, but I can't spot my best friend. He might have a clearer idea of what's going on between Guelman and Antonov. He usually does.

My heartbeat slows, and I relax into the corner, my eyes scanning the room as the stage lights illuminate a woman wearing a cloud of gold beads. Her cowboy boots shimmer under the lights. Gold streaks her long, wavy hair as well. She looks like a Russian icon with her olive skin and a cloud of golden-and-bronze curls framing her face. She bows her head as I take her in, and then she throws her arm out, pointing at me as she begins to sing.

"Break up, break down, breakout!" Her voice rings over the heads of the mingling Moscow nightlife. Most of them probably aren't listening, but I can't tear my eyes away as she sings about taking the walls down brick by brick until you can climb over the rubble.

She reaches into the darkness, and it feels like she's singing directly to me. I don't know what about her holds my complete attention. With her upward slanted eyes, sharp cheekbones, and that cloud of hair spun with gold, she isn't conventionally pretty, but something about her deep voice pulls at me.

I close my eyes and lean my head against the red velvet and let her voice caress me. I shouldn't allow myself to take this moment when I'm working, but I let myself breathe as her voice drops low like a suggestion, and I imagine building a world with just the power of the notes she sings.

I open my eyes as the last notes ring in the silence before the low hum of chatter begins again. Antonov is still goofing around like a court jester, and my boss is still standing behind him, probably waiting to slit his throat.

Satisfied that I didn't miss anything important, I let my eyes stray back to the angel on the stage. As she brings the microphone to her lips and stands silently for a moment, I see one hand move to the corner of her eye to catch something and wipe it away. A tear? And then she gives a bright smile, and her husky voice eases through the murmur of the crowd.

"*Spasiba, Moskva! Ya tibia llublu,*" she says.

There's nothing wrong with her Russian accent, but she's muddled up the verb. Instead of telling everyone in the room that she loves them, she's telling one person how she feels. For one blistering second before the lights go up and she leaves the stage, it's as if she's talking to me.

Then the lights come on, and she's gone.

CHAPTER THREE

Vadim

The red-roped VIP section empties out as Antonov plays the part of the Pied Piper and leads a parade of girls and drunk hangers-on down the stairs. One girl stumbles on her heels and he catches her, picking her up like a trophy and passing her to one of his friends. To him, she's a thing and not a person.

She doesn't object. The Night Governor has broken her in and trained her well. It makes my skin crawl, but it's not my job to worry about these things. I'm here to provide security tonight, and anyway, teenage girls aren't my preference. Not anymore. Nothing good can come from hanging out with someone that naïve.

I scan the room once more and find nothing out of the ordinary. Dima, Sasha, and Sergei patrol the other three corners of the VIP deck. Sasha catches my eye as he prowls toward our boss. My best friend always moves like a jungle cat, padding across the room like he's one move away from springing on someone and ripping out their throat. He waves at me to signal that I'm in the clear.

Time to make a move. I'll walk the rest of the club. Check the corridors. Clear the exits.

I rise from the bench, and a painful twinge sparks through my right knee. Damn fighting. I can still feel it in my muscles as I stalk toward the fire exit. I push the bar attached to the door, knowing I'll have to loop through the club and come back up the stairs and step into the darkened hallway.

Once I'm away from the main stage, the illusion of glamor falls away. Lighting and scantily clad teenagers make up the façade in the front of the house, but back here it's just plywood and dust.

Sticky carpet clutches my boots near the fire exit, likely from the spilled champagne and vodka that have soaked in from the club. Then the last evidence of parties fades to dusty gray fibers. The soles of my shoes slide against the surface as I open each door to check for people I don't recognize, anyone who's in a place they shouldn't be, or packages I haven't seen before.

Brooms and cleaning products wait behind door one. Door two leads into an empty conference room. A fluorescent-lit whiteboard smeared with the remnants of black writing dominates the back wall. Giggles float beneath door three, and I stand outside, listening to the sound and checking for my knife and gun before I open it a crack. Dancers move around the room and defer to Oksana, an auburn-haired stripper I sometimes sleep with when we both need to scratch an itch. Nothing to worry about here.

I open the door wider, and she grins at me. "Vadim, honey, have you come to pay us a visit?" she says, leaning back in her chair, her thigh slung provocatively over the side. The sight is tempting when I'm off duty, but not when I'm working.

Around Oksana, dancers pull off their lingerie and stalk

naked around the room, looking for sweats and sneakers as they journey back to normal life. One girl becomes a headless vision as she wrestles a sweatshirt over her bouncing, pink-tipped tits. Oksana catches me watching and offers a sly smile, but I shake my head and keep my hand on the door-knob. She winks as I close the door behind me and return to the gray corridor.

The girls' voices fade as I make my way past empty rooms, listening at doors for anything untoward. I'm about to head back to find Sasha and check in with our boss when voices with an odd rhythm catch my attention. They sound more American than Russian.

It's none of my business because she's not likely to be a threat, but curiosity propels me past the next few rooms in the hope of catching another glimpse of the little songbird. As I near the end of the corridor, I'm certain it's her voice. She has a southern accent that sounds like honey, and I tell myself it's not really eavesdropping as I lean against the wall and listen to the rise and fall of each word she speaks. I close my eyes and let the sound wash over me, but the thud of heavy male footsteps approaches the bend in the corridor, putting me back on alert. Alive to a possible threat, I slink into the shadows.

CHAPTER FOUR

Kesera

There's no hum from the crowd to lift me up and keep me buzzing as I return to the dressing room, and I have nowhere else to go. I don't speak Russian, so I can't just head off into the night. Wearing barely anything, I'll soon be trapped in this room with a man who wants to suck my talent dry before he starts on the rest of me.

I sit down at the mirror and begin removing my makeup, pulling away the heavy greasepaint to reveal the dark circles under my eyes. I was hoping to hang out with the other artists tonight. I'd heard Amy Vinelli is playing too, and I thought maybe the two of us could knock back a few drinks and talk about a duet. My music is just fast-paced party tracks to get the crowd dancing, but I like her blues style and would love to explore that. Combine a bit of her 60s vibe with a bit of my country roots. We've both got the vocal range to do it.

If I can ever get out from under the men managing me. I wonder if she's also controlled by someone who can't wait to sell her to the highest bidder. Jimmy got a clear million for

17

tonight. He's thrilled with himself, so I hope he'll be in a softer mood and let me go to bed without pushing for more.

I steel myself as the doorknob turns and he walks in.

He smirks, strolls to the wine fridge, and produces a bottle of chilled vodka. I've heard the billionaire who hired me tonight has a vodka distillery. The wall behind the fridge is stacked with bottles reflecting the harsh strip lighting.

"Great gig tonight. The crowd loved you," he says.

"Did they?" I skeptically raise my brows at him as I pause with the makeup sponge in mid-air. He walks over and puts his clammy hands on my shoulders. I remain as still as possible and try not to flinch away from him.

"Well, I met a booker who has a round of similar gigs lined up for the summer. Most of the Russian oligarchs summer in Italy or Cyprus. In six months, we could be on yachts with the wealthiest men in the world, playing as you perform at their birthday parties. You'd like that, wouldn't you?" He catches my eye in the mirror and grins before he tosses back the shot and pours himself another.

"You would," I say grimly, staring back at his reflection looming behind my shoulder. "I'll probably see as much of Rome and Cyprus as I've seen of Moscow."

"Don't be churlish. Moscow is a shithole, but that's not the point. There's so much money to be made at these gigs. These guys will pay top dollar for whoever is at the top of the charts, so we've got to strike hard while you're still hot." He bends down and puts his head on my shoulder, then looks at himself in the mirror before his eyes dart down the front of my dress.

My nose screws up as the sour smell of his breath reaches it, and I flinch as he moves closer, but that doesn't put him off. He's not reading my signals. Or worse, he's getting a kick out of ignoring them.

His fingers dig into my shoulders. I try to shake him off,

but he meets my eyes in the mirror and grins at me. It's not a nice smile. His hand tightens and slides down my arm, gripping hard enough to bruise. My mouth twists in disgust, which only seems to please him more.

"You are still hot, baby," he says, sticking his tongue into my ear. It feels like a slug, and I lean away, which only moves me closer to his other hand.

He reaches to grab my breast, squeezing hard enough to send a shock of pain through the sensitive skin before turning his attention to my nipple and pinching it like he's tuning a radio. I flinch and gasp. If this is his idea of foreplay, then it's no wonder he has to resort to harassing teenage girls under his employ.

He takes the gasp as enthusiasm and reaches for my other breast so he can knead them both. I'm caged in his grip as he stands behind me, my waist pushed hard against the vanity with no room to move. I go very still, hoping he'll realize I'm not into this, but apparently he likes his girls young, wooden, and unresponsive.

As he grips my breasts, his breathing speeds up, washing me in the sour fug of coffee, milk, and two shots of vodka. It turns my stomach and I retch, bending lower over the vanity and curling in on myself and away from him.

"Come on, baby, don't be like that. Let's have a little fun," Jimmy growls, gripping me tighter.

I slide to the side and knock over the chair in my frantic attempt to get away from him. I lift the chair as I stand. There are no legs to fend him off, but it places a barrier between us. I brandish it at his face and hiss, "I don't want this. There are lots of other girls here. Why don't you find one of them?"

"Because I want you. I *own* you. You do what I say, and I say that tonight is the night." Jimmy advances toward me.

I throw the chair at him and it lands on the floor with a

crash, but he remains between me and the door. I jump the other way and end up tripping against the sofa, and then he's on me. Wrestling me down. Tearing away the thin crotch of the dress as he settles between my legs.

"Come on, you little slut. Give it up. You're nothing special. There are a million more girls like you in Nashville. I made you. You're only famous because of me, and now you belong to me." Jimmy's not smiling anymore. He looks furious as he holds me down with both hands.

He's too far away to headbutt, so I spit in his face. That only makes him more furious, and he pulls back his arm and slaps me hard across the cheek.

That will bruise.

"You're not looking after the merchandise!" I shout, but he's not looking at me anymore. He's scrabbling at his zipper, a nasty smile on his face.

"I'm going to teach you a lesson, you jumped-up little piece of trailer trash," he says.

"Get off me!" I scream as loud as I can. I'm writhing against him, bucking against his iron grip, when the door opens.

"Is this a party anyone can join?" a deep baritone voice says.

I look up at the most beautiful man I've ever seen in my life. The scar on his left cheek only serves to highlight the perfection as his blue eyes blaze down at me.

CHAPTER FIVE

Vadim

When I heard a palm crack heavily against skin, I couldn't stop myself from opening the door. The sound brought back memories of my childhood. Now, standing in the open doorway, I blink my eyes shut, then open them again to glare at the man who's hastily doing up his zipper.

God, what a pathetic specimen. What kind of worm needs to backhand a woman to get her to sleep with him?

My golden-haired angel from the stage has a red mark on her face, and she's scrabbling away from him on the black leather couch, eyes wide and shoulders shaking. The man draws himself up to his full height, but I still dwarf him.

"Get out," he says. He has an American accent, but it's not pleasant to listen to like the singer's. It's too nasal. "This is a private dressing room. You don't belong here."

"Just checking that everyone is enjoying our Russian hospitality and having a good time," I say.

The man glares at my little songbird, and as he stops to

adjust his pants, I meet the girl's green eyes. Her gaze is like her voice. It's true and doesn't waver. She sits up, edging her way toward the corner of the sofa as she arranges the gold beads over her lap in an attempt to conceal her crotch. I'm curious to see more of her body, but she hunches over and continues covering as much of her legs as she can with gold beads. They clatter against each other as she struggles for modesty. It's such a contrast to Oksana next door.

The man takes a step toward me, and I cock my gun. "Did I say you could move?" I ask, putting a hint of granite in my tone.

He dusts his hands over his denim-clad thighs and tries for a practiced smile as he walks toward me, but his eyes shift nervously from side to side. "This is a private room, and I think you're in the wrong place, friend."

"I'm not your friend, *friend*." I move the barrel of the gun between them before settling the sights on the man. I look back at the golden songbird, who stares directly at me now. "As I said, I'm just checking that everyone is having a splendid time in our beautiful city. Are we?"

This time, the songbird shakes her head, slowly and deliberately, her gold-streaked curls catching the lights surrounding the dressing-table mirror. She looks directly at me and mouths, *No*.

"I think that the little songbird here might like to come with me," I say, raising my eyebrows at her.

She nods and steps toward me as I hold out my hand. The beads rattle as she walks, flashes of thigh appearing with each step. The less I can see, the more enticing it is. She places her hand in mine, and I twine my fingers around hers as I imagine those delicate fingers wrapped around other parts of me.

"I think there's some mistake," the man says, taking a step toward me.

I point the gun at him and he stops. He's big enough to bully someone smaller, but not man enough to even try to defend his territory. I know this kind of pathetic worm. He might be a big man in the US, but in Moscow, he wouldn't last a week.

"I don't think so," I say.

"We've got a flight to catch. We've got concerts to get to. Kesera is very important. I—"

I wave the muzzle of the gun in his face, and he stops. The girl's warmth sinks into me as she steps closer, wraps an arm around my waist, and leans her head against my side.

It's a strange feeling, playing someone's savior. It's been years since the last time I tried, and it didn't end well. My little songbird here doesn't know who I am. If she did, would she still stand so close?

I look down at her with a question on my face, and she nods again. Whatever she faces here, it must be pretty bad for her to take her chances with a gun-wielding stranger.

I lead her into the corridor and open the door next to her dressing room. Beyond it is a darkened room, but she steps inside without hesitation, still holding my hand. I follow her. Something about this room reminds me of the cupboard Sasha and I would hide in at the orphanage, which spooks me for a second.

I'm still gripping my gun, so I lightly touch her shoulder with my other hand. The darkness calls for lowered voices, the way it did when Sasha and I hid as kids. Back when I still believed I had the power to save people.

"Are you okay?" I whisper.

Her hair tickles the skin beyond my shirt's opening, and I suck in a breath as she nods. "Yeah, I will be. Thanks to you."

"Too early to be thanking me, zolotaya."

She squeezes the hand that isn't grasping the gun. "Why? Are you an axe murderer or something?"

I laugh as I lean my back against the door to prevent anyone from barging in, and then I pull her against me and let her drop her head into my chest. "Or something, zolotaya."

I can't see her, but I feel the tremble in her muscles as I stroke my hands up and down her back. Her whole body continues trembling, and her skin is ice against mine. All the signs of shock. I pull her closer, making a soft shushing noise. It's not much of a come-on, but I'm sure she wants to feel safe, and this is the best I can do.

"You keep saying that word. Zolotaya. What does it mean?" There's a southern twang to her husky voice, so different from the Americans I met when I was in New York.

"It means golden, honey. Because you're golden. Precious. Not the sort of woman a man should be knocking about."

She huffs. "No woman deserves that."

I expect her to step away from me then. When she doesn't, I let myself sink into the closeness as I stroke my hand from her lower back to the top of her spine and stop at the nape of her neck, circling her narrow throat. The reedy thrum of her pulse thumps beneath my fingertips. She is too delicate and fragile for a man like me.

I'm not sure how to reassure her. If she met anyone who knew me, they would do nothing to set her mind at rest, so I just hold her in the darkness and silence, feeling the gentle tremor of her small body. And she is small. She's not statuesque like the dancers, and she has tiny breasts.

Her head is level with my armpit as she burrows into me. I pull her into the circle of my arms, leaning down to bury my face in her hair.

Jasmine and roses.

I continue my rhythmic stroking of her body as I breathe her in. She smells of springtime and hope. It's winter in Moscow right now. The kind of winter that will stretch on for

24

six months until the snow turns to piles of dirty, icy slush that will yield the bitter fruit of dead bodies when the spring comes.

Her nose presses against my shirt as she moves even closer, and then her voice cuts through the illusion that this is the kind of woman I can pretend to deserve. "What are we doing?"

"Hiding from life. From work," I say, flicking on the light switch and bathing us both in a blue florescent glow. "We should get going."

She glances at my gun and then shudders and wraps her arms around herself. "I don't have anywhere to go."

I open the door and look into the empty corridor. "We'll figure something out," I say without really knowing what I mean.

CHAPTER SIX

Kesera

I must be losing my mind, but my god, the man I'd been leaning on felt familiar, and he smelled so good. Like salt and pine needles. For one moment in that dark room, I had to fight back a sudden urge to taste the triangle of skin beneath his spread collar. Instead, I'd rubbed my face against him and allowed him to pull me closer.

As we step into the dark corridor, my entire body tingles. I chalk this up to coming down from the high of being on stage. It has nothing to do with leaning on someone and feeling their solid arms around me, or having a handsome man pull me into his broad chest like I'm meant to be there.

I feel foolish, but I haven't felt anything in so long that I let myself shut out the world and snuggle up to a complete stranger.

A stranger who now strides ahead of me with a pistol in his hand.

Muffled women's voices filter from a crack of light beneath a door ahead of us, and a sudden burst of laughter echoes in the gray corridor as the door opens. I guess that's where he's taking me, but instead of relaxing, the tightness in my shoulders returns as thoughts clang around my head.

Jimmy.

The new album.

Demands from the label.

And who the hell is this man I'm following?

A cold shiver runs through me as I think about how I'll fix the mess I'm in. I have two days left with Jimmy in Moscow, but he'll be vindictive now that I've turned him down. Is a Russian stranger with a gun really a better option?

I trot to keep pace with the stranger's long strides, but my anxiety gets the better of me and I place a hand on his shoulder. He stops and turns slowly to face me, staring down at me with otherworldly pale-blue eyes. Like a wolf. Or an angel. He could be either, for all I know.

"Hey," I say, my voice sounding loud to my own ears. "Where are we going? Are you giving me back to him? Sending me back to Jimmy?"

He shakes his head in answer and watches me with those strange eyes, and I take him in. His hair is a warm sable color, and his sun-kissed skin stretches over slashing cheekbones, a square jaw, and lips I want to trace with my finger. Only the faded white scar on his left cheek mars the perfection.

"You saved me." I slide my fingers down his arm, and he shudders as if my touch almost hurts him.

"I'm no one's savior, zolotaya."

These words set off alarm bells in my brain. I step away, but he grips my hand and squeezes it, drawing me toward the open door. The tall Russian pushes me inside a room filled with half-dressed women. He keeps his hand on my shoulder, and there's something comforting about its weight.

"Oksana, is your bathroom free?" he asks a redhead wearing only a G-string.

A dozen women in various stages of undress turn to face us as he speaks. Some wear sweats, but the other half wear little more than rhinestones and sequins and platform heels.

The redhead appears to be their leader. She doesn't look embarrassed as she stands up, making sure the man at my side can see every inch of her large, creamy breasts with their rosy nipples. She smiles at him and spares me a brief glance.

"Vadim, honey. Did you bring a guest? Is she going to join us on stage?" She gives me a derisive look, taking in my swaying beads, my flat chest, and my scuffed boots. I'm not an Amazon like these women, and she's trying to make me feel small. From the way she faces forward, pushing her tits toward the man at my side, I have a feeling they've slept together.

"Not funny. Are you going to help me or not?" He clips out the words, holding back any hint of the tenderness he showed me. I'm an idiot, though, thinking of him like we've got some kind of connection when I didn't even know his name until she spoke it.

Vadim.

I'm losing it.

This Russian stranger can't save me from my life and the fact I'm being forced to work with a man who wants to break me. What am I thinking? That he'll hop on a jet with me to Nashville? I must be mad.

I look back at him, and he nods before pushing me toward a bathroom door. I close the door behind me and look into the mirror. The woman staring back at me looks flushed and bedraggled. My eye makeup has smudged, and I do the best I can with water and some tissues while I listen to the low hum of voices in the changing room outside.

I run the tap and turn my attention to my attire. Jimmy has torn the fitted panties of the short stage dress. I rub the ripped fabric through my trembling fingers and squeeze my eyes shut, listening as the sound of female voices fades to the click of heels and the slam of a door as the dancers troop out.

Opening the door a crack, I stand in the bathroom doorway and watch him for a moment. He's looking down at a phone, his head bent, long eyelashes casting shadows across his cheekbones.

"Vadim?" I question softly, stepping toward him. He looks up and stares at me, unsmiling, and I stop until he holds out his hand.

"Come on, little songbird. We need to figure out what to do with you."

We step into the dark club, listening to the beat of the music as we move down the corridors, past the backstage entrance, and into the curtained VIP area.

"Wait here for me." He leaves me in a dark corner and strides toward a handsome, dark-haired man on the opposite side of the room.

It takes a while for my eyes to adjust, but I scan the crowd until I see Jimmy. He's seated on a bench at the back, eyeing me malevolently. Once in a while, he lets his anger mar his nice-guy mask so everyone can see who he really is. He crooks a finger at me but gets distracted by a woman wearing a skirt so short that I can see the white flash of her underwear as she sits down and puts a hand on his shoulder. As he turns her way, I return to scanning the room.

Vadim remains locked in conversation with his dark-haired friend, their heads huddled together. Nearby, a tall bald man in a tux picks his way through the crowd and moves toward the bar. People part for him, and Vadim's eyes follow him.

I start to edge through the crowd toward the bar. I'll be safer out of dark corners where Jimmy can reach me unobserved, and if this bald man is important, perhaps my proximity to him will provide some protection.

I lay my hand on the bar top at the same time as the bald man. He waves at the bartender, who walks over with a bottle of champagne, pours a glass, and slides it across the bar top to me.

"That was quite the performance," the bald man says. "You've got a powerful voice for such a small woman."

He smiles, and a gold canine tooth catches a glint of light from the backlit bottles. He lifts the glass and hands it to me as his eyes run down my body, but it doesn't feel sexual. It's like he's appraising me to see if my power runs further than my voice.

My scalp prickles as I take the glass, every instinct telling me to keep control of my senses in this man's presence. Raising the glass, I let the bubbles touch my lips. Sharp floral liquid touches my tongue, but I don't swallow more than a touch. I haven't eaten since lunchtime and my stomach feels hollow. If I drink, it'll go to my head, so I raise it in a wordless thank you.

He takes my other hand and lifts it to his lips. "Yevgeny Guelman. Enchanted to meet you."

The touch of his mouth on the back of my hand makes my skin crawl. I have no idea why I felt safer with the man who burst into my dressing room with a gun than this well-dressed Russian who has been nothing but polite.

"Are you enjoying Moscow?" he asks.

"I haven't seen much." I let my eyes wander to Vadim, who's still listening to his animated friend, and across to Jimmy, who's watching me through narrowed eyes.

"Did Antonov not invite you to the after-party? Such poor manners." The furrows on his forehead deepen, and he purses his lips. "Of course, I'd be happy to take you."

"If that's where all the pretty dancers went, I'm sure my manager would love it." I raise my glass to my lips again, pretending to drink. "It's more his scene than mine. I'm a little tired."

Warm yellow light bounces from behind the bar and reflects off the man's lined forehead as his lips curve into a smile that doesn't reach his eyes. "I won't take no for an answer, especially not from a beautiful woman like yourself. The star attraction should really join the party."

There's something about the way he describes me as an attraction that spells out how he sees. To him, I am a pawn on a chessboard and not a tired, hungry woman.

Smiling tightly, I scan the crowd for Vadim. His back is turned to me, and the only man who catches my eye is Jimmy. He grins at me and draws a finger across his throat, so I turn back to the man looming beside me at the bar, who brandishes the bottle of champagne like a weapon.

"Come now, drink a little more. I don't like to see people refuse my hospitality."

I've gone from the frying pan to the fire, and I see no way out of the flames.

CHAPTER SEVEN

Vadim

A beer bottle rolls from under the red bench, and Sasha kicks it against the table like it's done him a personal wrong. When it returns to our feet, he follows it with his eyes, then delivers another blow to the glass. It cracks apart, creating a jagged wound at its opening. Sasha kicks it back under the seat and steps toward me, shards of glass crunching under his feet as he runs his hands through his dark hair.

"What's got into you?" I ask. Nervous energy comes off Sasha in waves that are strong enough to put me on edge too.

"Parties like this annoy me. Watching everyone else drinking and fucking while I'm trying to work out what the Night Governor's going to do next." He swivels his toe in a circle over the broken bottle fragments. "Makes me itchy."

"Yeah, me too." I glance back toward the dark corner where I left the singer, but I can't spot her through the remaining stragglers. "I don't think that clown Antonov will see out the month."

Sasha stares at the thinning crowd. The bulk of the

revelers have followed the richest man in the room to an after-party. "He's still useful. There's a deal going down on the China-Russia border, and the boss wants in on the smuggling routes." He grabs a bottle from the table and takes a swig of warming beer with a grimace.

"How do you know what the border deal involves?" I question.

"Guess who's going to spend two weeks in deepest Siberia in mid-winter if the deal comes off?" Sasha's mouth twists in disgust.

I clap a sympathetic hand on his back, glad I can't speak Chinese. I get sent to New York when the Night Governor needs errands run with his American business rather than Siberia. "Is that why you're in such a bad mood?"

"Yeah. I'm the only one he trusts to deal with the triad gangs near the border." He sighs, tossing the beer bottle from hand to hand before tipping the dregs onto the floor. "Or he doesn't want me around and he's sidelining me. You've got to watch my back while I'm away. I don't trust him."

I pull Sasha over to a sofa and fish around in a bucket of melting ice for some cold vodka. Once I've found it, I pour two shots in glasses that are none too clean. "No one trusts him, but you're the smartest guy in the room and he needs you."

Sinking to a bench, I hand my friend one of the shot glasses as I scan the throng of people for the singer. Now that the crowd has thinned even more, I see the corner I left her in is empty.

"That's probably why he doesn't like me." Sasha looks over, worry creasing his forehead. "If I have to leave town next week, you'll be here, right?"

"Where else would I be?" I let my head tip back as I watch the disco ball paint patterns of light on the ceiling.

"We both need to get out of Moscow. That fucker doesn't like anyone."

Sasha stares pensively at the bar, then he throws back his drink. "Looks like the boss has found some fresh meat."

I follow his gaze across the room and see my little song-bird talking to Guelman. The boss might be pouring her champagne now, but he likes to break women for sport, even when he's not selling them for sex.

She catches my eye and smiles. I wave and rise from the sofa, but my best friend grabs my arm and yanks me backward.

"Where do you think you're going?" Sasha looks over at the bar and sees the bottle of champagne our boss is pouring into his own glass. He goes to top up my golden-haired angel's glass, but she puts a hand over the top and smiles sweetly at him. Everything about her is sweet, from her hair that smells of flowers to her lilting southern accent.

"Leave her to the Night Governor. He'll take care of her," Sasha says, tilting his head to the side as he looks between me and the scene at the bar.

"Guelman has never taken care of anyone in his life. He'll use her and discard her." With a sense of foreboding, I look between the woman I've become fascinated by and the looming figure of Yevgeny Guelman.

Sasha's eyes rove around the room, taking in the drunk American music executive and the last remaining strippers before landing back on our boss, who flashes his gold tooth at us with a malevolent grin. "She's a star. She'll be okay. Anyway, what do you care?" He shrugs.

"I don't," I say, cupping the back of my neck and shifting from foot to foot until Sasha slaps me on the back and starts laughing.

"Fuck me. Little Vadim's got a crush."

"Piss off. She's not interested." I turn back toward the bar

35

and watch the way the light plays across her gold curls and olive skin. She's so fucking beautiful.

"The way she keeps looking over at you says otherwise, but I think the Night Governor's got his eyes on her, so you better move fast if you want any action." Sasha grins at me, his teeth flashing blue under the strobe lights.

Guelman slides his arm around the singer's shoulders, and she stiffens. Strange that she can sense enough to be afraid of him, but she needed rescuing from a man who must be much less dangerous.

As if on cue, her puffed-up manager starts making his way toward her at the bar, and I can't stand it another second. She's mine. I elbow my way through the thinning crowd until I'm right behind her, and her whole face lights up in a smile when she sees me.

"Zolotaya," I say, damning myself for not asking her name, but she steps into my side for the second time this evening. I slide an arm around her waist, pulling her into the shelter of my body.

Guelman looks at the pair of us, and I can see the wheels turning in his mind, calculating how he might use the connection to his advantage.

"Kesera was the star attraction tonight. Are you escorting her to Antonov's after-party?" Guelman says. The Night Governor gives me a pointed look, making clear this suggestion is only a little short of an order. It's an order the little songbird doesn't want me to obey.

She laughs and plasters herself against me, her fingers digging sharply into my waist. "I'm a bit jetlagged."

Sasha sidles up to the boss, leans near his ear, and says something under his breath. Guelman nods, glancing briefly at both of us before stepping away to talk with Sasha at the end of the bar. I continue watching as Sasha holds up his phone and points to a text. The boss shakes his head, then starts back toward us.

"Business calls me away. I will leave you with Vadim." He leans down to press a kiss to her cheek and looks at me from beneath hooded eyelids. She shrinks from his touch, and he smiles like her fear gives him a personal thrill. "I trust you won't make a mess of this. Do your best to show the talent some of Moscow's culture. I'm sure a lady like this would like to see more than your usual shabby haunts."

He stands to his full height and turns toward the door. Sasha follows him, stopping to talk to one of the girls before winking at me.

The singer at my side stiffens. I step around her, gently turn her to face me, and cup her shoulders, kneading her tight muscles and running my hands back and forth along the narrow line of her back, trying to transmit that I mean her no harm.

"I'm sorry. I shouldn't have left you alone. I didn't even ask your name." I smile and let my hand drift into the curls at the nape of her neck.

"Kesera," she says. Her head sinks into my palm, and she looks up at me with dilated pupils.

"Do you want me to drop you back at your hotel, or do you want to stay with me for a while? I can show you a bit of the city if you'd like?" I can't think why she'd choose to come with me, but for some reason, I hope she will.

She glances around the bar before her eyes drift shut, then turns her face into the heel of my hand, as if seeking comfort. I massage the back of her head with fingers that feel overly large and clumsy before she opens sleepy eyes and whispers, "I'll take my chances with you. If that's okay."

I pull her against my body and wrap my arms around her. "More than okay," I say softly into her hair before taking her hand and leading her to the corner where Sasha is pouring himself another shot of vodka. I watch him down the drink. He's on the road to oblivion.

"You off?" Sasha lapses into Russian, pulling car keys from his pocket and throwing them to me. "Where are you heading?"

I catch the keys, which he throws a little too wide so I have to drop my arm from Kesera's shoulders. "Out for a bit, but she's tired. Maybe I'll take her to the dacha."

"The dacha? We don't take anyone there." Sasha's brows draw together in a dark line when I bring up our house in the woods.

Is it wrong to want to steal a moment away from the dark energy of Moscow? I think about the snow and silence and the small wooden house in a clearing in the trees. The way the light filters through the branches and glints on the snow. The dacha is our sanctuary, and I don't take anyone there, because I don't want the place contaminated with anything that can follow me home. I haven't taken a girl there for years. Not since Sasha's sister.

But this is different. It will be over before it begins.

"We don't take anyone we might see again," I say. "This is temporary. It's clean. She's not part of our world, and when do I have time to meet someone like that?"

Sasha looks at me quizzically. "I didn't know you *wanted* to meet someone like that. Emotions are messy. Especially at a time like this."

"Fuck off, Sasha. I won't start getting sappy about someone I've just met." I look at the girl who's pressed against my side. "Of course, I could always hand her back and drink and fuck Oksana instead."

Sasha laughs. "Okay, you've made your point. More chance of complications and definitely more chance of a hangover with Oksana. If I'm away, you'll need to keep your wits about you."

"I'll take her out in Moscow first, but I need to get out of the city to clear my head. Is the dacha empty? Can I use it?"

Sasha narrows his eyes, but he lets his doubts hang in the air instead of voicing his objection. "If you know what you're doing."

"Always, brother. Always. When have I ever let you down?"

He smiles. "Go on, then. Have some fun. Clear heads next week and all that." He puts an arm around my shoulder and squeezes, but before I can make an exit, the singer's manager blocks my way.

"We've got to leave. I'll need Kesera to come with me," Jimmy says, looking up at me with a nasty smile on his face.

CHAPTER EIGHT

Kesera

When you don't speak the language, you've got nothing but body language to go on, and a month of concerts in Russia, Israel, and Dubai—plus trailing around after slimy Jimmy and the men he likes to hang around with—has sharpened my senses.

Vadim's friend doesn't like me.

His eyes keep cutting to me, and he jabs his finger at Vadim like he's trying to make a point when he looks at me. He threw the keys Vadim's way so he had to step away from me, and he flashed a malevolent grin when we were separated.

I must be too tired to think clearly. I was so focused on parsing the body language between the man I've chosen to go home with and his handsome friend that I missed the bigger threat. I didn't even notice Jimmy approaching. Now he's looming over me, pressing his fingers hard enough into my arm to leave a bruise.

I suck a breath through my teeth, but Vadim moves fast

for such a big man, gripping Jimmy's arm and twisting it behind his back until he makes a squealing noise.

"She's not going anywhere with you," Vadim snarls, and I smile. I shouldn't like the threat of violence, but it makes me wonder what he'd be like in bed. Would he be gentle or unleash some of that power on my body? What would that feel like?

I tamp down the thoughts and try to focus on the conversation, but I'm so tired that the volume of their words fades to a low buzz in my ears.

"Sasha here is in charge of booking flights. According to the roster, you aren't out of here until Sunday night, so if you want to take a straight flight back to Nashville, I would advise waiting for the use of the private jet. You are, of course, welcome to try Sheremetyevo airport, but you never know who you might meet." Vadim drops Jimmy's arm and slips his hand to his holster, fingering his gun.

"Well, look here, young man, I need you to understand that Kesera and I have meetings in Moscow tomorrow. I need to take her to see some promoters. We've got important business to do," Jimmy puffs out.

Sasha pulls a gun from his waistband and starts flicking the safety catch on and off. "No, little man, I believe that Vadim wants to take your singer out on the town. Am I right?" He cocks his head at Vadim, looking to see how his friend will react. I'm glad there's a new focus for the dark-haired man's dislike and all his venom is now directed at someone who deserves it.

Jimmy blanches at being called little man, but he's half a head shorter and at least two guns down on the two Russian men, so he doesn't argue.

Sasha glares at the man who has made my last nine months a living hell with his demands and threats. "I'm the one who deals with the promoters. If you need to talk about any of your artists, I know who's looking for headline entertainment in Italy and Cyprus. Vadim will have your little girl back at the airport in time for the flight on Sunday."

"But I—"

Sasha holds up a hand, halting Jimmy with a single gesture. Jimmy looks between the two men as Vadim pulls me against his side and wraps his arm around my shoulder. It's obvious Jimmy is out of his depth.

"Might I suggest that it would be in your best interest to do what I say?" Vadim says. "We are very generous hosts when our guests don't cause us trouble, but we aren't the kinds of men you want to cross, Mr. Ullrich. We aren't those kinds of men at all . . ." He looks pointedly down at his gun, his message clear.

Jimmy glares at me, but I seize the chance to get out of here. I stand on my tiptoes to whisper into Vadim's ear. "Let's go."

Vadim shivers as my lips touch his skin, then leads me out of the club. And I follow him, telling myself it's the right thing to do. So far, he's been kind to me. It's been months since anyone touched me, and his hands felt good.

We get in the back seat of a low black sedan, and the lights of Moscow shine against the car windows. Buildings slide past the glass, their façades lit up like wedding cakes, with snow banked against their doorways. The city is draped in white finery.

I press my face against the glass, watching the lights pick up the faded pastels of buildings that look ghostly in the darkness as I try to focus on something other than the presence of the man in the back seat with me. I lean my forehead against the window, closing my eyes and feeling the coolness of the condensation as I breathe in.

Now that I'm alone in the car with him, the exhaustion hits me and I'm questioning my judgement again. I let my attraction to this stranger overpower my common sense. He's so much bigger than me and can do what he wants with my body, and the thought is equal parts thrilling and terrifying.

"You're shivering." Vadim's Russian accent seems more pronounced without the thumping music in the background. His fingers paint a trail of fire down my arm, and the hair on my forearm rises to meet the heat of his touch. He cages my palm between his two enormous hands and rubs my fingers. "You're absolutely frozen. Come here."

He pulls me toward him, opening his coat and folding me, my beads, sequins, and thin jacket against the pine-scented warmth of his skin. I burrow into his side, nestling against his strength. I rub my forehead against the triangle of skin at his throat, and he goes still. I wait for a kiss, for something sexual, but the only thing moving is his heart, which thuds against his ribs and beats against my ear.

Reluctantly, I pull away and look out of the window. "It's beautiful."

"Better by night, when you can't see the grime or the scars."

I glance at him, and he lets his otherworldly blue eyes drift to my lips before they slide toward the window.

The car swings around the ring road, and the Kremlin's turrets loom into view, spires blazing bright against the darkness. I feel transported in time.

"It's like a fairy tale. Look at the castles, the towers, the houses of noblemen. I've never seen anything like it."

"What kind of fairy tale, zolotaya? A Disney story where the woodland creatures bring you breakfast and everyone lives happily ever after?" Vadim asks.

"What other kind of fairy tale is there?"

He settles back against the seat, fingers tracing mine as he tightens his grasp on my hands, but he doesn't meet my eyes. Instead, he looks out of the window, at the high red walls and dark green towers of the Kremlin. "The real kind. We killed all the noblemen in Russia. If you're looking for a fairy tale, we have only those where blood is spilled and there's a steep price to be paid for everything you gain. In our stories, Cinderella's sisters are tortured to death and witches' houses run through the woods on chicken's feet."

I snort with laughter and bat his chest with my hand, but he doesn't flirt back. He just keeps watching me with hooded eyes. "You're just trying to scare me. You've no more seen a house balanced on bird's feet than I've met a woodland animal that wants to have a chat while helping me out."

"You Americans," he sighs, gripping my hand again. "I'm just trying to point out that in the real fairy tales, it's an eye for an eye, a tooth for a tooth. The price for the happiness has to be paid."

"That's a grim view of the world."

"A realistic one, perhaps."

I stare down at our clasped hands and stroke circles on his palm. I want to curl up against him, but he doesn't look like he'd welcome the touch.

"You don't have dreams? Nothing you've set your heart on?" I ask.

"I've willed things to happen. I mark my territory, watch my back, and defend what's mine, but I don't dream. Dreams are for fools." He pulls my hands to his lips and presses a kiss to my fingers, sending a molten thread of heat between my legs. Every nerve ending in my body is attuned to the place where his lips touch my skin.

"What's the difference? I dreamed of being up on that stage, and now I am." My eyes fall to his mouth and I imagine kissing him, but he looks away, lowering our hands to my lap.

Vadim's thumbs draw circles on my wrists, tracing my pulse. "But there was a price to be paid, wasn't there? What was that I saw tonight? The price for fame?"

45

I sit up straight, pulling my hands out of his and shifting toward my side of the seat. As I look out the window, my back straightens. "I didn't sleep my way to the top, if that's what you're implying."

There's a soft laugh in my ear as Vadim moves closer and pulls me into his arms. He catches my hair in his hand and draws it away from my ear, pressing a kiss right beneath it, and I can't help the moan that escapes me.

"God, you smell like fucking springtime," he murmurs against my neck.

Part of me wants to lie back against him and bare my neck to him like an offering, but the other part of me feels prickly and offended. I pull away and turn in his arms, looking up at him. His breath comes faster now, and the blue around his pupils has narrowed to a faint ring.

"Didn't you want to help me tonight? Does everything have to be a transaction?" I stare up at him, waiting for his reply as the car pulls to a stop and idles at the side of an embankment.

Instead of responding, he leans forward to tap on the glass divider as he says something in Russian to the driver.

He opens the door, letting in an icy blast of air. "Come on. I want to show you something."

Stepping out of the car, he reaches back to pull me into the snowy night. Soft flakes fall around us, their dance lit by the glint from the gold domes above us.

"Where are we?"

Vadim smiles. "Have you seen anything of Moscow?"

"I walked around Red Square this morning, but I didn't go into St. Basil's, and they were repairing Lenin. Is that right? Can you repair a dead body?" I walk beside him up the steps of a huge church by the silent waters of the Moscow River.

"I think you have to replace the formaldehyde and touch up the wax. You didn't miss much. St. Basil's is dark and poky

46

inside." Vadim's lips curve up at the corners, and he holds out his arm so that he can help me up the slippery steps. "Lenin's dead. If you make it back to Moscow for another concert, he'll still be dead."

"So where are we?" I look at the lights moving in the water. The snow gives the air a hushed quality, despite the low drone of traffic in the background.

"I'm taking you to all my favorite places: a church, a bar, and a dacha."

I want to ask what a dacha is, but I'm stuck on the fact that the first place he's taken me to is a church. I start to hum "Going to the Chapel of Love" by The Dixie Cups as I smile at him questioningly.

Vadim shakes his head, a smile ghosting his lips as he pulls me against his body, folding me into his winter coat and guarding me against the cold and darkness. Before us is another wedding cake of a building, its bright gold domes spearing the night sky. It's a strange place to bring me, but I suppose I haven't been on many dates anywhere, and never somewhere as exotic as Moscow with a man as fierce as this. Perhaps this is normal here.

"This is the Cathedral of Christ the Savior. Stalin pulled it down. It was going to become a palace for the Soviets, but the Great Patriotic War got in the way."

"Which war?"

"I think you call it the second big war."

"Oh, World War Two."

Vadim leans down and tightens his arms around my waist. "Are you listening to my story, my zolotaya, or are you trying to teach me English?"

I lean back and snuggle into his body as his voice drifts through the dark air.

"The Soviets ran out of money to construct this church,

but when the USSR fell, the people of Moscow donated the money to rebuild it as beautiful as it ever was."

We hold hands and walk up the steps to the bridge, the lights of the cathedral bright against the water. He gives me his coat, which is warm from the heat of his body.

"It moves me whenever I come here. I like to stop the car on this side of the river and walk over to the bar on the other side and think about the million small sacrifices that went into every brick, every gold leaf on the domes." He looks up at the church and from this angle, his eyelashes cast shadows against his cheekbones.

"It was the late nineties when they rebuilt it. Things were tough for most people, and yet a million Moscow citizens put their hands in their pockets to resurrect it. You can knock us down, bulldoze our foundations, but we have faith that we will rise again." He squeezes my hand.

"And that's not a fairy tale?" I ask, gripping his fingers tighter.

"No, zolotaya, it's a million small sacrifices. At a time when people couldn't afford the basics, they paid to build this." He smiles at me, leaning down to brush his lips against mine. It's so cold and his touch is so soft that I'm surprised I can feel it all the way to my toes.

Against the bridge, the river curves away into the darkness, and my feet slide on the icy ground. Vadim steadies me, and I laugh as a group of beautiful women walks past us over the bridge. They look like a flock of birds, with short, bright dresses and long legs flashing above their towering stilettos.

"How do they do it? How do they balance on those shoes on this ice? Do they have magic powers? I can barely stay upright in my boots." I'm wide eyed as they sashay past us.

Vadim's deep laugh reverberates behind me. "The price to be paid for beauty. We understand these things in Russia, and we practice for them."

A couple of them look back at Vadim, leaning into each other and giggling. It makes me want to stick my claws into him—or them. I'm not sure who I want to lash out at first, but I have to remind myself that I'm only here for another couple of days. As he says, this is not a fairy tale.

He wraps his arm around me and pulls me into the shelter of his coat as we walk across the bridge and down wooden steps into a bar.

There's a wait as a pretty, platinum-haired woman in a white suit shakes her head at Vadim. He leans over and says something in a low voice, and her eyes widen as an older man who must be her manager appears behind her. He nods at Vadim and says something in Russian. I catch the words *face control*.

As we move through the door and into a curtained waiting area, warm air envelops me and I relax a little.

"What's face control?" I ask.

Vadim laughs. "You're pretty enough to come in, zolotaya, and I know the manager."

The people in here wouldn't look out of place in Nashville or Austin if we swapped out the cowboy boots for their shoes. There are no more G-strings, just the kind of beautiful people you find in any city on a Saturday night.

The muscles in my shoulders drop slowly away from my ears. I hadn't realized how much being surrounded by glamorous half-naked Amazons was messing with my head.

Vadim leads me to a table overlooking the river. Patrons turn nervous looks our way before whispering in hushed tones amongst themselves. The maître d' nearly breaks his thin legs as he scrambles to ready our table, and I have the uneasy sense that this may be a fairy tale after all. But instead of the woodcutter, I've chosen to go home with the wolf.

CHAPTER NINE

Vadim

There are a dozen different Moscows. The concert halls with cellists playing Rachmaninov, the private jets flown by billionaires, seedy clubs brimming with my friends, and a bar like this full of beautiful kids who think they can change the world. I brought Kesera here because I thought it was her kind of place, but it was probably a mistake.

The girl at the door wouldn't have let us in if the manager didn't owe me a gambling debt. The couples at the neighboring table keep slanting worried looks our way, now that the maître d' looks like he might be about to have a heart attack. My singing angel sits in front of me, knitting her fingers together like she's trying to find something hidden beneath the skin.

I reach over and take her tiny, trembling fingers in my large fist. She's so damn pretty and she smells like flowers, but she's way too good for me.

I have no idea how to romance a woman at all.

A heavy weight settles in my gut, as if I'm stepping around

land mines. If history has taught me anything, it's that women who get close to me end up shattered.

"What do you want to drink?" I look around the room for a waitress and wave at a woman with a nose ring and bleached hair who pretends she hasn't seen me. She begins to rearrange some cutlery on a nearby table.

Kesera rolls her neck, looks at me from under long, dark lashes, and gives me an embarrassed smile which makes me want to kiss her. "I know it makes me sound like an old woman, but I'd love a hot drink with some honey. It helps my voice."

I look over at the maître d', who glares at the waitress and says something that makes her rush over. "I've got an idea," I say, ordering a drink and rubbing her fingers with my thick thumbs to try to stop her trembling. I'm torn between wanting to wrap her in cotton wool and wanting to tear off her clothes.

I'm saved from my jangling thoughts when a flight of vodka appears. Little jewel-colored shot glasses balance on a piece of wood, along with a glass teapot containing a bright-orange drink.

"What's this?" She pulls her hands from mine and runs her fingers along the teapot's silver filigree handle, avoiding my eyes.

I reach to take the pot from her and pour her a small cup. The liquid glows like the sun on a polluted day.

"Try it. It's a berry that grows wild in Siberia." I grin at her like I've done something clever and then feel like a fool. I don't want to scare her, and the women who seek me out for a quick fuck usually do so for the cheap thrill of being scared.

Kesera lets her eyes fall shut when she takes a sip and moans softly as the drink slides down her throat.

"It's so gooood," she says, her southern accent caressing the vowels. It makes me think of other ways I could get her to make that sound. "It's like the drink the handsome prince in a fairy tale would bring thousands of miles across Siberia for the princess to try."

I can't help laughing when she smiles at me.

"You should laugh more often. It makes you look younger." She tilts her head to the side and watches me with those mossy-green eyes for a moment.

"You're determined to see everything as a fairy tale, aren't you?"

A shadow falls across her face, and she reaches for one of the vodka shots, picks it up, and drains it, wincing a little before she wipes her mouth with the back of her hand.

"God, that's strong." She stares at me and then says, "I got saved by a handsome hero and now I'm drinking a magic drink. Isn't that the kind of thing that happens in fairy tales?" There's a fierceness in the way she says it, like she can will it to be true.

"I'm not sure vodka qualifies as magic."

"The Day-Glo orange stuff. It tastes like magic."

She looks at me with those big eyes, and I run out of words. I reach for her hand and thread our fingers together. We sit in silence for a few minutes as the cathedral's gleaming domes shimmer in the water below the window. There's a strange kind of comfort in it, but I feel compelled to warn her.

"I'm nobody's hero, zolotaya. I'm not a good man, and you shouldn't put your trust in me."

Her smile goes brittle and doesn't crinkle around her eyes. "You keep calling me that nickname, and I'm no one's golden girl. Not anymore."

"Tonight, you are. You're mine." I bring her fingers to my mouth again, kissing them softly.

The vodka must have gone to her head, because to my surprise, she circles the table and slides in next to me. She draws my head to hers and kisses me so softly it feels like feathers or angel wings. Like every soft thing I didn't know I was missing.

When I open my eyes, she's staring at me.

"I know we don't have long. It's only hours, really. Can we suspend reality until I leave? Call it a fairy tale for a little while?"

I pull her tiny frame against me, wrapping her against my side and enjoying how small and delicate she feels. She sighs, shifts, and leans her head on my chest, and I watch the snow fall into the dark water outside as I explore the sensation of having this strange woman put her trust in me. I'm plucking up the courage to kiss her again when I hear a soft snore and she slides sideways into my lap. She's out cold.

The drink must have knocked her out because I can't wake her up and I have to carry her to the car, cursing myself for not looking after her better. Once we're in the car, the noise of the city fades as we pass the ring roads and reach the snowy countryside on the outskirts of Moscow.

This is the best time to leave the city. When the snarls of traffic calm to emptiness. It's the thing I fucking hate about Moscow, and it's one of the many reasons why I have to get out of here. Nothing works. Everything is a zero-sum game. You could have all the billions in the world and die of a heart attack before the doctors could reach you in an ambulance because the streets were clogged with cars. Money can't buy you out of the dogfights and the chaos. The only way out of this mess is to leave. China, America, it doesn't matter. Sasha and I need to be anywhere but here.

I look over at the sleeping girl in the seat next to me as we pull off the highway and into the woods. The darkness of the winter roads stills my mind as the white birch trunks flash past me. I've sent the driver home. I don't want to share these hours with anyone else, even if she's fast asleep.

She's curled in my coat, her wavy hair a gold-streaked cloud above her cheekbones. I don't know much about her and I won't have time to find out, but it's probably better that way. I wouldn't chance bringing her to the dacha otherwise. Too many painful memories.

This place belongs to the Night Governor, but Sasha and our friends use it. I never really understood what Guelman saw in a bunch of no-hopers from the same orphanage. He's a sick fuck, but in a twisted way, I'm grateful to him.

The only one of us that didn't belong in that godforsaken children's home was Sasha's sister, Polina. She was too beautiful and gentle for that damned place or this blasted city. I don't think we've brought a woman here since Polina. The house probably smells of men's socks and stale beer.

I look over at my little songbird. She's wearing my coat, but her legs stick out the bottom, amid a clatter of beads and chains. I'm just thinking about stripping off her layers when the phone rings.

"Vadim, you still in town or did you leave?" Sasha's voice stretches out across the darkness.

"I'm on the way to the dacha. Almost there." My eyes scan the lines of snow-crusted branches and the white flash of birch trunks. "Trouble?"

"Nothing has blown up yet. Antonov is talking with the Night Governor. I'm going to lie low and hope I don't have to go to the ass end of Siberia. It's probably good that you're out of town. Is she with you?"

"Yeah, fast asleep. I think the time difference knocked her out." I keep my eyes on the dark road as trees flash by the windows.

"What's the attraction? She's not your usual type. Since when do you hang out with sleeping women? Aren't you usually in and out too quickly for anyone to catch any shut-eye?" He chuckles to himself at his poor joke. Sasha's no better with women than I am, but he's a handsome fucker, so he's not spoiled for choice.

"Maybe it's a palate cleanser. I like it out in the woods, and it's not like I can bring Oksana or one of the other dancers out here. Sleeping or awake, there would be drama, and then they'd get ideas and I'd never be able to shake them off. This is simple. I'm putting her on a plane on Sunday. A nice, clean break. I can come back into town when I drop her off."

"I'll let you know," he clips out.

Hanging up the phone, I listen to the snowbound silence and the ticking of the engine. I can hear her soft breathing next to me. I'm playing at being someone else: the kind of man who does good turns for women without expecting something in return. It's a game, but it's a game I can play a couple of hands of this weekend.

I know it can't last.

I glance down at the sleeping woman at my side as night shrouds the trees. There's nothing but headlights on the snow and the soft sound of her breath next to me and the rapid beating of my heart. For the next twenty-four hours, I can be anyone. If that's not a fairy tale, then I don't know what is.

CHAPTER TEN

Kesera

I feel like I'm swimming into consciousness through deep, dark water as a giant hand rolls my shoulder back and forth.

"Wake up, zolotaya. We've only got about four hours of daylight left. The sun goes down early here in winter."

I screw up my eyes against the light. "Why is it so bright?" I croak.

"The light reflects off the snow. We need to get into the woods while we can."

I roll over to see Vadim towering above me like some ancient god of snow and ice. He's wearing only a pair of gray sweatpants as he swims into view through the haze of sleep, the sharp lines of his torso becoming more defined. His chest is marked by tattoos of stars and a cat's head, and a couple of sharp scars sweep down one arm and across his midriff. His body is different from the gym boys with their protein shakes back home.

Harder.

57

Sexier.

More threatening.

"Move over." He pats the sliver of white sheet at the edge of the bed, and I make room, staring at the ceiling. He lies beside me, not touching me. In the eerie light of the cabin, we're two strangers again, the intimacy of last night gone like footprints under fresh snow. The inches between us feel like miles.

My throat is scratchy with sleep and my eyes feel puffy, but I can smell the forest on his skin, mingling with the scent of soap and mint. It makes me want to burrow against his side, but he lies rigidly next to me, tense and waiting.

I take a deep breath and wrinkle my nose, coughing as the exhaustion of the days, weeks, and months catches up with me.

"What can you smell? Day-old vodka and men's socks?" He chuckles.

"Hmmm," I hum, inhaling deeply. "You smell of cedar and pine with an undertone of sandalwood and pheromones."

"Really? You got all that from one sniff?" He stills as my pinkie edges along the side of his hand.

"No. I just made all that up. I have no idea what sandalwood and cedar smell like, but it sounded impressive." I turn to watch a smile ghost across his lips, but I'm disappointed when he doesn't come any closer.

The ghostly light from the snow bounces off the walls. Outside the window, bare black branches bend under the weight of snow, and a pale gray wash of sky provides a backdrop.

"Where are we? Is this a house on chicken's feet that's about to take off into the woods?" I ask.

His shoulder is level with my eye, and I have the strange desire to lean over and taste his skin, to kiss every scar and tattoo, but he's studying the planks above us as if they hold the clue for the winning lottery numbers.

"It's a dacha," he says without looking at me.

"What's a dacha?" I reach over and touch his shoulder, and he inhales sharply, so I leave my hand where it is. I wait for him to wrap me up in his arms the way he did last night, but the space between us feels alive with something, and he doesn't bridge the gap.

"A Russian country house. Since Soviet times, a lot of families in the city have had one. During the week, everyone was all cooped up in a tiny apartment in the city, but on the weekends, everyone would flood into the countryside, grow vegetables, grill meat, breathe in the forest. There's not much else to do around here."

Great. I'm miles away from anywhere, stuck in the middle of the woods with a gangster I've known for a few hours. What felt like a great way to escape the situation in my dressing room last night seems less sensible in the cold light of day. A tendril of unease unfurls under my solar plexus, but I focus on keeping my breathing even.

Memories of last night filter back to me. The couples at the next table watching him with suspicion. The way the maître d' fumbled around. The bright-orange drink. But after that, the memories of the night are hazy. Did I kiss him? How did I get back here? I sift through the images of church domes reflecting in water and vodka shots on a table in flickering candlelight, but I come up blank.

I pull my hand away from him and run it down my side, over the huge t-shirt I'm wrapped in. I'm naked under the worn gray fabric, and I swallow down a ball of embarrassment and fear.

"I'm not wearing my dress. Did we . . . ? I'm guessing we didn't . . ." My voice trails off into the morning air and the snowy light beyond the window.

"Those beads didn't look like they'd be very comfortable to sleep in. You were like a rag doll. The time difference knocked you out once the adrenaline wore off." He reaches out and lets his knuckles graze my cheek.

"Is this where you spent your childhood?"

At the mention of his childhood, Vadim's hand stops moving. "No. Sasha and I didn't get to use this place until we were older. A man we know, a mentor of ours, lends it to us." He shifts on the bed, rolling so that we face each other. His eyes are such a pale, clear blue they look unreal.

"Who's Sasha? A girlfriend or a sister?" I watch the rise and fall of his chest and let my gaze fall on his mouth.

"No, Sasha is my best friend. You met him last night. Handsome fucker. Scary guy." He leans across to catch my hand, pressing it against his pec. His chest hair dusts my fingers.

"He didn't like me." I think back to the conversation in Russian and the way Sasha looked at me.

"Don't take it personally. He doesn't warm up easily." Vadim bites the tips of my fingers gently before smiling properly for the first time since he lay down. "I like you, though."

Does he?

Last night he was constantly touching me, threading his fingers through mine, pulling me against his side, wrapping me in his coat, aligning our bodies. This morning he's keeping his distance, and I'm aware of how little I know about him. He's gorgeous, but he's a man that scares people.

"I doubt I'm your type," I say.

"You're everyone's type."

"My god. You wouldn't say that if you knew what my life was like." I let my eyes drift across his perfect face, then reach out to touch his scar. His eyes flutter closed as I run my finger over it, down his cheek, and along his jaw.

"When I saw you on that stage, it sounded as if you were

singing to me. It was all I could think about. There were a couple of half-naked women sitting next to me, but I only saw you and that cloud of golden hair and that golden voice. You are luminous."

I choke as a tumble of words clogs my throat. He couldn't be further from the truth. I bury my head in his shoulder, and he slides his hands under the t-shirt, drawing it up.

"You shine so brightly. Men want some of that to rub off on them. I think I was looking for you last night when I went backstage and stumbled across you." He pulls me against him and buries his head in my hair, his words shivering against the skin of my neck and vibrating along every meridian in my body. "Fucking hell. A girl like you has no business with a man like me, but I wanted to snatch a few hours for myself."

His hot hands roam up and down my naked back, cupping my butt and drifting down my thighs as he licks my neck, sucking and kissing my collarbone and shoulders as he mumbles in Russian. He lowers the t-shirt until my hard nipple almost pokes out.

He sits up, looking down at me with pupils blown wide and his nostrils flaring. "Take it off. I want to see all of you."

I go for the hem of the t-shirt, but he's quicker, pulling it up to my neck. Running his hands up my body. Cupping my breasts.

He gently pinches one nipple, and I gasp as he lowers his head to the other. He sucks almost all of my small breast into his mouth as he draws the hard bud against his palate, and I make a mewling noise which sounds foreign to my own ears. I'm turned on, but there's an edge of fear as well.

He moans and starts sucking my other breast as he kicks my legs wide with his knees, running his hands up my arms until he's holding me down on the mattress.

"Vadim?" My voice sounds breathy and small.

"Show me how you are wet for me." He spreads me wider with his knees and looks between my legs. "Fuck yeah."

His breath saws in and out of his nostrils as he stares at my wet and swollen center. But he's not looking at my face. He hasn't even kissed me.

I screw my eyes shut and go still, turning my head to the side and telling myself it won't hurt. His hands run down my body and his warm mouth lands between my legs. I will myself somewhere else. I don't know when he stops, but he stills and presses a kiss to the soft skin of my inner thigh.

"Kesera?"

I don't reply.

"Zolotaya?"

I'm too embarrassed and scared to answer as he rises onto his forearms and puts space between us.

"Baby, what's wrong?" He's breathing heavily as he gazes down at me. Pale blue eyes search mine for something—something I don't understand.

I squeeze mine shut and turn my head away. When I open them, he's waiting above me.

"Forgive me." His arctic eyes search my face.

"There's nothing to forgive," I whisper. I mean it. It went too fast. I shut down.

He stares at me for long moments, and I look back, waiting. Waiting for him to come back to me, for that white fire between us to blaze back to life. But he wrenches away from me and sits on the edge of the bed, his back to me.

"What kind of a host am I?" He puts his head in his hands and shakes it as if shrugging off a bad memory. He doesn't look back at me as I lie back on this strange bed and look at his stiff shoulders hunched away from me. "There's hot water and towels in the bathroom behind that door. You're welcome to borrow any of my clothes."

He stands and paces to the door, and I stare at his retreating back until the door snicks shut behind him.

What the hell just happened? One minute, I was ready for him to devour me, and the next, he couldn't even look at me? God, I made a mess of things. Maybe I shouldn't have pushed him away.

Mumbling under my breath and feeling awkward, I walk toward the bathroom. I grab a towel from the stack of threadbare linen in a cupboard on the wall, then turn the tap and watch the running water until the steam begins to rise. What the hell am I doing here? Stranded in the Russian woods, miles from home, with nothing to look forward to but an argument with Jimmy at the airport.

I'm so damn tired. That moment when Vadim put his arms around me was the first time since my dad died that I felt like I could let my guard down. I just wanted to be loved so badly that I'm imagining things that don't exist with a man I've just met.

"I'm a fool," I say to myself as I step into the shower. My words echo against the tiles.

I step under the stream and let the hot water wash away the tears that begin to trickle from my eyes. I really thought I'd have control over who was in my life once I was famous. I thought people would flock to me. I thought fame was the answer, but it's just brought more questions and I'm lonelier than ever.

I don't know what I'm doing wrong with men. The guys in my band make jokes about not wanting to sleep with me. My manager wants to force it on me when I've made it clear I don't want him. Then, when I finally find a man I want, I can't handle him.

Tipping my head beneath the water, I scrub my skin, trying to wash away my shame, fear, and confusion. By the time I emerge from the bathroom, the house is silent.

"Vadim?" I call, walking through the empty rooms. My voice echoes back at me.

CHAPTER ELEVEN

Vadim

There wasn't much in the village shop this morning, but I found some rye bread and some eggs and butter. I've beaten them in a bowl with salt and pepper as I wait for Kesera to emerge from the bathroom.

I've got no business bringing a soft, pretty girl like this into the woods with me. She hasn't eaten for hours, and she's exhausted after flying halfway across the world to sing for a bunch of rich assholes, and what do I do? I ferry her out to the middle of nowhere and take off all her clothes.

God. Last night. What the fuck did I think I was doing? Stripping off that dress and looking at her tiny, pert little breasts pouting up from her chest and just begging for my mouth. She's so petite and she was so tired, flopping against the mattress. I'd had to put her arms into that t-shirt of mine like a rag doll.

I wanted to climb all over her this morning once she was awake. Fuck her. Claim her. Suck her skin till she's covered in bite marks so that everyone knows she's mine. I'm a fucking animal. But I won't touch her after what I saw in that room. I don't get my kicks from sex with unwilling women. I thought she wanted it. She was moaning and wet and swollen, and then she just froze.

Bending over the counter, I stare at the pale-yellow eggs. My fingers grip chipped Formica before moving toward a jar of dill pickles. I put them down idly and close my eyes as the tiny kitchen with its broken oven and rattling fridge fades out of view.

The sound of footsteps brings me out of my daze. Kesera edges into the room, her gaze darting to everything but focusing on nothing. A black belt winds around her slender waist, holding up a pair of my sweatpants beneath a massive wooly gray top of mine. She looks so scared as she stands in the bedroom doorway and looks up at me with her arms wrapped around herself.

"*Moya* zolotaya." I wave her toward a seat, and she pads over to the rickety table, gaze bouncing around the room. I tip the butter into the pan and watch it melt into brown bubbles. The eggs hiss when I pour them in, and I focus on that, trying to ignore feeling as if I've failed again.

"I'm so hungry, I could eat anything." Her voice is artificially bright and strained.

I plonk down a plate of rye bread and eggs that have crisped at the edges and slide it toward her, then pour us both some coffee. "That's good, because I'm not much of a cook. When did you last eat?"

She picks up a fork, her arms awash in the fabric of my old sweater, and waves it back and forth pensively. She's so tiny, swimming in my old clothes.

"Dunno. Yesterday morning, maybe. I can't eat before a show." She scoops a forkful of eggs into her mouth, closing her eyes and letting out a soft moan that makes me think of how she looked naked. I shift in my seat. My sweats don't

66

hide much, and the noise she makes sends all the blood in my body rushing south.

She opens her eyes and mechanically scoops up the remaining eggs as she watches me. My discomfort must be visible, but not for the reasons she thinks. She eats the last mouthful and points the fork at me.

"What's going on, Vadim? If you don't want me here, you can take me back. I've been on my own a long time, and I'll survive whatever Jimmy throws at me. He's worse when he's drunk, but he'll be sober by now. Look, I don't want . . ." Her voice trails off as she stares over my shoulder at the expanse of trees and snow beyond the window. "I don't want to put you to trouble, okay? You don't need to look after me. I'm a big girl."

She sits up a little straighter in her chair, pulling her shoulders back and trying to look brave. She just looks young and scared in clothes ten sizes too big for her.

I lean across the table and tuck a finger under her chin to tilt her face upward. "It's not you."

"Yeah, I've heard that one before." She offers a bitter laugh.

I cup her face in my hand and look at her. She's even more beautiful in my old clothes, with no makeup to shadow her big green eyes. "I'm out of my depth, okay?"

I walk back to the sink, bracing my hands on the side and looking out at the sun sinking lower between the bare branches. Breath saws in and out of my chest.

"I don't bring women out here. I don't sleep in a bed with them or lend them my clothes. I'm good for a quick fuck, but I don't know how to do anything more."

A spider crawls across the sink and makes its way up the wall, looking for a fly to trap. It starts to spin a line of thread and crawls along it toward a corner of the window. I return my attention to the sink, thinking about whether to drive her back to Moscow when I hear her footsteps and feel her tap me on the back. My heart tries to beat its way out of my chest as I slowly turn around.

She looks small and breakable as she stands in front of me, shifting from foot to foot, her eyes looking past me to the snowy woods outside. I want to pull her into my arms, but what if I scare her? I lean back against the sink and watch her.

"I'm not very good with men either." She chuckles and lifts her shoulder. "You tell me you look at me and think of sex. I find that hard to imagine, but I'll try to believe you."

"What else would I be thinking of?" I look down at her halo of bronze curls. Their colors shimmer in the light from the window, and I want to plunge my fingers into them and use her hair to move her body.

"Well, you were surrounded by beautiful women." Her gaze sinks to my mouth, and she licks her lips.

"Yeah, and I'm surrounded by half-naked women every time Sasha and I are in one of those clubs with our boss. Not to mention the brothels." I shrug and then wince. I shouldn't bring up brothels. She must think I'm a pig. I stare down at her. Her eyes are the color of the woods in spring, but they're clouded by doubt. "Why don't you believe me?"

She tries to turn her head away, suddenly shy. "It's just that . . . men, you know, they don't want . . . I can't. "

"Fucking hell, zolotaya. I'm the only man here, and I don't want to think about anyone else touching your body. I lost control because I want you so much. I did it wrong."

I give in to temptation, sliding my hand into her hair and pulling her head back until we're both breathing hard as we look at each other. I sink into her green eyes like I'm lost in a forest, giving in and slamming my mouth against hers, kissing her like a plundering army. She gives a soft moan and I reach down to cup her buttocks, pulling her tight against my erection as she winds her legs around me.

God, I want her so much it hurts.

She mewls like a kitten as her tongue slides against mine and her hands thread into the hair at the nape of my neck. When she starts to rock against me, I go still. If I start now, I won't be able to stop.

Drawing back, I press my forehead against hers, my breath coming in sharp pants. I can taste the mint from her toothpaste.

"Now do you believe me?" I breathe against her mouth, and she presses her lips to mine before she buries her face in my neck.

"You stopped," she whispers against my skin, sending electric currents along my vertebrae.

"Because if I didn't, then I wouldn't be able to." I lift her away from me and set her on her feet, spinning her to face the table where she's left a slice of buttered rye bread untouched. "Eat, please. You nearly collapsed on me last night."

She steps toward me and presses a kiss to my cheek before tiptoeing back to the table and jamming a large bit of bread into her mouth, chewing thoughtfully while she watches me.

"Why are you so hard on yourself? You're a good guy." She takes a sip of coffee.

"I'm about as far from a good guy as you can get." I sink into the chair opposite her.

"Well, you've been good to me." She reaches toward me, and I clasp her fingers. Her delicate hand with its gold-tipped nails appears so small in my huge, calloused paw. I could break her without even meaning to.

I squeeze her fingers. "People who love me get killed. I'm bad luck."

Throwing back the last of her coffee, she walks toward me and stands between my legs. For someone so small, her hands grip my shoulders with surprising force.

"Listen to me, Vadim. I don't know you, but I know enough. Maybe I see something you don't often show people. You aren't planning to hack me apart with an axe in the woods, are you?" She glances around the kitchen before smiling down at me. "Should I be worried? Is there something you're not telling me?"

"There are lots of things I'm not telling you." I grin sheepishly at her, and to my surprise, she laughs.

CHAPTER TWELVE

Kesera

The entryway is a tangle of shoes and dust jackets as Vadim kneels in front of me and sifts through the pile of odd shoes. He pulls out a pair of battered gray furry things that look like a cross between a Christmas stocking and a ski boot without a sole.

He hands them to me, and I finger the strange texture. "What are these? Fairy tale boots made of reindeer hair?"

"Nope, valenki. Russian snow boots."

"But they're not waterproof, are they? Are they made of wool?" I turn them upside down. The bottom is made of hair too.

"Nope, they're something better. They're cold-proof. Put them on. If your feet get wet with the snow, they will hold in the heat." He crouches beneath me, slipping my feet—which are already wrapped in two pairs of his giant socks—into the shoes. It's another tender gesture from a man who keeps telling me I shouldn't believe in his goodness.

71

A lock of hair slides over his eyes. I want to brush it away, but he stands and wipes his hands on his trousers before I pluck up the courage to touch him. He pulls me to my feet and holds up an old black jacket. It's huge and I'm awash in fabric, but it's warm. I pull it closed and jam an old beanie on my head.

"You said women don't come here, but these shoes look too small for you or your friend." I can't help my curiosity.

"Women don't. No one's been here with us since Sasha's sister, Polina." He opens the door and walks into the snow, head down and shoulders hunched.

The light is fading now, and the trees stand like sentinels. The energy between us ebbs again as he withdraws into himself, marching into the woods without me.

I trail behind him. My feet crunch in the snow, leaving small indentations that walk alongside his giant footprints as he strides through the trees. "Did Polina grow out of snow-ball fights and fun in the woods?"

"She died," he says without turning around.

He continues deeper into the woods, the eerie white light reflecting off the birch branches around him. I watch his back as he moves through the trees. There's something he's not telling me, but I don't have the courage to ask. If we're only together for now, I don't have the right.

The snow is deep and it's hard to keep pace with his long strides as I start after him. "Wait for me. I don't want to get lost," I call as he disappears between the trunks.

The woods are a silent etching in monochrome, the image stark against the fading afternoon sunlight. Even the trees are black-and-white.

He turns and stands under a spindly birch tree, watching me with a shuttered face. I catch up and reach out to touch him, but I drop my arm in mid-air. The snow wraps us in silence. Even the animals are hiding, and the cold has silenced the birds. There's no sound but our awkward breathing.

Vadim reaches for my hand, which hangs limply at my side. "I'm sorry. Let's catch the last of the light. I'll take you to the river, and then I've lit the banya so we can warm up."

"The banya?"

"Another new Russian word. It's a sauna." He points back at a small pine shed nestling against the eaves of the house. It's the first time I've seen the house in daylight. The wooden slats are painted a pale green, and the eaves are edged in scalloped white boards. It looks like a place Hansel and Gretel or Snow White might have lived in—a fairy tale cottage in the woods.

"Where did you learn such good English?" I ask, trying to lighten the mood.

"Disney movies."

"Really?" I breathe in disbelief.

"Nope, not really. Summers in Brighton Beach." He takes my hand and leads me into the trees, the snow crunching underneath our feet. He drops it again as he shoves his hands into his pockets.

I want him to put his arm around me like he did last night, but I've touched a nerve by asking the wrong question, so I keep my eyes on the snowy ground and trail after him.

"Brighton Beach. Isn't that near Manhattan?"

"Coney Island, yeah. Had a . . . mentor, I guess you could call him, who moved there, and I spent a few teenage summers with him. Guelman. You met him last night. I was a useful pair of hands in his . . . business in Little Odessa. It's in the US, but it feels like Russia."

"That guy is seriously creepy."

"Well, they don't call him the Night Governor for nothing."

Vadim stops as the trees open onto a winding river, its waters frozen hard and covered with snow. The wide banks slope down to the water, and animal tracks dot their edges. Further down, smoke curls from a cluster of houses beyond the next stand of trees.

"The Night Governor? That sounds like something from a video game or *Lord of the Rings*."

"He doesn't play games," Vadim says, striding ahead of me and not inviting further questions.

As the dwindling light reflects off the snow, I wonder what questions are safe. I saw the way people looked at him last night, and it feels like my words are full of unexploded ordnance. I want him to want me again, so I don't ask any more difficult questions.

"So how did you learn English if everyone around you spoke Russian?" I puff out as I catch up with him. Cold air stings my lungs with each breath.

"I wanted to. If you want something enough, you can make it happen. Just depends on how much you're willing to sacrifice for it." His breath forms a cloud between us as he looks down at me.

Catching hold of his elbow, I tug on it for leverage, and he crooks his arm so I can thread mine through it and walk at the same pace. We pick our way along the frozen river. The land is flat and the sky wide and white. The sun slants in wide, pale beams through the gray clouds. His manner is thawing, but there's still a chill between us. I chatter to fill the silence.

"That's something I understand. I always wanted to sing, so I put everything into it. Playing at clubs, finding people to gig with, hanging out in sleeping bags in the back of a rusting old van."

"So what do you want now?" Vadim looks down at me.

"To free myself from my management. I don't want to be

74

tied to Jimmy forever, but I've got a three-album deal, so I'll have to record what he wants and survive the experience. I'm only one album in." I lift my shoulders in resignation. There's no point hoping that anyone else will get me out of this mess. "I sold my soul to the devil when I started working with the label."

"Selling your soul to the devil? Now that's something I understand. But if you've got two more albums, it's not for eternity."

We stop at a copse of trees where someone has carved a bench out of wood. It's piled with a foot of snow, so Vadim bends to brush it away before sitting down and patting his leg.

"Sit here or you'll get wet and cold." He grasps my waist and pulls me down.

I gingerly lower myself to perch on his thigh. As soon as I do, he wraps an arm around my waist and lets me rest against his chest, but I'm prepared to spring up if he changes his mind.

"So, who did you sell your soul to?" I soak up his warmth and listen to the thud of his heart.

"You met him. I didn't know I had anything to sell when I traded my life. It's too late for me now."

I force a weak smile and another change of subject. "So what do you want?"

"To get out of Russia. The place is failing and there are easier pickings in America. I want opportunity, and the States is where the money is for people like us. Plenty of crime in Moscow, but the people who run the country have a stranglehold on the proceeds. If you want to make money as a person like me, you need to go to a society where people have grown complacent and forgotten how to fight. You barely have to work to steal from people in the US. You've made it so easy that we just have to reach out and take it."

I laugh nervously. "So we're all idiots, then?"

"Not exactly." His blue eyes scan my face. "But you're softer. It's what I like about you." He grips my hand through thick gloves and sighs.

I squeeze his hand back and nudge him until he slings an arm around my shoulder, circling my body, and we watch the sun sink lower on the horizon. The smell of wood smoke comforts me. I can't hear voices, but we aren't totally alone.

Vadim points toward the rooftops as the snow turns blue and gray in the fading light. Pinks and yellows streak the blank canvas where the sun dapples through the trees.

"Didn't bring skates, which is a shame. It's fun if you walk a bit further down, past the bend in the river." His eyes lighten as he changes the subject. "They usually clear the ice near the river. I wish I could take you."

"I don't know how to skate." I watch the line of red where the sun hits the horizon, relishing this closeness.

"I'd hold you up so you didn't fall." His voice rumbles in my ear, and I can't resist the temptation to press a kiss against his jaw. He sighs and stands, setting me on my feet. "Come on. Let's head back while it's still light. The banya should be hot by now. I lit it before you woke up, and it'll make us both feel better. Nothing like getting naked and rolling in the snow."

"Naked?"

He throws his head back and laughs. "That's the bit you get stuck on? Not rolling in the snow? Yes, naked. You can't enjoy a banya with your clothes on. You're lucky I haven't started cutting birch twigs to beat you with. Then again . . ."

He pulls a knife from his pocket and walks to a nearby tree, cutting a few branches off with a long, curved blade.

"What are those for?" My eyes widen.

"Stimulating your circulation. What else?" He grasps my hand, our arms swinging as he leads me back through the trees, the birch twigs trailing on the ground. I fixate on the movement of the branches through the snow.

"Are you really going to beat me with those?" I look up at him, and he grins wolfishly.

"Only if you want me to."

CHAPTER THIRTEEN

Kesera

When we reach the door of the little wooden shack, Vadim drops the branches and a smile crinkles his eyes at the corners. "Actually, these don't have the leaves on, so they're not right. I just thought it would be funny to worry you."

I step inside the shed, and heat and the smell of pine hit me. As I pull off the beanie and shake out my curls, Vadim strips off his jacket. He reaches behind him to pull his sweatshirt and t-shirt off in one move, leaving his scars, tattoos, and acres of bronzed skin on display.

"There might be some dry twigs in the banya." He looks at me questioningly. "If you're into that sort of thing."

"I don't really know what I'm into. Not much experience to go on. But I'm into you."

After shrugging off the heavy coat, I hand it to him. He hangs it up and sits on the bench, pulling off his shoes and socks. I stand before him, sweating inside my clothes as he sheds his jeans and reveals long, muscular legs dusted with hair. His skin still has the echoes of a summer tan, and the lines of swim trunks mark his upper thighs. I turn my head and face the pegs lining the wall.

"Shy?" Vadim comes to stand behind me, and his body heat overpowers the warm glow coming from the closed pine door of the sauna next to us. Leaving me my modesty, he stands behind me, and I hear a rustle of fabric as his boxers land on the floor.

"Very shy." I drop my head and look at my feet as I toe off the wet snow boots. It's like a game of strip poker where I could win with a poor hand because I'm wearing so many pairs of socks.

Sensing my nerves, Vadim crouches behind me and murmurs, "Put your hand on the wall for balance and give me your foot."

I lift my leg and he peels away the sock layers from one foot and then the other. He reaches for the belt holding up my sweatpants and slowly undoes the buckle, his hands sliding beneath my waistline to caress the skin of my hips. His thumbs draw soothing circles, and there's something erotic and sensual about being undressed by a man I can't see.

Sucking in a sharp breath, I lift my arms so he can pull up my t-shirt and sweater to press a soft kiss against the base of my spine. He's kneeling behind me naked as he removes my clothes, but he's the one in control.

I press my hands into the pine wall, my fingers tracing the knots in the wood as he lowers the sweatpants and I step out of them. I'm not wearing panties, so I'm bare beneath all the layers of clothing. His hands stroke up and down my legs, tracing soft circles under the cheeks of my ass, but not demanding anything more. I'm melting like the snow dusting the clothes pooled on the floor.

He raises my shirt an inch higher and presses his lips against the base of my spine again. I sigh softly, aware that

I'm bare from the waist down. His nose and forehead press against my lower back. He stops and rests his head against me, his hair tickling my skin as he allows me to get used to feeling this close to him. I widen my stance in invitation, but he pauses.

"You still with me, zolotaya?" he whispers through kisses against my back.

"Hmmm," I sigh, a cocktail of nerves and excitement fizzing inside me.

I want him.

I want him so much I ache with it.

So I push the nerves down, knowing how little time we have. He must take my humming as consent for more because his hands slide up the sides of my body and slip around me to circle my breasts. Featherlight touches skirt the area where I most want his hands—and his mouth. I rise on my toes, widening my legs a little further.

"You look so fucking pretty like that. Bend a little lower, baby, and show me."

I press my hands into the wall until I'm bent at ninety degrees.

His hands ghost around my breasts, stroking down my body until he reaches the delta of my thighs. He pushes my legs wider, and knowing I'm on display for a man I can't see sends a gush of arousal to my molten core.

"Please," I say as his hands stroke me gently from my thighs to my tits, avoiding all the good parts and making me crazy. "God, touch me please."

The hypnotic movement of his hands continues. I bend lower, rising on my toes, turned on by the knowledge that he can see exactly what he's doing to me.

"Keep still for me like a good girl, or I'll have to beat you with those birch twigs," he says as his hands finally cup my breasts, caressing and squeezing until he finds my nipples. He rubs and pulls on them gently. When he twists one, I moan. "Do you like that?"

His hair tickles my spine as his mouth brushes soft kisses against my vertebrae. I push against him, rocking back and forth and begging for more contact, for more anything. His hand drifts lower and slides into my folds, finding me soaked for him.

"Zolotaya. Is this all for me? You're so wet," he murmurs in that low, dark voice.

"God, yes, it's for you," I say. I push against him, wanting his fingers deeper inside me. Wanting his fingers *every*where. I want him to break me apart and put me together again.

He stands then, pulling the remaining clothes over my head and spinning me in his arms until we're chest to stomach, his hard length pushing between us. He lifts me and pulls open the door to the sauna.

Once inside, he sits on a pine bench and deposits me in his lap. His hard, hot length presses against my thigh as I wrap my arms around his neck and trail soft kisses over every inch of him I can reach. He tastes of the woods—salt and pine resin. I kiss his collarbone but avoid meeting his eyes. A dark rumble vibrates his chest as he laughs and wraps his arms tighter around me, our skin slipping against each other in the heat.

He lifts me away and tilts me back so I can look up at him, and I fall into his pale-blue stare. "Shy again, zolotaya?"

I feel the words vibrate under his breastbone as much as I hear them.

"You've got nothing to be shy about. You're fucking beautiful."

He kisses me, lips sipping at me like he wants to savor the taste before his tongue slides into my mouth, making me drunk on him. I pull my arms tighter around him and dig my fingers into his scalp, drawing a moan from deep inside him.

Hot lips slide lower against my neck, and I arch against him as he finally reaches my nipple. Every time he sucks deeper or scrapes his teeth against the bud, he draws pulses of sunlight out of me. I buck against him and cry out as he bends me backward against his arm, mouth painting streaks of fire against my tits, sucking one nipple and then the other until I'm burning like the air around us.

"I love these little tits. So fucking perfect, the way they sit up and beg for my mouth," he says, leaning down to devour me again as his other hand parts my legs and his finger thrusts deep inside me.

I'm wordless now, arching against him, bucking in his lap, riding his fingers as my whole body flames like a Catherine wheel. My core pulls tighter, and heat spins me into a dizzying whirl.

His dark voice curses in Russian before he says, "Fuck yes, ride my hand, zolotaya. Take what you want. Use me."

These words push me over the edge, and my core squeezes his fingers as I open my mouth in a soundless cry. Tears seep between my lashes as his fingers stroke gently between my legs and his mouth meets mine in a soft kiss. I keep my eyes tightly closed as his mouth owns me and comforts me, his tongue stroking mine.

The taste of mint and pine rush to my head like vodka. His strong arms cradle me in his lap. I've never felt so cherished. Or so wiped out. Spent. Boneless. Still floating in the heat.

His voice pulls me out of my trance. "Hey, beautiful. Open your eyes." That ice blue gaze shines down at me, his eyes warmer than I've ever seen them. "See? Nothing to be shy about."

I trace his cheekbones in wonderment. The cut line of his jaw, the strong brow, the way a scar breaks through the line of one eyebrow and travels down his left cheek. The imperfection only serves to enhance his beauty.

"You told me to use you, when I . . ." My thoughts fade as I look down and press a kiss to his chest where beads of sweat roll between his pecs, skin glistening in the heat. I'm losing myself in his body as much as avoiding his eyes.

He puts his finger under my chin again. "Give me your eyes. You've got eyes like the woods in spring. I can see a whole season in them."

His warm stare bathes me in something I haven't felt from a man before.

Acceptance.

And it makes me suddenly brave.

"I don't want to use you," I say. "I want to give you everything. Everything you've given me. I want to give it all to you."

"You will, zolotaya." He smiles. "You will."

Chapter Fourteen

Vadim

I can't stand it anymore. The way she looks at me. Her curls are damp and her whole body is covered in a fine sheen of sweat as she gazes at me like she's drunk.

Kesera turns to me with a smile so bright it could make me snow-blind, and I pull her to her feet and balance her against my body as I carry her to the door. She sucks on my skin and slides her wet pussy against me. If I don't dump her in the snow in the next five seconds, I'm going to lose it.

"Hold on!" I shout.

I open the door to the icy darkness and run into the snow, falling to my back and rolling her on top of me. She shrieks as I roll her to the side and land between her spread legs, the snow at her back and the heat of my erection cradled in her molten core.

"You bastard, it's so cold," she says.

The icy air clears my head and cools my blood.

Kesera scrambles out from under me and hurls a snowball

over her shoulder as she skips back to the heat of the sauna, a naked, laughing vision.

After another round of warming up and cooling off in the darkness outside, I've gotten some kind of control of myself. But more than that, I feel light. Joyful.

We're kicking off our clothes and boots, and grinning at each other like a pair of children by the time we get back to the house. Maybe it was rolling in the snow without clothes on or throwing snowballs at each other on the way back from the banya.

She shakes her hair out of the beanie and throws the snow-encrusted hat at me. "Catch."

It flies across the room but I let it fall, pulling her onto my lap instead, inhaling kisses from her mouth like air. I haven't been this boy since I was nine and got into the orphanage with Sasha. It's like wearing clothes that don't quite fit, making me feel pressed out of shape in my own skin.

I lean down and swallow her kisses whole, thrusting my tongue into her mouth, knocking back her little moans like shots of vodka. "I need to fuck you now, zolotaya."

She stares up at me with a dazed look as I carry her to the bedroom and drop her on the bed. I'm surprised as she tears at her clothes, stripping off the layers until she's kneeling in front of me. Her damp bronze-and-golden curls float around her shoulders, her tiny breasts peeking up at me through her hair. Her pretty nipples have taken on a deep plum color, sore where I've sucked and bitten them till she cried out.

Seeing where my eyes drop, she pulls her hair over her shoulders, places her hands underneath her tits, and cups them, though there's not enough to fill her hands. She lifts them like an offering and arches her back.

I don't move. I want to fall on her like a wild animal and bite and mark her skin, so I hold still, quivering as I listen to her breathe. She lies back against the pillows and spreads her legs, her glistening pink pussy opening like a flower in front of me.

"Vadim, I need you. I want you so much." She's opened her body like a present, stripping off the wrapping and gifting it to me. Her fingertips twist her nipples.

And it's too much.

I don't think. Not about her pleasure, not about a condom, not about a thing. My mind is a blank field of fresh snow as I fall on her and push deep into her wet heat. She tenses, adjusting to me, and I still above her.

"You're so big," she says.

I lean down and suck her neck, marking her skin like the animal I am. "No, baby, you're so tiny. But take me, my love. You can do it for me, can't you?"

Her hair tickles my forehead as she nods.

"Tell me."

"Yes. All of you. I want everything."

With her permission, I let go and rip into her, slamming into her tiny body again and again. I'm a fucking animal, making her scream as I bottom out inside her, pressing all the way and tearing another strange noise from her throat.

"Christ, yes, take it. Take all of me," I shout in Russian.

She shouldn't understand, yet she does, twining her limbs around me like ivy and pulling me closer than I've been to anyone.

I must be hurting her, but I can't stop. I want to eat her alive. Kissing, sucking, biting. I want to mark every inch of her as I push into her.

The sounds she makes. Keening noises. Each time I hit the heart of her, she breathes out a soft little mew, like a kitten. It sends me over the edge, and I bury my face in her neck, inhaling the scent of summer flowers as I get drunk on her. I groan into her shoulder and bite the soft skin of her neck as I wind my arms under her tiny body and lift her by the waist. I raise her hips so that I can sling her ankles over my shoulders and get deeper.

Her hands grip the sheets as I move faster, harder. The room echoes with the sounds of the bed banging against the wall and her breathless gasps as I drive into her like a monster. She's gripping the headboard and pushing back against me, urging me deeper. It makes me want to break her apart, but it's me who's breaking as her back bows and her pussy contracts around me, pulling my soul out of me as white light explodes behind my eyelids. Snow, ice, nothingness. I'm nowhere and everywhere as I collapse on top of her, crushing her tiny body with my weight.

I move to pull away from her, horrified at the way I've brutalized her, but her arms hold me tight. The fingernails of one hand dig into my shoulder as her other hand winds through the hair at the nape of my neck.

"Not yet, darling," she whispers in my ear. "I feel so close to you. A few more minutes."

I don't meet her eyes yet. I'm too stunned to speak, let alone look at her, so I balance my weight on my forearms and breathe into the perfume that rises off the skin between her neck and shoulder. Her hands map rivers and forests over my scalp, and she presses her mouth against my hair.

Lifting up, I stare down at her in stunned wonder. "Are you okay, zolotaya?" I ask, fearful of the response, but her smile rips a hole in my chest. She looks lit up from within.

"I've never felt better in my life."

She pushes my shoulder and I roll onto my back, taking her with me and looking up at her. A red crescent marks her shoulder where I've bitten her. I don't speak, just trace the edge with my thick fingers, a question in my eyes as I scan her irises. I'm close enough to see the marks of bronze and gold that break up the green. Even her eyes are golden tonight.

She's like a woman transformed as she crawls over me, pushing her tits against my mouth, nudging my lips with the berry of her nipple, willing me to swallow her down again. I wrap my mouth around her and suckle, drawing more mewling noises from her.

"I want to come again. You make me crazy," she says, rubbing against me and purring like a cat.

I suck her nipples until the skin has gone a deeper shade, devouring her tits until she's writhing against me. This time, I can go slower, so I lift her until all of her melting softness lies against my cock.

Her hands rest on my shoulders as she rises and lowers herself onto me with a soft sigh. Pushing her down slowly, I grasp her hips and stop her movement as I look up at the goddess impaled on my cock. Her hair surrounds her like a golden cloud, but she's covered in red marks where my mouth and fingers have bitten into that unmarked skin.

"Zolotaya, use me to make yourself feel good. I don't want to hurt you." I pull her down on me, bottoming out against her cervix as my finger traces a bite mark underneath her breast.

She grasps my hand and draws it up to her mouth, sucking my finger to the back of her throat before she lets it slide out.

"I. Will. Not. Use. You." She leans down to punctuate each word with a kiss before sliding up and down on my hard length. "I want to show you how I feel about you. I want to give you everything you gave me. All the pleasure."

I look up as she rides me with her head thrown back and her hips moving to the rhythm of a song only she can hear. I pour myself into her. All my worries and fears dissolve into her tight heat as she collapses on top of my chest and I pull her closer.

I'm not sure when we fall asleep or when we wake up. I only know the night is a symphony of lips and hands, finding every corner of each other's bodies, twisting each other into every shape we can to get closer than we've ever been to anyone. I drift into darkness amid a haze of pleasure, more content than I've been in years . . .

Then the sound of a banging door tears me from sleep, and I jackknife awake.

Chapter Fifteen

Vadim

"Wake up, asshole." Sasha's voice echoes from the porch, and the screen door rattles as his heavy footsteps thud past the bedroom and into the living room.

A heavy sigh seeps from my lungs as I pull a t-shirt over my head and look longingly at the warm, sleeping body under the covers next to me. A bronze leg tipped with pink toenails pokes from the nest of blankets.

I circle her toe idly with my thumb, but she doesn't stir. I press a kiss to her cheek, breathing in the scent of flowers and looking at the way her eyelashes cast shadows on her sharp cheekbones.

I pull on some boxers and stride into the living room, where Sasha sprawls on the sofa, a pile of takeout boxes from our favorite Georgian restaurant stacked on the table next to him. The delicious scent of cheese and toasted bread wafts from one of the boxes.

"Khachapuri?" I ask, pointing to the pizza box.

"Probably cold by now. I had a long drive in from the city." Sasha glares up at me, his face thunderous.

"Why the cavalry?" Cupping the back of my neck, I rub my eyes blearily. "What time is it?'

"It's midday, asshole." He shoves the box toward me with his foot, and I collapse onto the old chair opposite him, a spring coil digging into my leg from under the stack of Uzbek blankets we piled onto the threadbare furniture.

I open a box and shovel a slice of the cooling Georgian pizza into my mouth, watching Sasha quizzically. He doesn't usually turn up unannounced when I'm here, but then again, we're usually alone here together, grilling shashlik, playing cards, shooting the shit.

"Where's the fire?" I ask. "I thought I had the rest of the day. I've got to get her to the airport at about five thirty, right?" *I want more time. I need more time with her. This can't be over yet*, I think as I scan the dark ridge of his brows over the takeout boxes. Sasha is spoiling for a fight, which is never fun for those around him. "What happened? Do we need to pack up and leave now? Is something going down in Moscow?"

He shakes his head. "Nothing you didn't already know about. I think Antonov and the Night Governor hashed things out, so the China-Russia trade route should be open by next month." He reaches down for more khachapuri and jams the slowly congealing cheese bread into his mouth. He continues, talking around a mouthful of food. "The Night Governor hasn't decided what he wants to do with us foot soldiers yet. I'll probably be in the ass end of nowhere, but maybe you'll get New York and Dima will get London."

"Well, as long as we all get out of here, it's all good," I say, leaning back in the chair and watching him. "So what are you doing here?"

"Why? Haven't you finished playing happy families?"

"Who's playing happy families? She's asleep. We fucked. I

spent the night with her. What's the big deal?" I wave my second slice of khachapuri at him, hoping I'll feel more coherent with some food inside me. Sasha is my best friend and I'd die for him, as I've proved on more than one occasion, but sometimes he gets on my last nerve. "Since when are you so interested in my love life?"

He snorts. "Love life? You've never had one. You fuck girls like Oksana and it's nothing for me to concern myself with, but this . . . ?" His eyes stray to the bedroom door, which remains shut. "That guy your little songbird came out with is a grade A asshole. Since you decided to play white knight, he followed me around the whole night, talking about which stars on his roster I can hire. As if I'm interested in American pop stars. I'd half a mind to pistol-whip him to shut him up, but I don't need the drama." Sasha stares out of the window, mulling something over. He gestures toward the bedroom door. "You don't need the drama either."

"What drama, Sasha? I've been here less than twenty-four hours. I'm having some fun."

I bend down to sift through the takeout boxes. Rolls of eggplant, pomegranates, and walnut paste. He's brought all the good stuff, and it makes me wish I could just picnic alone with Kesera instead of deal with him.

"Good of you to bring us both lunch, but there's a lot of food here."

"I asked Dima to come along too, and maybe his brother. Not sure if Marat can make it, but we need to discuss our next steps."

"Now?"

"Why not?" He points at the closed bedroom door. "You got something better to do?"

"Well, actually, Sasha . . . since you mention it . . ." I let my voice trail off as I stare at him. "And I'll ask you again. Why are you so interested in who I fuck?"

He pulls out his gun and throws it down on the table as he glares at me. "Because you're not just fucking her, are you? You've brought her out here where we come as a family, and you're doing what? Playing mommies and daddies?"

And this, ladies and gentleman, is why I can't have something good. Because there's always a complication and something always goes wrong. I just didn't imagine in a hundred years that the complication would be Sasha. He's always had my back.

I run my fingers through my hair, pulling at it as I look at the shut door. "Don't be a dick. I brought her back with me because I needed a break." I point at the takeout boxes and try to make light of this situation. "Sometimes you want shashlik, sometimes you want Georgian food. Maybe I just wanted a taste of something different. Why are you so wound up about this? She's going home tonight."

I might wish she wasn't, but if I'd been entertaining any ideas of seeing her again, Sasha's stormy mood and petulant behavior quickly disabuse me of the notion. I don't need to drag a nice girl into our drama, and if we're opening up new trade routes, there's bound to be drama.

"What is the Night Governor doing? If you're on edge, then there's more." I jam a roll of eggplant into my mouth and chew on it, crunching on a pomegranate seed. The sour juice explodes on my tongue as I grind it between my teeth and watch Sasha.

"He's a fucker."

"Guelman? Come on. You don't rise from being a professor to controlling the Moscow underworld unless you're a fucker."

Sasha scowls at me and pulls out his curved knife, spinning it in his hands. It's a nervous tic. "He's going to fuck us."

"What?"

"Leave us all here. Pull the money out and leave us to face

the music. We've got to get out. All of us. If we're out of Russia, we'll have a chance to build a power base that doesn't rely on him. I don't trust him, and I need you to focus."

When Sasha said he wanted me in the States, I had a brief moment imagining a few more nights like this one, but let's face it. Wherever she lives, it'll be a long way from Little Odessa and Brighton Beach, which is where I'm going to land. We'll be worlds apart, even when we're in the same country.

Kesera had looked at me like I'd placed the stars in the sky above her instead of spending most of last week chasing some Georgian gangsters who'd ripped off the Night Governor around a series of sleazy strip clubs in downtown Moscow. I tracked down the bastards who'd been skimming a five percent cut off the club proceeds.

I shot the manager who skimmed the money, but I'd kept his colleagues alive to send a message. I shot the first one in the ankle, the second one in the knee, and the third one in the thigh. They'd have matching limps to show off around town so that everyone knew what happened when you crossed us.

I don't enjoy that part of the business, but you have to send a signal. If you mess with any of us, you mess with all of us. And it will cost you. I think they got the message loud and clear.

The girl sleeping in the next room is so damn beautiful inside and out, and I wish I had longer, but she isn't part of this world. She's a dream. Sasha is the brother who will fight by my side through the nightmares. I owe him everything.

He pulls a stick of wood from the basket near the fire and begins whittling it with sharp strokes, the blade sending splinters across the floor.

"Come on, brother. You know I've got your back." I lean over and point a finger at him. "You were the one that told me fucking would clear my head. I was just following orders," I add with a grin.

"You weren't. You're not just fucking her."

"Come on. It's been a day. What are you talking about?"

"The only woman we've ever brought here is Polina." His words fall like bullets, digging into the floorboards and ricocheting off the walls.

The death of Sasha's sister sits between us in the silence. I release a long sigh and nod at him as he whittles the stick into the figure of a man before snapping off its head with his fingers.

"Who's that?" I ask. "Guelman?"

His lips twist into a rueful half smile. "Don't we both wish."

I don't tell him it was a dick move to bring up Polina. I'm sure he knows. We're bound by cords of death and missed opportunities. There aren't many certainties in this life. Sasha's loyalty is one of them.

Another is that anything good ends up like the snow in Moscow by the end of February—a gray slush encrusted with grime that hides things you'd rather not know about. Then it melts, only to freeze again into sheets of black ice that deliver nothing but broken bones and black eyes.

He's right. It's intoxicating to be so close to someone, and I let myself get carried away because it felt so damn perfect, but it's risky. And I'm getting *too* close.

CHAPTER SIXTEEN

Kesera

L ow, masculine Russian voices drift from the next room as I open my eyes. A soft, pale light bathes the room. The snow makes everything more beautiful. Or maybe it's the way I'm feeling.

My body is sore but humming and alive. Muscles I didn't know I had, stretching and burning. Red bite marks mar my skin, as do the bruises where heavy fingers gripped me, but I feel so energized that I could skate down a frozen river in my bare feet or take flight and whirl through the trees with one jump.

The door opens and Vadim steps in. I smile and hold out my arms to him, but slowly let them fall to the sheets as he stands at the door and watches me silently. I wait for him to make a move toward me, my hands starting to knot the bedclothes to stop from reaching for him again. Then I sit up slowly and pull the sheet around me to cover my body.

"Party's over, zolotaya. Sasha's here. I'll have to meet with the guys. I wanted . . . I'm sorry." Vadim stares out of the

97

window, unable to meet my eyes, and his shoulders droop as he shakes his head. "It doesn't matter what I wanted."

He looks like he's weighed down by something. I don't want to add to his burden, so I smile brightly at him and reach for the t-shirt tangled in the pile of bedding.

"S'okay. I get it." I pull the t-shirt over my head. If someone's going to give you the brush off, then it's better if you've got clothes on to face them. I cast my eyes about for more clothes to wear but come up short, so I pull the covers over my legs. "Can I go clean up?"

Vadim steps toward me, sits on the bed heavily, and resumes looking out the window as he reaches for my hand. He avoids my eyes as he threads his fingers through mine, but he brings our joined hands to his lips and presses a soft kiss against my knuckles.

"Sorry, zolotaya. I'll get you a towel and when you come out of the bathroom, there'll be guys outside, so get dressed."

He walks to the cupboard, pulls out a couple of threadbare towels that feel like cardboard, and comes to stand in front of me, throwing the towels on the bed as he takes my face in his hands. My eyelids shutter and his lips feather across them before landing softly on my mouth and teasing across my lips.

"Zolotaya," he whispers. "I've got to go."

I slip from the bedroom to the bathroom next door with my head down, trying not to catch the eyes of any of the men. I take a quick shower to the sounds of more footsteps and voices. Clearly, there won't be much privacy.

When I pull myself together, I edge into the cramped living room. Four guys lounge over the old sofas, and aside from Vadim, I only recognize one of them. Sasha, who was talking to Jimmy last night, glowers at me and nods. A younger guy with black hair doesn't meet my eye—he's too busy playing a handheld computer game—and a tall, burly man who resembles the younger computer player talks to Vadim.

The burly man strides over, holding out his hand. I reach out for a handshake, but he picks up my fingers and kisses them. "I take it you are Vadim's little songbird. No wonder he hid you away from all of us. Never mind, we've found you now."

He grins, but there's no malice in it.

Despite that, Vadim slides past him and wraps an arm around my waist, marking his territory. "And since she is *my* little songbird, she'll be with me," he says to the smiling joker, who holds both of his hands up and backs away, shaking his head and laughing.

"I'm Dimitri, but you can call me Dima."

Sasha looks up at me from the coffee table and pushes some takeout boxes toward us. "My friends call me Sasha, but you can call me Alexander," he says, glaring at me. The dislike that I felt the night we met has grown into outright hostility.

Vadim's arms tighten around my midriff, and his low voice rumbles in my ear. "Ignore him. He's in a foul mood and spoiling for a fight."

"Something you want to share with us, Vadim?" Sasha sneers.

"Sure, Sasha. I told her you're an asshole and she should ignore you." Vadim pulls me across the room and onto his knee, then begins piling food onto a plate.

I'm not sure I can eat now. The atmosphere in the room is curdling my stomach. I've walked in on an unspoken conversation, and I sense that Sasha isn't happy about me being here. Dima seems to think the tension is funny, and the younger guy remains glued to his game.

"If I'm in the way, I don't mind taking a cab," I say.

"There aren't any cabs out here. We're miles from town," Vadim bites out.

"Sure there are," Sasha says. "I'll bet there's some old guy in the village who wouldn't mind earning a few rubles. We can send Marat out to look."

Vadim's fingers dig into my thighs. "Not funny, Sasha. Marat would probably stir up some trouble by saying the wrong thing, and I don't need our neighbors playing taxi service. I'll take her and we'll leave now. If these discussions need to happen tonight, we can talk when I'm back from Sheremetyevo. I won't be long. There's not much dacha traffic on the road at this time of year."

I nod at the rest of the men, grateful to get into the bedroom as Vadim produces my suitcase and leather backpack. At least Sasha got my stuff from Jimmy, but I have the feeling I've stumbled into something I shouldn't have. There was a gun on the table, and I'm sure I saw a holster on one of the other guys. Whatever they were talking about, I probably don't want to hear it.

CHAPTER SEVENTEEN

Kesera

The drive to the airport is silent but not uncomfortable. Trees flash past, the black marks on the birch trunks creating a hypnotic pattern. I sink into a trance as I watch them go by.

After about an hour, Vadim switches the radio on and a mournful voice echoes between us.

"This is beautiful but sad." I lean forward in my seat to concentrate. "What do the words mean?"

Vadim leans over and grasps my hand, pressing it against his mouth before he answers. "How I love you. How I fear you. It seems I met you in an unlucky hour."

"Does this apply to us?" I say, trying to frame a bigger question I'm too afraid to ask.

"Well, it's about a man with dark eyes, and my eyes are blue." He hums the refrain under his breath as the miles of birch trees zip by, their pale trunks white against the gray sky.

I wish I had more time with him, and the questions jostle for space in my head.

Can I see you again?

Would you like to fly halfway across the world and come to one of my concerts?

Vadim's voice breaks the silence. "Will you be okay?"

I shrug and smile, though it doesn't quite reach my eyes. "I'm used to flying."

His deep voice vibrates in the small space, and his fingers grip my hand. "That wasn't what I meant. Who will protect you?"

I close my eyes and soak up the comfort of his touch, babbling nervously to fill the space. "Thank you for looking after me. No one has done that for a while. When I started out in Nashville, I always had the boys around."

"Boys?" Tension radiates from his stilled fingers.

"The guys in my band. Jimmy cut them loose."

"Pretty little songbird." Vadim keeps his eyes on the road but lifts his hand to dust his fingers down my cheek, the tenderness of the gesture at odds with his size and the life he must live. "Perhaps you can get them back. We all need someone in our corner, as long as you can trust them not to manhandle you like that bastard who's managing you."

It must be nerves because I blurt out, "Stevie, our bassist, once told me that the idea of sleeping with me made him laugh." I clamp my hand over my eyes and screw them shut. "God, I'm embarrassing myself."

"He was lying," his dark voice says definitively as his finger strokes back and forth, sending shivers along my nerve endings.

"I doubt it." I roll my eyes at Vadim.

He's surrounded by curvy Amazon women, and I bet he takes dozens of them home. I've known him less than twenty-four hours and I've known the way women look at him like they want to eat him up.

"I don't doubt it for a minute. Did Stevie get a record contract, or did they just want you?"

"They just wanted me."

Vadim laughs, taking away his touch and focusing on the road as the trees give way to grimy buildings. We must be almost there.

I watch his profile—the blade of his nose, the faint dusting of stubble on the hard line of his jaw—and wish I could kiss him again, but he's driving and doing that thing where he shuts off.

"You need to believe in yourself or you will get eaten alive. Men will always circle you."

I sigh and mull over what he said as the parking lots and the gray tarmac come into view as we near the terminal building. "Honestly, I'm just not most guys' type."

Vadim leans over and pats my hand as he parks, asking me to stay put, and then he circles the car and holds the door open for me. I step into the harsh winter air, and he cages me against the car with his arms. I feel tiny but protected.

"You are so damned beautiful, and the fact you can't see it makes you more alluring. I promise you everyone can see your beauty, though maybe not everyone is brave enough to reach for it." He leans down and kisses me. His lips are warm against the icy air, and the burn of his mouth makes me feel dizzy and alive.

I nurse the faint hope this could be more as he pulls me against his side and wheels my suitcase into the private jet terminal. I was excited to travel by private jet, but like most first-class amenities in airports, it's all bland and soulless. Everything is greige, that colorless hue that seeks not to offend. At least it's quiet, and I have a few final moments to drink Vadim in with my eyes as I sit down.

You could cut glass with the angles of his cheekbones. I want to map the lines of his face with my fingers and memorize every ridge and dip of his muscles with my hands. To press my lips against every inch of his scars.

But I'm out of time. And inspiration.

Stuck for words, I stare down at my boots. I was wearing them the first time I saw him, when he walked in on me and Jimmy, and now I have to leave him behind and return to a world where there's no one in my corner. I haven't felt held and so wrapped up in the comfort of being cared for and seen since my parents were alive.

"Zolotaya." Vadim squats in front of me so that I'm staring directly into the pale fire of his irises, searching for some future I wish was there. Did that last kiss mean anything?

"I wish we had more time," I whisper against his lips as he presses his mouth against mine. His kiss is so soft. How can such a hard man touch me so gently while the people who are supposed to protect me are harsh and twisted?

"I do too, golden songbird." His voice is low and soft, caressing me. "I do too."

"Will you ever come to America?" I let the question fade away, lacking the courage to ask for more.

"Maybe." He gets up and sits down next to me on the bank of chairs, putting his arm around me and drawing me to his wide chest. I rest my head against him and listen to the steady thud of his heartbeat. "I might."

And for a moment, I feel a bright flare of hope.

He balances his chin on my hair, and his breath dances across my scalp. "But if I did, my life would be a world away from yours. I wouldn't want to draw you into all my chaos."

"If you did. We could try. Maybe. I wouldn't mind. Do you think we could?" I draw circles against his chest with my fingers, and my words spin in circles that match them.

His retort is quick, cutting my musing short. "No,

zolotaya. I don't. You don't know what you're asking." His words land like stones at the bottom of a well.

"You make me feel safe."

His laughter reverberates against me. "Christ. I shouldn't."

"But you do. You don't know the music business. It's full of creeps like Jimmy. The power lies with pervy old guys in suits."

His arms tighten around me. "You think men like me can't send a signal to little worms like him? He's a coward, and I have contacts in America. Why do you think I came to the airport with you? I won't let him leave Moscow without a little chat about how things are going to work from now on."

I sit up and trace the harsh lines of his face with my eyes. "Then why? If you care that much, why can't we be something more?" I whisper.

He grips my arms and gives me a gentle shake. "Because this was beautiful. Wasn't it? You felt it too."

The weight of his gaze sears into me, and I nod, tasting the emotion on my tongue, feeling my throat clogging with tears.

"And that's why it has to end. Sharp and sweet. It's all I can give you." He closes his eyes and shakes his head. "Please. Don't sully it. Don't ask me to ruin you."

He looks up as Jimmy walks into the airport, wheeling his bag behind him, and he rises to stand. Before he can pull away, I wrap my arms around him and whisper in his ear.

"You are worth everything, Vadim. Everything. Don't forget."

"Oh, zolotaya." He stares down at me with a rueful expression. "If you knew me, you wouldn't feel that way."

He walks over to Jimmy and talks to him. I count down the minutes on the clock as I watch their body language. Jimmy shrugs and puffs up his chest, but as the conversation passes the three-minute mark, he hunches in on himself and looks wildly around the terminal, searching the shadows for something or someone he can't see.

Vadim nods at him and walks away. Back toward the bank of chairs where I stand to meet him. But he doesn't stop. He doesn't say goodbye. He doesn't look back. He just walks into the snowy darkness and out of my life.

TEN YEARS LATER

SONGBIRD STAR FILES LAWSUIT AGAINST ROCK PRODUCER

"Breakout" singer Kesera files sexual-abuse lawsuit against producer Jimmy "Jimboi" Ullrich

Kesera, singer of last year's top 10 hit "Breakout," filed a case against rock producer James Ullrich, alleging a campaign of sexual and emotional abuse. She claims the producer, also known as "Jimboi" Ullrich, attempted to rape her on a tour of Moscow and subjected her to a campaign of sexual harassment, inappropriate touching, and emotional abuse that left her shaken and unable to work with him again. She's suing her record label and asking to be freed from the three-album deal.

Kesera herself has yet to comment publicly, but she is scheduled to speak with Oprah to discuss the court case once the initial hearings are out of the way.

Producer James Ullrich has countersued for libel, alleging reputational damage, stating, "If everyone could make up abuse allegations and free themselves from legally binding contracts, then the music industry would collapse."

CHAPTER EIGHTEEN

Kesera

Stevie isn't just my bass player. He's my oldest friend and he's called in a favor, which is how I find myself in the VIP area of a Russian nightclub in Brighton Beach. I haven't been to one of these dives in years. Not since I stopped searching for Vadim.

Stevie cradles the guitar like it's an extension of his anatomy, fingering the strings and peering into the crowd below. Looks like fun down there. The DJ mixes an anonymous club track with a bit of old-school pop, and the crowd downstairs goes wild. Two hundred arms shoot into the air simultaneously as the beat drops and Madonna's nasal vocals ring out. She sings about the people coming together. There's a shout of joy, and the track speeds up.

It doesn't surprise me that no one on the top level jumps up and down. They're all pretending to be cool or they're too jaded to have fun. But like it or not, these are my people now. Rich, successful, too bored to enjoy themselves.

I miss the old days when we were broke, but we had fun

trying to get noticed. I wish I could disappear into the crowd and lose myself in the music, but I'd get mobbed for selfies by people who probably aren't even fans and just want a picture for their social media.

In the middle of the crowd, I spot a pretty blond girl in a plastic tiara and sash that says 21 TODAY. She bounces up and down in the middle of a crowd of friends.

I guess this is Stevie's new conquest—only just old enough to drink and not interested in anything more than a private gig from someone famous.

She hasn't glanced up here once since we came off stage. Yet again, Stevie has picked the wrong girl, but I'm not one to talk. I haven't gotten laid in so long I've almost forgotten what sex feels like.

I sink down on the leather bench next to him, nursing my soda water with lime. "Ready to head off? I can give you a ride back to Manhattan." I reach over and twang one of the strings to get his attention. "I'll take this back with me if you're going out clubbing."

He grins, his forehead shining under his thinning hair, and nods as I stand to shrug into my jacket. He doesn't stand a chance with this chick, but no one likes to hear that shit from their friends, and I'm not gonna be the one to break it to him.

Rising to his feet, Stevie slings an arm around my shoulders. He's too thin, probably from snorting too much coke, but I've given up lecturing him about that too. I lean into him as we pick our way through the chairs to the exit, but he crashes into me from behind as I stop short and stare across the room.

It can't be.

Not Vadim.

Not after all this time.

But I can't help looking.

Stevie follows my eyes to the booths at the back of the VIP area. "Not that guy. Please tell me you're wrong."

He pulls on my elbow and drags me toward the velvet rope separating the high-rollers and poseurs from the people actually having a good time downstairs.

I stare at the corner where I thought I saw the man who is the subject of a hundred song lyrics I've written. I've spotted Vadim's shadow in nightclubs, on street corners. Once I even thought I saw him at my daughter's school drop-off. I must have had a particularly poor night's sleep before that imaginary sighting.

Stevie pulls me around to face him and spits out his next words. "I thought you were over all this nonsense. You stopped taking these crazy gigs. You're not still looking for him, are you?" He tilts his head toward the corner of the balcony, eyes narrowing.

"Don't patronize me, Stevie. I only came tonight because you asked me to give you a bit of moral support. I stopped searching years ago, and I'll probably be wrong this time too, but . . ."

"You promised me." His biting tone sinks through my skin as he looks at the crowd of men standing close to the balcony. "Everyone knows who you are, Sera. If that bastard had really wanted to find you, he'd have found a way."

"Don't talk about him like that. It's harder when you're famous. I'm not always easy to reach."

I look at the men in the corner. There are five of them, laughing and joking with one another in a tight huddle. They're all muscular and vaguely threatening, but one of the men stands apart.

His back faces us, and I can only see the wide set of his shoulders and the way he bends his head to his friend, but there's something familiar about the way he moves, even when I can't see his face. The strength and the silence. No drama. Just an implicit threat.

"He's had ten years. Trust me, if he didn't come for you, it's because he didn't want to." My best friend looks at me with pity in his eyes. "It's not like he didn't hear the songs. They had constant airplay for two whole summers."

"You don't know that."

"I do, babe. I know men. If he'd wanted—"

I hold my hand up to stop him, lips tight. I know what he's going to say. I'm the one who wrote a whole album about a man whose last name I didn't know in the hope he'd seek me out. I don't need another reminder that it didn't work.

I glance back to the other side of the balcony. Most of the other customers have given the men a wide berth—there are two empty tables next to the group—but a huddle of girls who look barely out of their teens flutters around them like butterflies in short dresses. The man I'm watching is the only one who doesn't put his hand on the girls.

Fixing Stevie with a hot stare, I set my jaw. "It's not for me, okay? I have to ask. If there's a chance, then I need to know."

I start toward the men, my friend trailing in my wake and muttering under his breath as he follows me. I don't need to hear what he's saying to get the gist of where he's going with this, but if it ends with embarrassment and me apologizing and buying a round of drinks, then it's nothing I haven't done before and it won't kill me.

I tap the tallest of the six men on the shoulder and put on my brightest, most confident voice. "Excuse me. You look like someone . . ."

He turns. There are a few more lines around the eyes, but . . .

It's him.

I can't stop the smile from bursting across my face.

"Vadim," I whisper, and reach for him. My hand freezes in mid-air as I wait for him to smile back, for his face to mirror the joy I feel.

His lip curls and his brows pull together in a frown. He's looking at me like I'm something he scraped from the bottom of his shoe as he mutters something too low for me to catch. And I'm still smiling at him like an idiot, my arm held aloft and the grin frozen on my face. To let the smile slip would be to admit that Stevie was right all along.

I'd know him anywhere. I always knew I would. Cheekbones so sharp they cast shadows on the planes of his face, wide shoulders, and a body that moves through air like a knife cutting through flesh. His whole being is a study in perfect geometry, and his eyes are a pale blue that makes me think of ice flows.

His stare is just as cold.

It's galling to admit to myself that the pity on Stevie's face was justified when Vadim repeats the phrase I didn't quite catch the first time.

"This is all I fucking need." His eyes roll to the ceiling, and he clenches his fists.

The force of his words pushes me backward, and I trip over my feet in my haste to recover my pride. I suppose I'd never really admitted to myself just how much I still hoped Vadim had been waiting for us, hoping to find me the way I'd been dreaming of finding him.

Stevie steps closer behind me and puts a hand on my shoulder. "I think we should get out of here."

I remain frozen like an animal in front of a predator, watching to see if the hands that Vadim has balled into fists at his sides will unfurl and reach out to me.

"Come on, Sera. It's time to go," Stevie begs, tugging me, but I'm rooted to the spot, as if a few more moments will change the reality in front of me.

Hope is the cruelest drug. I should know. I've been mainlining the stuff for years.

Vadim leans down to the redheaded girl. She's a few years older than my daughter, but she's not too old to wear the same convent-school uniform. I'd ground Nadia for life if I found her in a place like this in six years' time. The kid is curled up between him and his friend on the sofa, and Vadim leans down and strokes the hair away from her forehead, looking concerned. She nods, gazing up at him with a dazed expression.

That small act of tenderness stabs at a raw place under my breastbone. I didn't publicly admit to dreams of a happily ever after, but Stevie knows.

"Poor, poor Sera," he says, rubbing my shoulder.

I don't need to turn around to see the expression on his face. My band knew the album I wrote must have been about the man I met in Moscow, but Stevie was the only one who knew how many gigs I'd booked at private parties in mafia nightclubs until Nadia was three. I finally had to concede that spending nights away from my daughter so I could chase a shadow was stupid. She needed stability, and that had meant getting a grip on myself and only touring when it was absolutely necessary.

No more private gigs for Russian billionaires, which did nothing to burnish my reputation. No more chasing shadows.

"I'm fine, Stevie. It's just us. We're all the family we need," I lie, swallowing down the stone of hope that's lodged in my throat. My eyes sting so I turn to the side, hoping Stevie can't see me as I drag my sleeve across my face.

I watch Vadim as he pats the girl's red hair absentmindedly and turns back to me with an empty stare. I don't know if he's sleeping with her or just watching out for her, but he's not giving me a fraction of the care he's doling out to the younger woman. The gesture makes me nauseous enough to admit I've spent ten years in love with a man who doesn't exist. A phantom I'd conjured out of one part wishes and two parts desperation and stupidity.

Vadim turns to a younger man standing in the shadows and tilts his chin at me. The skinny boy with a neck tattoo, sunken cheeks, and a mess of dark blond curls walks over.

"Andrei, take her out back to the Night Governor's office. I'll deal with this situation later," Vadim says.

I keep my eyes on the boy's bony hands as he pushes a security bar on a fire exit next to the bar and beckons me over. My back straightens and I don't turn back toward Stevie as I hear him tell Vadim, "I'll come with her."

But I hear Vadim's response. "I know exactly who you are. You're the guy who's always wanted to fuck her, and you can stay right here."

I let the door slam behind me on the knowledge that if he knows who Stevie is, then he's known who I am for a long time. And he didn't come to find me.

CHAPTER NINETEEN

Kesera

My anxiety is a physical thing. It's stupid to wear tracks in the carpet as I pace the room, but I've got to move. Walking, even if it's in tight squares around the desk and in front of the bookshelves lining the walls, is a welcome change from sitting in the chair and trying not to crawl out of my skin.

I'll give Vadim credit. If this is his office, it's a cut above most of the nightclub back rooms I've been in over the years, which are usually a symphony of plywood and chipboard, with torn and faded posters on the walls.

Books in Cyrillic script line the bookshelves. Tracing my fingers over the curves of the letters, I make out Dostoevsky, Tolstoy, Pelevin. Names, stories, histories that I only half grasp.

I taught myself to read the Russian alphabet after I had Nadia, and I read a lot in translation when I was pregnant with her, but I don't spot my favorite novel on the shelves. Of course, Anna Karenina was a silly woman in love with the wrong man, so it's no wonder the book spoke to me. I don't suppose Russian gangsters spend a lot of time worrying about lost love.

I kick the table leg, but all I achieve is a stubbed toe. I hop up and down on one leg, sucking in my breath for a minute before collapsing in a heap in the chair opposite the bookshelf. I'm bent over my sore toe with one boot off and my head bowed—consoling myself that at least I didn't throw myself under a train with a broken heart like poor Anna—when the door opens.

The air changes as Vadim steps into the room. He closes the door behind him and leans against it, regarding me warily. His eyes are drawn to where I'm cradling my foot, and I keep rubbing circles on my toe. I'd rather stare at a hole in my sock like it holds the secrets of the universe than look up at him again. One quick glance was enough to see that he's not delighted to see me.

"Zolotaya, time has treated you kindly, I see."

He still uses the pet name he gave me the weekend I met him. Zolotaya. Golden one.

"You remembered what you used to call me, then?" I ask, squeezing the offending toe to get the blood flow back to my aching foot. I hope it will draw some of the heat away from my cheeks, which I can tell are flushing with something. Lust? Shame? Could be any number of a tangle of emotions Vadim pulls from me.

"I couldn't forget. Not with all the songs on the radio."

I look up at him, and the hope must be written in my eyes so clearly that he shakes his head as he looks down at me.

Great. Now I know it's humiliation coloring my face.

"I heard you tell Stevie that you knew who he was," I say, "so I'm guessing that you've been in America a while."

"Yeah, I've been here almost ten years."

Guts twisting, the question I've been bottling up for a decade tumbles from my lips.

"So, you knew I had a daughter?" I slowly let the air out and watch his carved features for a trace of one of his rare smiles, but there's no hint of emotion.

God, did I know him at all?

He shrugs like it's no big deal as I sit straighter and steel my spine. There will be plenty of time for crying later. For now, I'll pretend it's as cut and dried as the former "love of my life" seems to think it is.

"I see."

My eyes roam the spines of the books behind the desk so that I don't have to look at him. Teeth digging into my lip, I suck cool air into my nostrils before I pull back my shoulders and meet those pale wolf eyes with the bravest stare I can muster. I do it for Nadia if not for me.

"Well, if the songs on my album didn't make it clear . . ." I pull out my stage persona and smile at him brightly. "She's yours. Our daughter. I'd be happy to take a DNA test if you have any doubt, but I think it will be pretty clear when you meet her. She looks just like you."

"There's no need."

My shoulders drop half an inch. He believes me. That's a small comfort, but it's something that he doesn't doubt my honor.

With his next words, he takes my heart—which is already a bloody mess on the floor at his feet—and grinds it under the heel of his expensive Italian shoes. "You don't have to take the test. I won't ever want to meet her."

I have no idea how I keep looking at him. Where I find the strength not to crumble. But I nod slowly. "You've made yourself very clear. Thank you. I can't imagine that we have any more to say, but you asked me to wait for you back here, or you . . ." I wave my hand vaguely to indicate the way he described me, not as a woman, but as a situation.

He walks over to the desk, sits down, leans his chin on his steepled hands, and watches me. The minute feels like an hour as the silence stretches between us.

"It's very unfortunate. But I'm going to need you to disappear." He lifts his shoulders as if he's apologizing for being a bit late for dinner, and not like he's just said he wants me to vanish.

"What?" I'm staring at him like he's got a second head. "Disappear? What are you talking about? I can't just disappear. I've got a daughter in school, a court case to fight, and a career," I splutter.

Vadim raises an eyebrow. It's a perfect parabola, questioning my sanity. Obviously, it's an everyday request in his world.

"A child in the mix is all I need. I'm not sure who saw you here, and I don't know who I can trust right now, so you'll have to lie low. The only blessing is you didn't mention that the child is mine in front of anyone."

He stands, picks up a bottle of cognac, then pulls out the stopper and pours two fingers into a glass. He hands it to me over the table and leans back in his chair before pouring another glass for himself.

"*Na zdorovye.*" He lifts his glass at me, eyes like frost as they regard me over the rim. "Your health, Kesera. Let's drink to you both staying alive."

A gulp of brandy goes down the wrong way and burns as it trickles into my nose. I put the glass down and bend double, coughing into my knees and allowing my hair to fall around me in a cloak.

I'm still in the brace position, waiting for the impact of his next statement, when I feel him move around the desk and come to lean against it next to me. I can see his long legs and the shiny black leather of his shoes and the way his suit pants cling to his wide, muscular thighs.

I wrap my arms around my legs and fold in on myself, gulping in breaths of air. He doesn't reach out to touch or comfort me, and his next words scrape at my skin like sandpaper.

"I'm sorry it has to be this way. It would have been better if you hadn't found me."

He walks to the bookshelf and pulls out a leather-bound copy of *War and Peace*. Inside the book are a handful of old Nokia handsets, and he throws one across the room at me. I'm not quick enough to leap for it, so it falls with a soft thud into the carpet at my feet.

"Burner phone. You'll need one to keep in touch." He takes out another one and tosses it at me. This time I reach out to catch it. I turn the narrow rectangle of plastic round and round in my fingers as if the keys can tap out a text message telling me what's going on here.

"What's happening? I don't understand."

Vadim leans on the bookshelf, one foot crossed over the other at the ankle as he lounges against the books and regards me with some amusement.

"I think you do."

I shake my head at him, but he carries on.

"I was hoping you wouldn't find me, but fate always catches up with you, I suppose." He shrugs as if he's not talking about blowing up my life. Our daughter's life.

"I'd stopped looking." I've had enough pity for one evening, so I look down at my feet. I'm wearing boots. Just like the night that I met him.

"I know you did. I let my guard down. I used to make sure I was out of the picture if you were playing a gig in one of our clubs. Sasha used to think it was funny. He even booked a few to mess with me." He smiles at me, like this is a joke I might enjoy. "Still, it can't be helped. I've got the money and the logistics for you to go on the run. I'll be in touch. You keep the burner phone on you. Give one to the kid too."

"If you're not planning on talking to her, that won't be necessary," I bite out.

He shrugs, strides toward the door, and looks back over his shoulder, folding his lips together in a rueful grimace.

"Are you going to tell me what's going on?"

He shakes his head. "For your safety, the less you know, the better. I'm sorry, Kesera. I told you I wasn't a good man when we met."

The door opens and Stevie's shouts echo from the corridor. I catch my name and Vadim's and some expletives, and then Vadim steps out of the room and shuts the door behind him, blocking out the noise. I'm left with nothing but an old Nokia handset and a head full of questions.

CHAPTER TWENTY

Kesera

Ten missed calls. All Stevie. No doubt he's up bright and early, ready to serve me a helping of humble pie with an ice-cold scoop of recrimination before I've even had my coffee.

He can wait.

I throw my phone down on the bedside table. I don't need my bassist to tell me what I already know. I'm crazy to have believed I was in love with a man I knew for less than forty-eight hours. I feel dirty, and not just because I haven't had a shower. My eyes are caked in mascara, and I've left streaks of last night's makeup smeared across my pillow.

I stagger into the bathroom to wash off the thin film of humiliation that's settled on top of my skin. Vadim doesn't feel the same way. Stevie was right. I'm an idiot.

I haven't found the hook yet, but doesn't heartbreak make for the best albums? I'm sure I can crowbar some hits out of the wreckage of last night's meeting once I've figured out what Vadim means by making me disappear. That's if he's planning on keeping me and Nadia alive.

I pick up my bag and scrabble through the notebooks, lipsticks, and pens for the singular Nokia handset I took from Vadim, but there are no messages. I don't know if that's good or bad. If he's planning to kill us, at least he hasn't scheduled it for early this morning. There's still time for coffee.

It's a grim thought, and I wish I could tell myself it's entirely unrealistic, but the last few hours have really hammered home that I don't know the man who fathered my child. Those hours in Moscow were etched so brightly into my memories, but they don't mean what I thought they did.

I'm pouring coffee for myself when Nona enters the kitchen. She hip-checks me as she walks past and pushes me into a seat. Our nanny hums a Russian folksong as she pulls out the pastries she made last night.

"Eat." She slides a plate of sticky honey-and-pistachio-laced baklava in front of me. "Too thin."

"You're the only one who thinks so." I look up at her, sipping my coffee and licking a crumb of honey-laced pastry off my thumb. I don't usually tuck into her sweet treats, but if there was ever a morning to comfort myself with sugar, it's today.

Nona shakes her head at me. I hired Nona, but she's more like a mother to me and Nadia than an employee. Less drama, more fabulous cooking.

"Yesterday. Good night? Stevie . . . he find his girl? I like him." Nona's English is broken, but she gets her point across. She's been hinting that I should pair up with Stevie for years.

I look down at the flakes of pastry, wishing it were that easy, but if the chemistry's not there, you can't fake it. I love the guy, but there's no part of me that wants to climb him like a tree. And men get frustrated when they know you don't want them. Then they take it out on you. God knows I

128

lived through it once with Jimmy producing my albums. I wanted to hold out for the kind of love I wrote about in my songs.

I laugh to myself, and Nona looks over at me with her eyebrows raised in question.

"Stevie's girl is too young for him. I think that's a wash. But I found the man I've been looking for."

Nona watches me over the table. She's got no idea what I'm talking about. Last night is still so vivid that I almost feel like I shouldn't have to explain. There ought to be a neon sign flashing over my head.

"Nadia's father was there," I say.

Nona's lips turn down in a grimace. She scowls at me, her face pulled out of its usual smile. "He no good man?" she asks shrewdly.

"How did you know? That's what he said."

There's a crash from outside the kitchen and then the patter of footsteps as Nadia comes bowling into the kitchen, her long hair wafting around her head. She's still in pajamas and she's carrying a brush.

"I need braids, Mom. Nona has to do the Wednesday hair for me." She throws the brush down on the table. We haven't even hit the teen years, and already every other thing is a challenge.

"Wednesday hair? It's Friday." I pick up the brush and turn to her.

"No, Mom. You are so . . . duh."

She doesn't even have the words for what I am, and her eyes roll so fast they could knock over bowling pins. Her expression reminds me of last night, when I told her father he had a daughter, but I still pull her into my lap and inhale her toasted-bread smell.

She slings her leg over mine and snuggles into my neck, her words muffled as I squeeze her tighter and rain down kisses on her hair. "Wednesday Addams. Not the day of the week. Don't you know anything?"

Apparently not, I think to myself, *if last night is anything to go by*.

My stomach twists when I consider how the reality of meeting Vadim will square with the stories I've told Nadia about her father. That she was conceived in love. That the man who helped create her made me feel protected and cherished, even if he lived in a country far away.

Was it a fairy tale or more like telling children about Santa, making them believe in the magic of life before all the golden things get tarnished by time?

Nadia picks up the brush and jumps off my lap. "Nona does better braids than you." She walks over to Nona and hands the brush to her. "My eyes don't go with the look. Can I get black contacts?"

"What? No. You can't. And you can't be Wednesday either. She hates her mom." I stick out my tongue at Nadia.

She pulls a face back. "I don't hate you, Mom. I just think you're embarrassing."

"Okay. Get Nona to do your hair, then go get dressed. We've got twenty minutes to get out the door, and you haven't eaten anything." I stand on weary legs and get ready for the walk to school.

That's the joy of New York—you can walk everywhere. I promised myself that if I was in town, I'd be the one to take Nadia to school myself, even if the bitchy throngs of moms at the school gate offer a cold welcome and Nadia would prefer to be driven in a town car like the cool kids. It's hard to give your kid any sense of the real world when you have money and staff, but not being chauffeured to school is a start.

I'm pulling on my shoes when Nadia walks out with perfect braids, and I point her to the sensible flat school shoes when she tries to pick up the Wednesday Addams style clunky platforms. Walking keeps your feet on the ground.

As I'm heading out the door with Nadia, Nona puts her hand on my arm. "You come back. We talk."

The walk to school is a blur. Nadia's chattering away about how Wednesday Addams doesn't care about what people think and why she needs to dye her hair black if she and her friends are going to form a detective club. Her braids bob as I walk behind her.

How much of the way she bounces on her feet is me and how much is Vadim? With her blue eyes, she looks so much like her father. I'm almost tempted to invest in a pair of black contacts for her as she ambles through the school gates, talking to a bunch of kids I don't know. The days when I had a grip on her friendships are drawing to a close. She doesn't look back as she walks through the wide oak doors, and I turn toward home.

I'm saved from further dark thoughts when the phone rings.

"Stevie. Did you get home okay?"

There's a dark laugh as I walk past the deli and a string of coffee shops. "Yeah, no thanks to lover boy. Kept going on about how he knows I want to sleep with you. His goons manhandled me out of the club." He sighs. "What are you going to do now? Does he want to play a role in Nadia's life? When are you going to tell her?"

I just hold the phone to my ear as I walk past the commuters on their way to work, the moms in their lululemon, and the occasional clubber coming back from a night out. I wonder how many of them had their lives upended last night.

"What's the plan?" He keeps firing questions like bullets as I wait for the lights to change. Red, yellow, green.

"I don't know, Stevie. I don't think he wants to play an active role in Nadia's life," I say, stalling.

"Well, that's good, right? Nothing needs to change."

"What?" I splutter. "How is it good that Nadia's father doesn't want to get to know her? On what planet is that good news?"

"Well . . ." There's a pause as Stevie breathes heavily. "He could be suing you for custody or asking you guys to move so that he has more access. He could be all up in your business."

I think about the burner phone which sits in silent reproach in my purse. I don't tell him that Vadim will probably be so up in my business he'll turn my life upside down. Just not in a good way. And he's not even offering a relationship with Nadia.

I nod at our doorman as I walk to the elevator, head bowed. "I'll call you later, okay? We need to talk about the court case. Jimmy is suing me for libel, saying he loved me like a daughter and never laid a finger on me. I could use some moral support right about now. I don't need another lecture."

"Kay." Stevie has known me long enough to know when I've reached the end of my rope, and I'm right down to the frayed edges this morning.

I let myself in and pad past the kitchen. I have a meeting with the lawyers later today. It's a whole parade of assholes with no letup, and I'm about to put on a suit and my battle-armor makeup when Nona steps in front of me. As if she knows what's going on, she holds her arms wide and pulls me into them. I sink against her round shoulders and soft chest. Nona is all soft curves, and she smells of honey and pistachio.

"*Devuchka*." She uses the Russian for little girl. "Now, we talk."

"I've got to get ready." I pull away from her, but she follows me into the bedroom and sits on the bed. It's like when Nadia was little and Nona had to follow us into every room in the house to make sure comfort was always on hand.

"This man. Nadia's father. I know men like him. Back in Moscow." She reaches for my hand and pulls me to sit next to her, stroking my arm for comfort. "If he find you. Probably trouble. You tell me what he say."

I pull out the burner phone and hand it to her. It sits in her hands like a bomb that's engaged to explode. "He gave me this. He tried to give me one for Nadia too, but I wouldn't take it."

Nona just watches me. Waiting.

"He wants us to disappear." I search her face as she nods. "What does that mean?"

"In Moscow, when I was refugee and I needed work. I work for men like them. He want you to disappear?" She regards me with dark, solemn eyes. "It means he in big trouble. Means you and Nadia in big trouble too."

A text lights up the phone, and we both look down.

7pm. Be Ready.

Nona goes to the closet and starts pulling out bags and laying clothes on the bed. I don't know what it all means. Or maybe I do, but I don't want to admit it. But she's in motion like she's done this before, opening my bedside drawers and pulling out medication and phone chargers.

A second text comes in. There's no emotion. Nothing to soften the words.

Nadia too.

CHAPTER TWENTY-ONE

Vadim

A daughter. A little girl. The words echo like a drumbeat in my head as I walk down the street to the banya, head down and shoulders hunched. I turn the thoughts over and over in my mind, trying to wrestle them into a shape I can control.

"Yo, watch where you're going, man!" I feel the weight of a body slamming into my shoulder and turn to see a skinny guy with tattoos. He's too jittery from a night out to notice that I'm not the sort of man you shake your fists at. Even in broad daylight.

Last night's news has made me lose my edge to the point that strung-out clubbers don't think I'm a threat. What about the Italians or the Albanians? What about my boss?

Plunking down on the gray stone steps of the Russian baths, I cup my head in my hands. We usually meet here on Sunday, and it's not good news that Sasha has broken our routine and asked me to come down here on a Friday.

What the fuck will I do if the Night Governor finds out

I've fathered a kid with a celebrity? Ten years ago in Moscow, he was powerful and dangerous, but now he's terrifying. He owns half the earth: mines, banks, shipping lines, congressmen, members of the FBI and CIA. There's not a thread of American life the Night Governor can't pull if he wants to. A few words in the right ears and Guelman can make anyone's life unravel.

I tug on my hair and try to catch my breath before I go upstairs to see Sasha. The stone beneath me has been worn by the feet of a hundred years of Russians like me feeling lonely in America. When I didn't seek refuge in the banya, I lay in bed listening to Kesera's voice singing about that lost weekend in the woods.

Fuck. I thought she was safe. And now she's fucking found me.

Rising wearily to my feet, I trudge up the steps to meet my best friend. Nausea swirls in my stomach. Maybe I'll feel better after I sweat it out. You can tell what a man's about when he's drunk or naked. Less to hide that way.

After stripping off my clothes, I head into the steam and the silence. The first session is about to start, and Sasha is already lying on the top bench, ready to bake as the heat rises. There are only two other people on the tiered pine benches.

Lev, the old, paunchy guy from Belarus, wears a tattered bathrobe around his body and a fuzzy felt cap on his head to keep the heat off. It gives him the look of a demented goblin as he pads to the door, his flip-flops slapping against the tile.

He turns to the room. "Last call. I'm closing the door, so if you want to leave, do it now."

I slap Sasha on the arm as I lower myself next to him.

He opens one eye with a dark glare. "I need to talk to you, fucker."

My head falls back against the pine, and I shut my eyes.

Fucking great. I need to ask for Sasha's help with this Kesera situation, and he's already agitated. Not that I say anything as Lev scatters eucalyptus oil across the room and the sharp tang of the trees rises from the pine benches.

The whirl of the bath towel reaches my ears. Lev stands in the center of the room, working the air. My shoulders and forehead burn as the steam rains down like fire. Let it rinse away all the bad ideas and leave me clear enough to figure out a way out of this mess. The only other sound is the heavy breathing of men alone with their thoughts in the stillness as the heat encloses us.

"Ice pool," Sasha says as the door opens and the other two men file out.

We walk straight to the freezing water, and I hold my nose and jump straight in. A hand pushes down on my head, and I look up and see Sasha standing over me, holding me down. I try to slow my heartbeat and wait him out, but he keeps his hands on my shoulders, pushing me lower. A muffled string of curses cuts through the water.

Sasha's mean when his temper is up, but he won't kill me. Without me, there's no one who actually knows the boy from the orphanage in Russia—no one to keep him real as the money, hookers, and private jets bend him out of shape. Without him, there is no one who will have my back in the Night Governor's world.

But when you can't breathe, the body starts to override the mind. I start by counting the seconds and focusing on the tiles lining the plunge pool. After what feels like minutes but may only be seconds, my lungs burn and I start to claw at Sasha's arm. He pulls his hand away, and I burst out of the icy water.

"What the hell? That wasn't funny."

After clambering out of the pool, I stagger to a bench outside the sauna, bent double and coughing like an old man.

I let the heat from the open door fan my aching and icy muscles, and I keep my eyes on the floor until I can gather myself together to face whatever Sasha is ready to dish up.

"What makes you think I'm trying to be funny? Did that look like stand-up comedy to you?" Sasha glowers at me. I've known him too long not to engage when he's spoiling for a fight like this.

"Clearly not." I raise my head to meet his eyes, which are bright with anger. "I didn't think you'd be so pissed off about her finding me. It's not ideal timing, I'll admit, and there are some complications you should know about."

Sasha grasps the towel slung around his waist as he looks at the murals above us. "God, give me strength. Are you in even more shit than I thought? Who the hell found you?"

I balance my forearms on my thighs and scrub my face. I'll have to tell Sasha there's a kid, and he's not going to like it. "The pop star. The one I banged in the old dacha in Moscow."

"You motherfucking idiot. You mean that we have to deal with not one, but two women that you've dragged into our business right as I was about to pull us out of drugs and into tax fraud where the real money is?"

Shocked, I look up at him. "How did you know about the kid?"

"What kid?" Sasha spreads his hands. "The girl you rescued from the brothel? This savior complex of yours is going to get us all killed or torpedo the business."

Sasha still thinks he can go solo and pull away from the Night Governor, but I'm doubtful. Guelman has eyes and ears everywhere.

"I haven't rescued any kid." I meet his narrowed eyes with a blank look.

"Sure you did, Prince Charming. You went into one of that psycho Spataro's brothels to talk with the Italians and picked up a red-haired teenager who asked you sweetly for help."

"Oh, her." I'd been so focused on the fact that I'm a father that I haven't been thinking about all the other pieces on the chessboard.

"Yes, *her*, asswipe. That pretty little thing is Spataro's daughter. He was going to marry her off to the Night Governor. Daddy sent her to the brothel so she'd know that there are worse things than an arranged marriage."

Then it clicks. "Spataro? The 'Ndrangheta don?"

"The very one. So now the boss is pissed off and the Italians will be baying for your blood."

"She looked like . . ." I stumble over the name.

"I know who she looked like, okay? Polina was my sister, but picking up teenagers in brothels and taking them home won't bring her back. Do you think I don't know that? Who knows that better than me?" Sasha's fists clench and he's pawing the wet tiles as if he wants to charge at me.

"No one. Which is why I was going to ask you for help with the other kid before you tried to drown me." I throw the words back at him. Sasha might be angry with me, but he's my brother in other ways than blood.

He throws his hands in the air. "What other damn kid?

"My daughter."

Sasha stands for a moment and looks at me like I've stunned him with a blow to the head before turning his back on me and walking toward the door. Slinging a towel around his waist, he heads for the stairs to the rooftop restaurant.

"My god. How big is this clusterfuck, and what have you dragged us into? We're going to need beer for this," he mumbles as he walks away.

By the time I've pulled on a robe and staggered up to the rooftop, Sasha is eyeing me warily over a steaming plate of Russian dumplings, a bowl of pickles, and a couple of pints.

"Ten years." He shakes his head. "Ten years of work and just as I'm pulling the threads together, you decide to pick up a teenager who looks like my dead sister and kick off a mafia war."

I pick up my beer and take a sip as my gaze wanders over the rooftops. "It might not be that bad," I say, sticking my fork in a dumpling.

"No?" His black brows rise. "You planning to drop her back over there and say you made a mistake?"

I grin crookedly. "Would it work?"

"No, you fucker." He punches me in the arm. "It wouldn't. And that's before we've even gotten started with the fact that you fathered a kid with a pop star—one who's all over the papers because she's in court every other week."

He gulps down half his beer and swipes a hand over his mouth. He picks up two dumplings and stuffs them into his mouth, his cheeks bulging as he watches me.

"What part of 'let's lie low for a while and let the money start rolling in' didn't you get? When did you find out about your daughter?"

"I don't know. About six years ago, when they moved to New York."

"You've known about them that long and now you suddenly have an urge to pretend you're *The Brady Bunch*?"

"No, she found me at a nightclub. With the Polina look-alike, as a matter of fact, and I'd have been able to keep a lid on the whole thing if this angry little fucker in her band hadn't started shouting in front of the boys about what a shitty father I am. I got one of the guys to kick him out of the club." I sigh, closing my eyes and tipping my head against the seat before adding, "But not before he made a lot of noise and I had to tell her I might need her to disappear."

He laughs darkly. "Oh, and how did she take that? Ready to give you a father-of-the-year award?"

"She didn't say much, actually."

I remember how she looked at me with her heart in her eyes. The way her face lit up when she saw me, her voice all breathy as she caressed the word *Vadim*. It hurt to see her like that. I had a minute to imagine what it would be like to have a woman who looked at me like that all the time before I shut it down. I wouldn't be so stupid.

Looking at Sasha, I take a sip of my beer and blow out a long breath. "I gave her a burner phone and told her I'm not a good man."

"Hmmm." He regards me over the rim of his drink. "You're one of the best, actually, you sentimental fool."

"Well, with the company we keep, it's a pretty low bar." I roll my shoulders and dig my fingers into the knotted muscles of my neck. "You're right. This is a clusterfuck. I knew I'd want the singer and my daughter out of town."

Sasha puts down his drink and just watches me, waiting to see how I'll explain the mess I'm in.

"I didn't realize the redhead was anything more than a pretty girl who needed help. I thought it would be easy to do her a favor." I look at the handful of people sunning themselves on the roof as Sasha waves over the waitress and orders more beer.

"Well, it won't be easy. You kicked a wasp nest, and we might have a mafia war on our hands if we're not careful." The waitress drops off fresh drinks, and Sasha draws a pattern in the rings the beer mugs have left on the table. "Even if we're careful, it's going to be a mess."

"Don't you ever think about your sister?" I ask, unable to meet his eyes as I ask the question. "If you'd seen someone who looked like her, are you certain you wouldn't have reacted?"

Sasha reaches over and turns my head toward him. "You are the only family I've got left. You and the other guys from the orphanage. Polina is gone." Taking a swig of beer, he downs what's left in his glass and stares into the bottom, avoiding my eyes. "Love killed my mother. She was a fool who took in her husband's bastard, and other than proving my dad preferred fucking white women, raising Polina gained her nothing."

I've heard this speech before, but Polina was his sister. Somewhere under all that bluster, I know he feels the pain of our failure to save her, so I let him jab the table knife in the air like it's a weapon.

He slams the knife on the table and spears a dumpling with his fork. "Remember that. Remember who we are and what we've built. Love is a liability."

"So, you won't help me if I need to save my daughter?"

Sasha sighs. "Of course I'll help you. What choice do I have?"

"There's always a choice, brother."

He shrugs like it's no big deal, but I know it will cost him. "We always choose each other. Nothing has changed. I'm just pissed off." He spreads his hands wide, as if he doesn't have words for the mess I've created, and then adds, "They aren't your family, though. You've just met them."

"You know the Night Governor will never see it that way. I'll have to protect them like they've always been mine. How safe are our safe houses?"

Sasha twists his mouth as he thinks about it. "Not as safe as they were last week, no thanks to you, but I can think of a couple of places you can use."

My best friend's temper is as violent as a summer storm but passes just as fast. Our boss is another matter. And now that I've ruffled the Spataro family's feathers by spiriting away the don's daughter, we're in deeper shit than I could have realized.

Which also means Kesera and our daughter are in there with me.

If the Night Governor figures out who they are, he'll use them against me. Keeping everyone safe seems nearly impossible, but I have no choice. If Sasha won't help, I'll take matters into my own hands, but I pray to god he'll come through for me like he has in the past.

CHAPTER TWENTY-TWO

Kesera

How much makeup is just enough? I look at my face in the mirror, painting over the shadows that ring my eyes after the last twenty-four hours, and consider the issue carefully as I wave the hairbrush at Nona.

I could have asked a stylist to come to the house before the meeting with the lawyers, but I wanted the comfort of someone familiar.

The Mary Poppins clone in the mirror looks back at me wearily. Long dark skirt. High-necked blouse, with Nona bent over my head as she pins the braids to the crown of my head. I look like a Victorian schoolmarm.

Nona presses a kiss to the braids, and I touch up my lipstick. Wear a full face of makeup, but make sure people can still imagine that you woke up like this. Be a good mother, but make sure you look like you never had sex. Oh, and don't forget, dress like a hooker if you want to sell records.

Even if this is just an initial meeting between my lawyers

and Jimmy's, I need to play it safe and look like a good girl. But balancing those conflicting signals gets exhausting.

"I'm so tired." I wave the makeup brush at Nona, whose smiling eyes twinkle back at me in the mirror. She pins in the last hairpin and pats my head.

"Men," she says, and shrugs. The word stands alone, but I know what she's getting at. Jimmy, the judge, the press, the executives at the record label, and now Vadim. Stevie is the only one in my corner, and he's too weak to defend me.

A final swipe of blush on the apples of my cheeks, and my war paint is on. I resolve to remain numb as I pick up the briefcase and steel myself. My PA has printed out the press coverage. I flick through the printouts. The headlines could be summarized in one line: *Poor Jimmy*.

Poor Jimmy loved me like a little sister (pity his siblings if this is how he showed his love).

Poor Jimmy worked so hard to drag me out of the gutter, and this is the thanks he got.

Poor Jimmy didn't have a public profile until I named him as an abuser.

I wrote those damn hits. I sang the songs. I made two of his three albums, and I made him a lot of money. Now I'm taking back my life, my words, and my power. He won't get another cent from me, and he'll pay for what he did so that he can't do it to anyone else.

Breathing in deeply, I exit the apartment and head to the car waiting for me outside. After a short drive, I walk up the steps to meet Maxine Reinhart, my defense. I might be dressed like a nun, but Maxine wears towering heels and a suit the color of blood. She's slashed her lips in the same color. She grins, showing teeth she's never bothered to get straightened, and holds out her arm for me to take.

"Ready to do battle?" She slides her arm through mine and looks down at me, and I nod at my outfit.

"This is my armor." I smooth a hand down the high-necked blouse and try to force a smile, but my lips won't follow instructions. I pull my shoulders up and march in next to Maxine.

Jimmy is still the same slimy little fucker. He gives me a grin from across the room. I remember his sour breath and his hands groping my breasts and pulling off my underwear. I remember being pregnant with another man's baby when he bent me over the sound mixer and pushed inside me. I was dry and it hurt, but I could feel my body warming up to let him in. Protecting me. Deluding him. I can still feel the edge of the table digging into my hip bones and the knobs of the mixers pushed against my swollen breasts as he slammed into me from behind.

And that voice. *"You love it. Yeah, you love it."*

It took years of therapy and thousands of dollars to unspool the tight web of shame that incident left. And now they're saying I have to make another album with him and hand him my therapist's notes.

Fuck that. Fuck him.

I'll sell everything and never record a note rather than give him another cent. And if I have to burn his business to the ground to be free, then I'll do that as well.

I glare at him and shake my head. I won't cower and I won't give him one smile that he can use against me. I'm not a teenager anymore, and he needs to know we are enemies.

I look at Jimmy's lawyers with a cold smile. "Good morning, gentlemen."

My eyes drift to the taller of the two lawyers. He's a good old frat boy. I bet he went to the same kind of college and pledged the same kind of fraternity. Alpha Asshole Gamma Douchebag. If Jimmy ever grows up, he'll look just like the man in front of me—a football player run to fat. Why is there

147

no one in the legal profession who graduated from the school of hard knocks with me? Figures.

Mr. Douchebag Frat Boy gives me a smile and brandishes a piece of paper. "We are here to consider the case of Jimmy Ullrich versus Kesera Mariko Smith. Mr. Ullrich is suing Miss Smith for libel and destruction of professional reputation. Before we take more of everyone's time, I would like to give both parties an opportunity to consider mediation and remind Miss Smith that commercial life would cease to function properly if we had to renegotiate all contracts based on allegations of sexual assault."

There's a snort from my left, and Maxine leans forward on the attack. "Really, Marcus. We've had the Me Too movement, and the legal system is still standing. In fact, your client appears to be making very good use of it."

Jimmy smirks at me like he's holding all the cards, but he's unaware I'm meeting with some of his other artists over the next month. I can't be the only one.

Jabbing her pen toward Jimmy, Maxine grins, baring her slightly crooked teeth. "And I would like to remind the plaintiff that my client would be very happy to produce another album for the Yamamoto Label as long as she no longer has to work personally with Mr. Ullrich. This lawsuit is entirely frivolous."

Douchebag frat boy's colleague, who is a little more sharply dressed than the other man, leans back in his chair with a performative sigh. "Mr. Ullrich has brought this case against the defendant because her refusal to work with him personally, and her subsequent public allegations, have resulted in trial by the court of public opinion. We are here in court today to stand for the rule of law." He sits down with a smug expression on his face.

Oh great, I think to myself. *Nice one*.

This isn't about a rich, entitled older man bullying a

talented younger woman and wringing her dry for as much money and sex as he can get. It's about justice and the rule of law. Sometimes I wish I was a big, brawny Russian guy with a gun.

Jimmy looks over at me. I can see him smiling from the corner of my eye, but I try to remain serious and look straight ahead.

"Miss Smith. I see your full name is Kesera Mariko Smith. Are you Japanese?"

Maxine frowns, but I put a hand on her arm.

"I'm American. My father met my mother in Okinawa while serving our country, but I was born and grew up here," I say, trying to keep my voice level despite the personal and irrelevant questions. In a case involving sexual misconduct, personal and irrelevant questions are the order of the day.

Douchebag pipes up from next to Jimmy, who sports a sly grin. "We plan to subpoena Miss Smith's therapist, as well as her phone records and any journals or diary entries. We also need further disclosure regarding the father of her child. We think she's hiding something."

I pull my handbag against me, feeling the square block of the burner phone pressed against my leg, and thank the Lord that Vadim left me nothing but silence and inspiration for a string of hit songs instead of a paper trail or a series of text messages. I clutch the bag and finger the outline of the phone like a talisman.

My lawyer stands. "In light of your requests for further disclosure, I would like to request an adjournment for more mediation, as Mr. Ullrich's legal team has suggested. We would like to be respectful of the court's time."

Jimmy looks like he's just shat a gold egg. Nausea rides up my gullet, but Maxine shakes her head and puts her hand on my arm.

"We are amenable," she says, rising and tapping my shoulder, and I follow her out.

Jimmy walks ahead of me, but he glances over his shoulder and winks. I want to punch the smile right off his mouth.

We file silently out of the office, and the car pulls up once we get down the steps. Across the road stands a boy with sharp cheekbones and blond curls. He looks like Vadim's sidekick from the nightclub. He watches me as he buys a packet of cigarettes from a vendor. As he turns, I catch a glimpse of the tattoo on his neck and shiver.

Getting into the car, safe from prying eyes, I turn to Maxine. "What the hell was that about? What's left to negotiate at this stage?"

"We're not going to give an inch. We're going to escalate our demands."

"How?" I lean forward.

"When you sued him, the burden was on you to prove that you are above reproach. If this goes to trial, conversations you had with your therapist could be fair game." She widens her eyes, willing me to consider what that means.

I bite my lip and nod at her.

"But now that he's the plaintiff, I'm going to ask for every phone record Jimmy has. Every possible conversation I can find that might buttress your case. He'll regret this, I can promise you." She smiles and leans over to grasp my hand. Her cool, papery fingers rest against my clammy skin, and she grips me harder.

"I want him to regret it. I want to stop him in his tracks." My voice comes out sounding ragged and fierce. "I can't be the only one."

"I do have one warning, though. You may regret this too. I know you say you don't know Nadia's father, but if you've hidden anything, phone records, conversations, I need to know."

I nod, reaching into my bag and running my fingers along the keys of the phone that Vadim gave me, as if a genie might appear and grant me three wishes if I keep at it.

"If you're hiding anything, then he'll find out."

I lean back and stare at the skyscrapers filing past and the people scurrying between them as we drive uptown. "There's nothing to find. I lost track of him years ago, and I couldn't even tell him about his daughter."

What I'm saying is technically true, but Maxine must smell my evasiveness because she taps on the barrier once we near her office. "Let me out here," she says, picking up her briefcase as the town car slows near the curb. "And think about what I said. They will use Nadia's father against you. It'll be a bare-knuckle fight, so I want you to think about what you're getting yourself into."

She gets out of the car and the door slams, breaking my circling thoughts. Vadim is a wildcard. How can I predict what role he'll play in all of this?

CHAPTER TWENTY-THREE

Vadim

The burner phone in my pocket vibrates. I suppose when you issue orders to a woman you have a child with, she doesn't just say, "Yes, boss."

Still, as I pull the phone out and look at the reply to my text ordering her to be ready at seven p.m., I'm still nursing the hope that it'll be a one-word affirmative.

The screen lights up in green.

> Your daughter is 10 years old. I don't want to frighten her. Would you call me so we can discuss this?

It's a reasonable request, even though I feel a surge of irritation I have no right to. I don't have much experience with children, but I suppose a crying and hysterical kid won't make this easier. Gritting my teeth, I reluctantly dial the number.

"Vadim." Her voice is soft, breathy, and tired. "Can you tell me what's going on?"

Another reasonable request. Not that I can afford to indulge her, but I'm impressed that she's keeping her cool.

"I'm sorry. The less you know, the better."

A long pause stretches out before her weary sigh comes over the line. Like she's dealt with dozens of assholes like me. I remember that sound. Funny, I remember the whole weekend we met. Those two days in the snow were a glimpse of another world. One that I'm not stupid enough to drag any more women into.

I had a couple of weak moments in the years after I first arrived in America. I hovered at the edges of her life and toyed with the idea of tracking her down, but how would that work? I even walked by the Blessed Heart Convent to watch her drop off our daughter in the morning a couple of times to catch a glimpse of her, but it just hammered home how far apart our worlds are. She's constantly in the media, while I'm flirting with getting thrown in jail.

"Okay," she says. "I thought you might say that, so let me lay out how things look from my end. We don't have to be back in court for a few weeks, as we've been asked to go back for another round of mediation, so that buys me some time. For Nadia, it's Friday night before spring break, and we planned to go to our place in upstate New York. If there is any way we can keep to the original plan, I would be very grateful."

"You're not in a position to make demands," I snap, and she huffs out a shaky laugh. I wait, gathering my thoughts and looking out at the water. Oil-slicked waves slam against the dock, reflecting my grim mood.

"It wasn't a demand. It was a request. Nadia is your daughter, and she thinks . . ." Her voice cracks and she gulps. There's another long wait. "You said seven p.m. Would you be able to meet me a little earlier so that we can discuss how best to make this look like . . ." Her voice trails as if she's groping for words, followed by another deep inhale and sniffle.

Is she crying? God, now I've made her cry.

I look up at the storm clouds gathering overhead and pinch the bridge of my nose.

"Can we make this look like something that won't frighten a kid? She's a good girl. Smart. Brave. Loving. Let's keep her that way. Please. Even if you don't want a relationship with her, can you . . . would you . . . ?" There's a long pause, and I listen as I walk out of the warehouse.

I pass a container of weapons that sits on the side of the dock at Sheepshead Bay and wave my hand at Andrei, the best young mobster on my team. He looks over at the cars, and I nod. That's the kind of wordless communication I'm used to when I give orders. I wave my hand and my best men know what I mean without me telling them. They pull out a gun or pick up the car.

Andrei pulls the car around, and the back door slides open. I step in and sit down. "What? Would I what?" I bark, regretting the tone as soon as the words are out.

"Would you be kind? She's a little girl and—" Her voice breaks now. "Everyone who is meant to love her has loved her."

There's a long silence. What the fuck do I say to that? If I decide to love her, then something bad will happen to her. The only person left that I care about is Sasha, and he can look after himself.

Reluctantly, I blow out a breath. "I'll be there at five thirty."

Hanging up the phone, I sigh and scrub my face. The Night Governor's intended bride, safe houses, Sasha. It's all a mess that I don't want to drag that poor woman into. This is exactly why I stayed out of her hair.

"Can we head into Manhattan right now?" I ask.

The car pulls away from the curb. Andrei does just what I tell him. The drive is a blur. I'm barely aware of the time going past when we pull out in front of the building. I tap out a text.

I'm downstairs.

The phone bleeps.

Pull around to the service entrance. You'll have to circle the block, but it's often overlooked.

We pull up at the entrance to a dark alley. She must have been waiting because she appears almost immediately. She's a tiny figure swamped by a gray hoodie, with her hair tucked into a baseball cap pulled low over her eyes. She wears dark glasses. She could be anyone, and that intrigues me.

I'd forgotten just how tiny she is. It was one of the things I liked about fucking her that weekend. The way I could pick her up so easily. The urge to protect her. I stuff those thoughts down. This is a big enough clusterfuck without pulling sex into the mix.

"Already in disguise, I see," I say as she steps into the car.

"Years of practice." She pulls off her glasses and gives me a wan smile. "When avoiding the paparazzi, you either wear the same clothes every day so the picture is too boring to sell, or you dress so they can't see what's under all the layers. Usually I try to do both."

She's wringing her hands, knotting and unknotting her fingers. Her nervousness is so jarring that, on instinct, I reach over and pull her hands into mine. This is what got us into this mess—my urge to protect her, which is only a few steps away from the pull to rip off her clothes and destroy that tiny body with my hands, my mouth, my cock.

Her small fingers curl around mine and she squeezes my hands, her legs turning toward me until she faces me in the back of the car. She raises her head, and her eyes search mine.

"You said you didn't want a relationship with her." She just holds my hands and waits, her gaze steady and brave.

"I don't," I confirm.

She swallows, but she keeps her composure. There's something touching about her bravery in the face of all of this.

When I got to the US, I did what I needed to do to protect her, and then I'd pushed her to the back of my mind. When I did think of her, it was as a star belting out love songs in skimpy clothes. I got used to walking out of the room when her songs came on so that no one could see how I felt. But I didn't give in to the temptation to think about her often, and only when I was alone, at night, under the covers.

She's still just as beautiful.

Maybe more so.

"I've been a good mother. She's brave because everyone in my world has her back. Since you don't want to be part of that, I won't tell her who you are."

Sighing, I drop her hands and lean back, looking at the roof of the car. I want to touch her as much as I ever did. All the layers just make me want to strip them away, but I need to put her off.

"It's a shame you didn't tell lover boy back at the club that he needed to keep his mouth shut. No one would have known she was mine if he'd had the sense to keep schtum, but he was ranting about what a bad father I was."

She nods, and her lips thin. She's working hard to keep it together, so I resist the temptation to keep touching her, but god I want to. I want to so much.

"Okay. I'll tell him he'd better not say another word. He'll listen, but I gather you don't wish us ill, even if"—she takes a deep breath and sits up a little straighter—"you don't wish to be part of our lives."

"That's right. It's all bad timing. There are some . . . Well, the less you know. As I said."

"Was it anything to do with the pretty redhead I saw you with?" She's a quick study to have taken in so much that night. Or perhaps she's just jealous. Either way, I don't respond to her question.

"If you give me the address of your place upstate, I can have one of my men look it over to see if it's safe."

"It'll just be the three of us."

"Three of you. Who else is there?" I've kept tabs on her over the years. Surely there's not a man I don't know about.

"Nona, our housekeeper."

"Oh, the Georgian woman? Okay. Well, the food will be good if she's with you. I suppose she can come to the safe house with you if it comes to that." I shrug, pretending I had nothing to do with who she hired to look after the kid I hadn't admitted, even to myself, was mine.

"How did you know she was Georgian?" Her green gaze holds questions. I don't tell her that Nona worked for Antonov back in Moscow and we've crossed paths before. I don't tell her that I was the one who paid a visit to the Upper Westside Nannies and made sure that Nona was at the top of the list of recruits for the nanny job.

"I've had a few guys watching you since we met at the club. Checking to see if there was any danger. So far, so good, but we don't want to push our luck. If we can get you to a safe house or out of town for a week or two until some of the tension dies down, that would be better."

"I'll tell Nadia that you're Nona's nephew."

"Hopefully I won't be there and it won't matter."

I don't ask what she's told my daughter about me. I've listened to her album about gold and beauty and love bringing her back to herself. It doesn't tally with my recollections of her meeting a rough gangster who ravaged her body in a run-down cottage in the woods.

She doesn't say anything more, but her eyes are shiny. She looks out the rear window and swipes a tear away from one eye with the sleeve of her gray sweatshirt. If she'd been angry or crying hysterically, it would have been less moving. There's something about her quiet dignity and her attempt to keep her feelings under wraps that twists my guts. I can't help myself as I pull her twined hands up to my mouth and press a kiss to her knuckles.

"I'm sorry, zolotaya. You don't deserve to have your life turned upside down. I'll do my best to be kind. For the kid's sake."

She nods and inches away from me on the back seat, but I grip her hands tighter.

"And for yours. Truly, I'm sorry," I say. "I never wanted you to be part of this mess."

I lean over and press another kiss to her forehead, and she stills. We sit like that for what feels like an hour but is probably only a minute. Then she pulls away from me. Her scent of jasmine and roses lingers in the air between us.

"Be ready to go in the morning," I say as she opens the door.

She exits the car and walks away down the alley. I follow her with my eyes until I see the door open at the base of the fire escape and light floods the dark street. She steps inside, back to another life. One I should never be part of.

"Drive."

Andrei pulls away. "Where to, boss?"

"Bolshoi. The Night Governor wants to see me, and it can't be good news."

CHAPTER TWENTY-FOUR

Kesera

I open the door and walk toward the service elevator. My reflection flashes in the mirror at the back of the grimy space. The person who stares back looks the way I feel. A small figure in sweats and a ball cap who could pass for a teenage boy. No hint of sex appeal or star power. My mouth is bracketed with lines of pain and my eyes circled with rings of insomnia.

Maybe that's why he doesn't want me. I'm no longer the young singer in gold beads and cowboy boots he took to bed in Moscow. The body under the sweats isn't quite the same either. My lower stomach bears a C-section scar, and while my boobs are a little bigger from having breastfed, they aren't quite as perky.

I shake the thoughts off, looking at my head turning from side to side as the elevator rises to the twenty-fifth floor. I thought when I won a Grammy and had a platinum-selling album that all my dreams would come true.

I open the apartment door and drop my keys into the

bowl next to a smiling picture of me, Nadia, and Nona. Nadia's about five in this picture, her blue eyes the same color as her tattered Elsa dress, the one she wore so much it fell apart and was covered in stains by the time she could no longer wriggle into it.

Humming the tune to "Let It Go" under my breath, I pick up the silver frame and look at the three of us. Nona has her arms around us, her gray hair in a bob and her smile wide enough to swallow all of our worries. Nadia sits on my lap and grins, her mouth missing teeth and the frayed sleeves of the nylon dress practically up to her elbows. Her eyes are the image of her father's. I'm looking down at her and smiling.

I slam the picture down next to the St. Petersburg china bowl I bought for my keys. Another attempt to fill the house with reminders of the man I made a child with. Another attempt to link Nadia to a heritage she's not likely to embrace now that her father has shattered the last of the illusions I clung to.

The keys ring against the porcelain as I shake the table.

That brief glimpse of tenderness was almost more painful than his coldness in the club the other night. The beautiful curve of his mouth. On my fingers. Against my forehead. His strong hands twined around mine. It reminds me why I fell for him and how it felt to be protected and cherished.

I look down at my watch. Six thirty. I have half an hour before Nadia gets home. I kick off my shoes and pad down the corridor in my socks. I can't face changing. I can't face the thought that I'm the one who has to do all the protecting and cherishing. Even Nona, who looks after me, relies on me for her wages.

I'm so tired as I sink to the bed. I tried to replace Vadim, but I didn't know how to do it. The nights out with people who just wanted to be photographed. Relationships that were little more than a series of photo ops. I'd taken a couple of

162

them home and had sex that felt like counting sheep. Part A goes into slot B. Disengage heart and mind.

Why does the touch of his hands on mine and the press of his lips on my forehead make me feel swollen and achey between my legs? Why didn't any of those other men make me ache the way Vadim did? What the hell is wrong with me?

I put my arms around the pillow and burrow into the covers. I turn until my back is against the throw cushions and pretend there's a man behind me who will fit my body into the curve of his arms, curl his legs around mine, and wrap his arms around my stomach.

I pretend this pile of cushions is Vadim. That he still wants me. And I let the tears come. Hope, fear, and longing fight for space behind my eyes. Heartbreak comes up behind them all and floods me until the tears leak from my tightly shut lids.

My shoulders shake and my eyes scrunch into tight balls. No one is here to see me crying like a five-year-old whose Elsa princess dress doesn't fit her anymore.

No one cares.

No one is going to wipe my tears away.

I've got nothing but an empty bed and a pile of pillows and a stack of packed bags in a penthouse on the twenty-fifth floor.

I'm crying for all the things that I can't have. Things that are close enough to touch but so far out of reach they might as well be half a world away in the frozen woods outside Moscow. I cry because I wish he loved me the way I once believed I loved him.

My phone chimes on the nightstand. It's not the burner, so I know it's not Vadim, but I don't know who else would be texting me right now.

I pull the phone to my face and blink. It's my lawyer. She's been in touch with five other stars who wish to pursue legal action against Jimmy, and at least three more who have admitted to misconduct but are afraid to come forward. If the mediation goes well, if these girls see that justice can prevail, they might be willing to speak out as well.

I have a chance to help these women, to give them the courage to take those first terrifying steps. But how can I do that when I have to hide in the shadows to protect myself and my child from the other monsters encroaching on us?

There is only one answer. I can't.

CHAPTER TWENTY-FIVE

Vadim

Oksana perches at the nightclub bar, nursing a luridly colored cocktail, when I arrive at Bolshoi. The after-work crowd is trickling in. A group of loud American guys in suits howls about Russian strippers and shots, and I worry they might be trouble.

I sidle up to Oksana, who narrows her blue eyes when she sees me. "He's upstairs, waiting for you."

Glancing around the room, I survey the exits out of habit and check the empty seats. "They won't be a headache?" I jerk my chin toward the table of braying suits.

"Nothing I can't handle, sweetheart. Get upstairs. The Governor has his storm-cloud face on."

Nodding, I make my way to the back, to the small library the Night Governor keeps as an office in our Brighton Beach club. My feet feel like lead as I climb the stairs and think about Kesera sitting in the Governor's office. I hope against hope he hasn't figured out who she is to me.

My phone vibrates in my pocket, and I pull it out to see a coded text from Sasha.

Got you covered. Two birds in the hand.

Thank god. I let my forehead thunk against the door frame, my hand stilling on the handle as a sigh gusts out of me and my shoulders drop half an inch. Sasha has secured more than one safe house for us.

Pushing on the door handle, I step into the darkened room. The smell of books, leather, and the faint whiff of cigar smoke lingers in the air as Yevgeny Guelman watches me with gray eyes from behind the desk.

He waves to a chair, and I sit across from him, waiting for him to speak, but he doesn't. He just watches me.

The deep lines in his forehead and his big, mournful eyes make him look like a man who carries the sadness of the world, not a monster who feeds off other people's pain. I don't say a word. I just lower myself to the seat and watch him, waiting for him to speak. I didn't know the redhead was important when I picked her up, but his first words don't surprise me.

Guelman lifts a Montblanc pen and waves it at me. "You do know ignorance is no defense in the eyes of the law."

"Or the eyes of the Night Governor?" I sit back in the chair, spread my legs slightly, and fold my hands over my stomach, trying to look as relaxed as possible when my whole body is alert. He won't kill me here, though. He likes to keep his office as a sanctuary, a refuge from the murder and chaos he creates. I'll meet with an accident: my brakes will fail, or I'll suffer an unexplained heart attack.

Guelman presses his lips together and then stabs the pen into the blotter in front of him, letting the dark ink bleed into the paper. "Your little stunt with the Spataro girl has caused a huge headache. Vincenzo Spataro is livid, and I am not best pleased either. So, where is my lovely bride?"

I blow out a breath, thanking every god known to man that he's not asking about Kesera and my daughter. "I left her with Sasha. She looked like—"

"I know exactly who she looked like, which is why I wanted her." He draws a picture of a knife on the blotting paper and licks his lips.

Why the fuck does Guelman want a woman who looks exactly like the nine-year-old girl he rescued from an orphanage? I know he didn't have fatherly feelings for us, but my skin crawls at the thought that he might have put his hands all over the first woman I ever loved and now he's looking for a young, nubile replica.

"So, what would you like to do?" I lean forward with my hands on my knees like I'm hanging on his every word, but I'm silently vowing that Guelman will never get his hands on any other woman I care about. Even if I can't let myself love Kesera or be any part of my daughter's life, I'll die before I let the Night Governor touch my family.

"You'd better get Alessandra Spataro back to her father within the next few days or there will be hell to pay. Tell Yaponchik that he'll deliver the girl back to the don himself if he knows what's good for him."

I watch him with a poker face, not reacting to the fact he calls Sasha, who's half-Chinese, Yaponchik. "You don't want us to deliver the girl to you?"

He grins, and his gold tooth flashes next to elongated canines that look like they could rip the flesh from any woman stupid enough to get into his orbit. That girl must have sensed the threat and tried to run. "She's a lovely little package, but this marriage is, first and foremost, an alliance with her father. Do him the courtesy of returning his daughter for him to punish first."

The way he says the word *punish* makes me wonder what he has planned for the girl. Before I can say anything or rise to leave, he continues.

"Spataro controls all the cocaine that comes into New York, and I'll be stronger than ever if I marry his daughter, but it's his business that matters." In a move that turns my stomach, Guelman reaches down to adjust himself in his pants. "The girl is just a nice bonus. A little gift for me to play with."

Nodding with an expressionless mask on my face, I don't show how his words make my skin crawl. The way he describes the woman he plans to marry is frankly creepy, but it's also concerning that the bride he's chosen looks like a child he brought up. The image of Polina's dead body springs unbidden into my mind, but I push it away as I rise to my feet.

My shoes slide on the expensive Persian carpet as I put some distance between myself and the monster who controls the Russian Mafia. I thank god Guelman hasn't mentioned Kesera yet. "I'll see what I can do."

"You understand the consequences," Guelman says in an oily voice as I open the door and listen to the music drifting up the stairs.

I turn and nod.

Sasha is my best hope now. He likes to pretend he doesn't have a heart, but I'd be surprised if he plans to hand the girl back to her father so that she can be a toy for Guelman to break.

And if he protects the girl, we're going to be in a world of trouble. Trouble I'll need to shelter my family from.

CHAPTER TWENTY-SIX

Vadim

There's a buzz of activity around the docks as I pull up in my car. Three heavily tattooed Chinese guys—strangers I've never seen before—are lined up, moving boxes of rifles in a human chain to another lorry.

"It would be quicker to use a forklift. This isn't the dark ages." Sasha's voice rings out from inside the metal containers as I climb out of the car. My eye is drawn to a muscular Asian guy with an air of authority.

Sasha emerges from the shipping container with a box of guns, which he passes to one of the men with a grin before walking up to the man I was watching . He pulls him into a one-armed hug, but the Chinese guy's lips twist and he shrugs Sasha's arm off his shoulder.

"Kai, this is Vadim, my right-hand man. Vadim, Kai saved my life when I first got to China. We're old friends."

They don't look particularly friendly, but I raise a hand in greeting.

"What's with all the manpower? You checking all this by hand?" I nod at the men moving weapons.

"They don't trust you. You're not one of us," Kai says, and I catch Sasha's wince before he beckons me toward the container at the edge of the dock where a desk and a couple of stools balance unsteadily on the metal floor. Not Russian enough for the Night Governor, but not accepted by the Chinese either.

Once we get inside, the smile drops off his face and lines of exhaustion bracket his mouth.

"I've got you two places to hide if you need to. One of them is linked to Kai, so Guelman won't know about it. I called in a favor." Sasha pulls a crumpled packet of cigarettes from his pocket, drawing one out with his teeth before throwing it my way.

I snatch the packet as it flies toward me, and then I light it up and pull out a stool. "I owe you."

Sasha walks over and drops two sets of house keys into my hand. "You don't. I fucked up with Polina. The fact the Night Governor wants a woman who looks like my sister . . ." He shudders.

Unsaid words hang between us in the smoky air.

Sasha takes another drag, blowing the smoke in a ring that breaks as it rises higher. Then he looks up at me and purses his lips. "I'm sick of pacifying the boss. He's a monster and he's never going to let us out from under his thumb. Kai is my best hope. Everything's shifting, which means it could be an opportunity or . . ."

The silence is pregnant with all the ways this could go wrong. I close my eyes, and images jostle for space. The Night Governor grinning as he talked about the new toy he planned to marry. The woman in the back seat of my limo talking about the child I never wanted our boss to find out

170

about. Christ. The ways this could blow up in our faces are endless.

"Do you trust him?" I ask.

Sasha doesn't get a chance to reply before the sliver of sunlight from the doorway is blocked and footsteps ring on the metal floor. There are a dozen unfamiliar gangsters moving guns around our docks. The Night Governor is making threats. I'm losing control of everything at the worst time.

Sasha won't trust anyone who won't drink with him. Kai must know him well enough to know that because he walks silently to the table and slides the bottle of vodka toward Sasha, but I've got no idea what's going on.

Sasha watches him as he pours, and Kai throws the drink back and then looks between us without saying a word.

"The chess pieces are moving on the board, and I need the Spataro girl out of the way." Sasha slides his glass toward his so-called friend and watches the spirit glug into it.

Kai picks up the drink and twirls it in his hands before confirming my instinct that nothing about this is a done deal. "You're not Gary Kasparov. What's in it for me?"

Sasha watches his friend's face until Kai finally puts the glass to his lips, and then he seems to come to a decision. "Do those guys outside trust you?"

Finally, Kai cracks a smile, leaning his forearm on his knees. "You know they don't. If you don't speak Wu dialect like the rest of the snakeheads, you aren't one of them."

"Well, the Night Governor doesn't trust me either, and if he marries this girl, he'll be unstoppable, so . . ." Sasha pauses to inhale. "I'm asking you to gamble on me." He hitches a thumb toward me. "On both of us. To see if we can't become more powerful."

Kai doesn't answer the question. He places the shot glass

on the table and rises to his feet. "I'd better get back to the men outside."

Once Kai's out of earshot, I stand. "The triads? You sure that's a good idea?" I step toward the door, but Sasha's fingers circle my arm and he drags me backward.

"You got any better ones?"

Turning to my best friend, my stomach twists and I blow out a long breath. I've got nothing to offer, and Sasha is doing what he always does. Finding a way out.

He shrugs like it's no big deal. "Kai always comes through. He just needs a while to think about it. The Italians will be looking for the Spataro girl, but they'll be following you. If we can get the Italian chick out of the way while I figure out exactly who is pissed off and how much, perhaps we can come out of this with a way to make more money."

He pulls me back to the table and pours another vodka shot. It's warm, but I sling it back like it's the best thing I've ever tasted. Then I pull my knife from my pocket and run my finger over the blade. "I need to get my kid and the woman out of the way."

Sasha's eyes follow the blade I'm spinning in my hands. It's something I do when I'm nervous.

"You worried?" he asks.

"Hell yes. What am I supposed to do with a ten-year-old?"

Sasha sputters and doubles over with laughter. "He's started a fucking mafia war, and what really freaks him out is babysitting." He's wheezing as he wipes his eyes. "Fucking brilliant, man. This is brilliant."

"Why?" I regard him over the knife blade. "What's so funny?"

"Come on. It's absurd. You've got to see the funny side." He's still chuckling to himself as I glare at the table.

"And if I get my own daughter killed? I stayed out of their

lives to prevent this kind of shit from happening. Now that I'm back, it's exactly as I predicted."

"Only because you decided to go and play savior."

It's my fault. Yet again, my best intentions are warped by the world we live in.

Sasha senses my anguish and grips my shoulder, giving me a shake. "We've put men on them, and so far we haven't seen anything. Get them to a safe house outside the city. If it comes to it, grab a go-bag and a suitcase of cash and take them on a road trip."

"Kesera said she had a place we could use in upstate New York. One of our guys is seeing how well we can secure it. Perhaps a couple of days on the road wouldn't hurt." I'll pick her up in the morning and text her with the new plan.

I listen for the sound of a truck door slamming and the Chinese pulling out with the guns.

"Can we get out of here?" I say. I feel itchy and when I get that feeling, I know it's time to move. Listening to my gut has saved me on more than one occasion.

"Give me a second. I'll just check the guns are gone."

Sasha strolls out to the dock and looks at the concrete. I follow him, and it's empty. I breathe a sigh of relief, but before I can ask my best friend about the safe house, a screech of tires breaks the soft slap of the tide before a burst of gunfire rings out. He's scrabbling for his gun as he runs out and ducks behind my Mercedes, frantically looking around for the source of the shots.

Exactly how vulnerable I am hits me like a fist to the gut. Because I'm not helping my friend shoot the intruders. I'm fishing in my pocket for the Nokia, trying to reach the woman I can't stop thinking about. I lie on the floor, one hand on my gun and the other on my phone.

Come on. Come on. Pick up. Don't mess about now, I pray.

Her soft voice comes over the line as another crack of bullets rings through the twilight.

"Kesera. Take the kid and Nona and go to the deli across the street. Don't wait. Take what you can carry and look for the kid with the spider tattoo. It's not safe. You need to get out of the house right now. Andrei will get you out of town."

The sound of shooting drowns out her reply.

CHAPTER TWENTY-SEVEN

Kesera

I'm done. Done with taking orders from men who don't have my welfare at heart. Fuck that shit. The only people I can seem to trust these days are the people on my payroll. It sucks that it's come to this, but I will not blindly follow orders from a man who says he doesn't want a relationship with his own daughter.

I look at the bags stacked by the door. I inhale deeply, willing myself to be calm after hearing gunfire on the other end of the line. "What have we packed?"

Nona picks up a list and starts counting off everything she's prepared. "Passports. Money. Phones. Nadia's asthma medication. Clothes. Cards from your Japanese bank account. Harder to trace."

I smile at Nona. Always five steps ahead, whether she's making dinner or packing to go on the run. God knows, she'd be the CEO of something if she hadn't had to flee a war when her kids were young.

175

"Okay. Let me call the security guys from the last tour. I need someone I can count on," I say.

I stroll into the bedroom and pick up the phone. Nadia's making a video in her room as she chatters to her dolls. One minute she wants black contacts and the next she's playing with a dollhouse and wanting me to rock her to sleep.

Taking a deep breath, I dial Double Canopy, the ex-military guys who ran security for my last tour. Dex served with my dad in Okinawa before he set up his own gig. If I trust anyone's advice, it's his.

"Double Canopy," the deep voice booms down the line.

The tightness in my shoulders softens when I hear his voice, and I'm centered once again. Even if he can't run security for us right now, he'll know what to do.

"Dex. Thank god you answered. I'm in a pickle."

"How serious? Cornichon or cucumber?"

I snort. I don't want to start thinking about penis-shaped vegetables. "Well, it's a kind of Russian pickle. Remember I told you about Nadia's father?"

"What? You found him?"

"Stumbled across him, more like. I was out with Stevie at some club in Brooklyn and after ten years of searching, there he was. Suffice to say, he wasn't pleased to see me."

I laugh bitterly as I run through the last twenty-four hours. The burner phones. The instruction to go down to the deli and find the man with the spider tattoo. I skip the part where he pressed his lips to my forehead and I could taste how it had been between us.

Dex is wheezing with laughter now. "Seriously? He asked you to go to a deli and meet a man with a spider tattoo? That sounds like one of those movies where you're shouting at the screen, 'You idiots are too stupid to live!'" His voice levels off now, and he sounds more serious as he says, "I really shouldn't need to tell you this. You do not leave to go to a second location with a man you don't know."

"Right, Dex." I smile, imagining his face right now. "Nona has packed go-bags. but I honestly don't know what I'm dealing with here. I don't know who knows about our connection to this man, and I don't know what kind of trouble he's in or might bring to my door. What are my next steps?"

"For starters, don't get in a car with a strange man. And don't accept any candy from strangers either." He chuckles again. "Sorry, this is serious. Do you have proper wheels and gas?"

"Yeah, I've got the SUV. Where should I go? I'm scared, Dex." I hear my voice shake, but I swallow the tears down. I don't add that I'm heartbroken too. Scared is bad enough.

"Head upstate to your place. Nadia will be far less freaked out. Change the code when you get in, and send me the number on the secure line. The house isn't impenetrable, but if anything happens, you just head straight to the panic room in the basement and wait it out. Don't mess around. Just hang there and one of us will break you out. I'll get moving right now."

"How far away are you?"

"If I drive all night, I'll get to you by first light."

"Okay. We're going now. I'll get the bags and tell Nadia. Love you, Dex. Thanks."

"Roger that, kiddo. We've got your back."

I place the phone back on its receiver. Honestly, I don't know what I've been thinking for the last twenty-four hours. I was so emotional and shell-shocked that I was just nodding at a man who asked me to disappear.

Get in a car with a kid with a spider tattoo? With my ten-year-old daughter? Vadim must think I'm a moron as well as unlovable. One of those things might be true, but I didn't get this far in the business without a good head on my shoulders.

I stride down the corridor. "Come on, kiddo. We're heading out for the weekend."

Nadia doesn't look up from her screen.

"We're going to the Gingerbread House. If there's anything you need for the next few days, it needs to fit in your backpack. We might have to go on a road trip."

"Mom!" It comes out as a high-pitched whine. "It's free dress day on Tuesday. We can't go on a road trip. Anyway, Sister Hayes says that children of celebrities shouldn't get special treatment."

Poor kid. I've tried hard to make her life normal, but it isn't and there's nothing I can do about it. I take her hands in mine and squat on my haunches so that she's looking down at me.

"Sorry, baby. Sister Hayes is right, but remember Dex, mom's friend who does the security for our tours? He thinks there might be a security issue for us."

Nadia nods at me, her eyes going wide.

"So I need you to do what Mom and Nona say. Okay?"

Nadia nods again and throws herself into my arms. "Can I take Mr. Doggie?" she says, plucking her crumpled stuffed dog from the floor. Mr. Doggie is gray now, despite repeated washes. All the love has bleached him of color, but he's still Nadia's favorite.

"Sure you can, baby. Dex will be with us in the morning, and we'll be fine, okay?"

I blindly stuff clothing into Nadia's bag, unable to concentrate on packing because of the thoughts swirling around my mind. I'm still locked in my own head as we start for the SUV and venture into the night.

THE DARK FEELS cold and unwelcoming by the time we pull up at the gates of the countryside place we call the Gingerbread House. I push the code on my phone to open them.

Nadia is asleep on Nona's lap in the back seat, and Nona's drifted off too. I'm alone with my thoughts in the darkness when the burner phone beeps in my bag. I drive to the house and wait for the gates to close behind me before I pull it out.

The green screen lights up with a text from Vadim.

> Please tell me you're safe. Andrei said you didn't come and there's no answer at your place.

I don't reply. I just stare out at the trees around the house that looks exactly like the little Hansel and Gretel cottage in the woods where we made Nadia. There are no tears left to cry at this point.

> Your doorman wouldn't tell Andrei anything.

Seriously? He sends a young hoodlum with a neck tattoo to ask about me, and he wonders why no one has said anything? Is he an idiot too?

> I'm going out of my head with worry.

Oh, so *now* he's concerned? Well, too fucking late, Mr. Mafioso. We're gonna be just fine without you.

The phone rings, but I toss it into my bag. Let him sweat. He doesn't want a relationship with either of us, so what do I care if he's out of his head with worry?

As I open the car door, a prickle climbs my spine. It's as if someone is watching me. The phone goes silent as I pull our bags from the trunk. I shake Nona awake, then step out into the darkness. The smell of pine and dew fills my lungs as I scan the trees. Shivering slightly, I let the car door close, alert for some unseen threat.

The velvet darkness of the woods surrounds us. An owl calls as I walk up to the high iron gates and run a hand down them to ensure they're closed. The gravel crunches underfoot, but mine are the only footsteps I hear. There is only the quiet of the trees at night. And the nagging sense that I'm not alone.

Chapter Twenty-Eight

Vadim

Birdsong and the cold kiss of a blade against my throat wake me.

"Don't move if you know what's good for you," a low American voice says. Sunlight filters behind my eyelids as I listen to the accent. Southern. Not New York. Not an Italian hitman, then?

Slowly, I open my eyes and look at the figure in black that looms over me.

"I don't know what you're doing here, but you'll find its better for your health if you put the car into reverse and leave now," the man says.

I look up into the weathered face of a bulky guy with a military buzz cut. He's built like a fighter—six foot four of solid muscle, but he looks light on his feet.

Kesera's gates stand just beyond the woodland area where I parked the car last night. I search the trees for Andrei and come up empty. While resisting the temptation to stretch, I silently damn Kesera for not answering my calls as I drove up here. I also curse Andrei for leaving me so exposed.

"So, you'll be happy if I just pull out and drive home before I've had a chance to talk to my woman?" I keep still and look at the man who has offered to let me leave. He keeps the knife to my skin, and the steel warms as it rests against my neck. His hand steadies the blade.

"If she was your woman, she wouldn't have called me to drive through the night to get to her at first light. I've dealt with dozens of men like you on her tours. You might think you have a unique connection, but I'm telling you that you're nothing special."

After hearing more of his southern drawl, I'm sure he's not one of the Italians or connected to the Night Governor. This means Kesera came up with this on her own. I almost smile at the thought that I underestimated her.

"Bit difficult to go anywhere with a knife to my throat, don't you think?" I say carefully. Let's not antagonize the big guy with the weapon until Andrei gets here.

"Which is why I'm going to take the knife away from your throat very slowly. And when you sit up, you're going to remember that I've got a gun pointed at your back and it's aiming at your heart. Hard to miss at this range." He gives a soft chuckle and sounds even more like he's from Texas. Despite the fact that he's got a gun pointed at me, that's good news.

We haven't been compromised. Yet.

He steps back, keeping the gun pointed at me. After waiting a couple of beats, I sit up slowly, raising both hands in the air before I turn to face him. My shoulders loosen at the sight of Andrei creeping toward us from the other side of the gates, gun drawn.

"Put the gun down or I'll shoot first and ask questions

later," Andrei bites out, firing a shot wide of the car to make his point.

I'll give the big fucker facing me some credit. He doesn't even flinch. He keeps his gun pointed at me and raises an eyebrow in question.

"Let's see if we can avoid dead bodies before breakfast," I say. "Kesera probably wouldn't like it."

"And exactly how are you an authority on what Kesera would like, my friend? If she'd been thrilled to see you, then I wouldn't be here with your wake-up call. So do you want your sidekick to put the firearm down, or shall we play musical guns?"

I nod at Andrei, who steps from the brush so the tall man with the military build can see him. The man lowers his gun, watching us both.

"She's not answering her phone," I say, tilting my head to the old handset.

"We'll see about that, shall we? If it's not too much trouble, I'll call her."

I nod at him, and he pulls a phone from his pocket. She answers after only a few seconds.

"Morning, kiddo. I'm standing outside your gate with a couple of gangsters from central casting. Scar face and spider tattoo. Do you know them?" He nods. "Uh huh. Okay. I can. You want spider tattoo as well, or just the dude with the scar? Right you are. See you inside." Shaking his head, he steps back from the car and waves his hand at me. "You can go on in. God knows why, but she's happy to talk to you."

I'm about to smile at that, but he quashes the emotion.

"As long as I'm there. I don't think she's too keen on any one-on-one time with you two, so do as I say and nobody needs to get hurt."

Reaching slowly toward him, I hold out my hand. "The name

is Vadim, and my friend over there is Andrei. You're welcome to use our nicknames, but if you're trying to make Kesera comfortable, that might not be the best way to go about it."

"Well, telling her to take her kid and meet a guy with a tattoo on his neck in a diner wasn't the best move either. You need to work on your technique, man." He grins at me, walks to the gate, and taps in a code.

Great. I didn't peg this guy for a love interest. He's at least a decade older than me, but he's in good shape, she answers his calls, and he's got her door code. It makes me antsy. I don't know what kind of men she likes. I don't know nearly enough about her.

Andrei walks over to the car, and I fire up the engine and slam the door. As the gates swing open and I drive up the winding road to the house, my headache returns and my heart starts to race. It's not just the fact that I didn't get enough sleep, because there in front of me, clearly visible through a copse of birch trees, is a pale-green and white wooden house that is a near-exact replica of our cottage in the woods outside Moscow. The dacha where I spent hours learning the taste and feel of every inch of Kesera's body.

CHAPTER TWENTY-NINE

Kesera

The screen door bangs and feet pound the floorboards as Dex stomps across the room, takes me by the shoulders, and gives them a squeeze. I slant my eyes toward the doorway where Vadim stands looking stunned, his gaze bouncing between the Russian fairy tale prints on the wooden walls, the Uzbek embroidery thrown over the sofas, and the central Asian rugs on the floors. I designed the whole house to look like an upscale version of the cottage where we conceived Nadia.

Vadim swallows hard, and the color drains from his face. He looks like he's seen a ghost.

"You okay, kiddo?" Dex's kind eyes look down at me, their edges crinkled with years of sunshine and smiling.

I glance between him and Vadim, glad I have someone in my corner too. Whatever he's seen in the army and since, I'm always happy that Dex was around for me once my fame blew up. It's been good to have someone I trust run my security, and right now it's even better to have a big burly man run interference between me and Vadim.

"Yeah, I'm doing fine. Nona's in the kitchen making coffee and breakfast, and Nadia's either still asleep or glued to a screen." I look over at the corridor and the closed bedroom doors as Dex pulls me toward a sofa and presses my shoulders. I sit, and he takes his place beside me.

"Why don't you gentlemen come in, take a seat, and we can have a chat about the security situation." Dex picks up his gun and waves it at the two armchairs facing the sofa.

Vadim walks slowly over to one, collapsing into it and scrubbing his face with his hands like he's trying to wake up from a dream. Or maybe he feels like it's a nightmare. Either way, it's not my problem. My only concern now is our daughter.

I glance at his friend and wave my hand to the younger guy with the spiderweb climbing up his neck. "Take a seat," I point at the armchair, and he grins back at me.

"This crib is totally sweet. It's so cool. I bet the head of our—" He stumbles over the next word. "Organization . . . would lose his mind if he saw it. It's just like the village houses near Moscow." He looks thrilled, while Vadim looks like he might throw up.

Vadim shakes his head at me. "What's going on, Kesera?" His arm sweeps in an arc, pointing at the Russian décor. "What is all this?"

"This is our weekend place." I play it straight, deliberately ignoring his point. "But we aren't here to talk about my taste in furnishings. I called Dex because he's my head of security and he runs things on our tours. He helped me design the setup here, and if there's a threat to myself or Nadia, then I'd like to plan the next steps with someone on my payroll."

My voice sounds firm, stressing the word payroll in the hope that I come across like a strong businesswoman and not a lovesick fool who built a shrine to the bastard who fathered her child and then never got in touch.

I'm clasping my hands together to stop their trembling. I have no reason to feel shaken after the shocks of the last few days. I could simply be worried about security and not feeling heartsick. The less I give away at the moment, the better.

I remind myself I don't know who I'm dealing with. The man who made me feel so cherished in Moscow has nothing to do with the man sitting on the chair opposite me, looking shell-shocked.

"I don't understand." Still looking slightly dazed, Vadim shakes his head.

Okay, I need to stop this nonsense. "No, I'm the one who doesn't understand. If you're serious about keeping us safe, then we both need to know what's going on."

Vadim looks over at Dex, assessing him coolly before seeming to come to a decision. He nods to himself, then addresses the man sitting next to me on the sofa.

"I made a sentimental decision to help someone the other night. In doing so, I set off a fight with a very senior figure in the Italian Mafia. My boss is a very dangerous man, and he's angry too. Exactly what that might mean, we aren't sure yet." He pauses and looks over at his young sidekick, who shrugs.

"Nadia has school, and I have an ongoing court case in the southern district of New York. Do I need to make a plan to leave town on Monday, or can we sit tight and try to disrupt Nadia's life as little as possible?" I'm pleased with how composed and businesslike I sound, but that falls apart with his next words.

"It depends on how many people know she's my daughter."

"Will you keep your voice down?" I hiss. "The most important thing at this juncture is that she doesn't know, and unless you're planning on sticking around, I'm not about to tell her."

Vadim's face is a picture of horror, and I turn to see where he's looking. Nadia stands in the doorway, her legs sticking out of fluffy pink pajamas that are too short for her. She adjusts her grip on her favorite stuffed dog toy.

"Whose daughter am I?"

CHAPTER THIRTY

Vadim

I never understood America's obsession with the film *Star Wars*, but at this moment, staring at the trembling kid standing opposite me in the doorway, I feel like Darth Vader.

I look over at the little girl, whose head is swiveling between me and her mother, an expression of distress etched on her face. "Good morning," I say.

"Is it?" She fixes me with a pale-blue stare that reflects my eyes back at me, and then she looks between her mother and me. "Whose daughter am I?"

Without thinking, I answer. "Mine."

"Wow, Mom. You suck so much." The kid turns tail and runs back to her bedroom, her footsteps thudding down the corridor as she drops her stuffed dog in the doorway. It lies there, looking balefully at me from the floor.

Kesera's shoulders droop, and she drops her face into her hands, muttering to herself. "And of course, it's all my fault."

"No, zolotaya. It's entirely my fault." I stand and catch Dex's eye.

"I'll give you two a moment," he says as he walks toward the doorway and beckons Andrei to follow. "Why don't you come with me, and we'll go and check on that coffee."

Dropping next to Kesera on the sofa, I put my arm around her shoulder, trying to shelter her with my body, but she remains rigid and edges away from me.

"I need to check on Nadia. I have to go." She tries to rise.

I tighten my grip around her shoulders and circle her small frame in my arms, holding her until I feel some of the tension ease as I rest my chin on her hair. "I'm sorry I've made such a mess of this. I wanted to keep you safe, and I haven't even done that. Let me do my best to not make it any worse."

"I really need to go and see my daughter." She tries to rise again.

"Our daughter," I say softly, tucking a finger under her chin and tilting her face to mine. "She's ours."

Kesera's green eyes rove over my face before she shakes her head as if it doesn't matter. "You've been out of our lives for a decade. She's mine."

I regard her carefully, keeping my arms around her. "She'll always be yours, first and foremost. I know I've messed this up." I run my hands up and down her trembling arms as she tries to hold it together.

She gives me a wry smile. "You sure have. But I need to go to her."

"What will you tell her?"

"The truth."

"And what's that?"

"That I looked for you for ten years and I didn't find you until I'd given up. She'll like that. It's like one of the fairy tales I read her, where the answer only comes when the hero gives up." She gets up and starts toward the bedroom. "The dark kind of fairy tale where there's a price to be paid."

"What will you tell her about me?"

"That we met, did something beautiful, and made the most beautiful thing in my life. That's also the truth."

I get up to follow her as she turns away.

"The kitchen's that way." She waves to her left, her back to me. "Go find Dex and decide what our next move should be."

I reach out and grasp her hand. "What was the price?"

She stills, but she doesn't turn around as I finish the question.

"In the dark fairy tales, there's always a price to be paid. What did you pay for the most beautiful thing in your life?"

Her shoulders hunch toward her ears and then drop in defeat. "I got the fame, the money, and the child. But no man will ever love me." Her hand shakes loose from mine, and she walks toward the bedroom, her footsteps sending echoes of regret along my nerve endings.

I wish it was safe to love her. If I could love anyone, it would be her.

CHAPTER THIRTY-ONE

Kesera

Nadia's huddled under the covers. One foot sticks out of a duvet with moons, stars, and other magic symbols on it, evidence of a fast-fading Hogwarts phase. Now she's graduated to Addams Family style teenage angst.

"Go away," a muffled voice says from underneath the heap of bedclothes.

I perch next to her on the covers, running my hand up and down the outline of her shoulders. She's still so small. Still my little girl.

"I'm sorry, baby bear." I keep stroking her.

"You lied. You said that my father would love me if he knew me, but if he loved me, then why didn't he come to find us, Mommy?"

My heart breaks for her as her little tear-streaked face emerges from the bedding. If it were in my power, I'd shield her from all my heartbreaks.

I climb next to her and curl my legs behind her knees,

wrapping her in my body. "I don't know, bear. I don't know why he didn't come."

"Did he just find us?"

Pain spears through my guts, landing deep in my womb. How do I tell her he wasn't looking?

"I found him."

"Was it a quest? Like *The Hobbit*?"

"Not exactly. I looked for a few years. I wrote songs that I hoped would be magic spells to bring your father back to us. And then I decided that maybe I should just look after you and Nona and he'd find us when he was meant to."

"Is that what God wanted?"

These questions. How do you start to answer them? Sending her to a Catholic girls' school left me with more than I bargained for.

"That was what I decided. And then I found him last week, and now he's here."

"Did he come for me?"

The pain in my stomach twists and churns. "I don't know, honey. I do know he's worried about us, about our safety, which is why I called Dex. We might have to leave town for a while and do schooling online like you do when I go on tour."

"But we've got free dress day, and I'm supposed to make gingerbread cookies in cooking class." She looks despondent, and I twine my arms around her more tightly, squeezing her small frame.

"If there are some bad men looking for us, then we have to protect ourselves and follow Dex's advice."

"What about my dad? Will he come with us? Is he going to protect us too?"

"I don't know, Nadia. It's been many years since I saw him, and I don't know who he is today. Time can change people. Sometimes life is difficult and people get scarred by that." I don't add that I didn't know him at all. That I saw something in him that wasn't there.

She wriggles out of my grip and grins at me, looking animated all of a sudden. "Hey. Do you think my superpower will work?"

My brow furrows. "Which superpower?"

"You and Nona said that I could make anyone love me. Do you think I can make my dad love me? Do you think I can make him love all of us?" She pokes her head out of the duvet, hope animating her features, and I reach out to trace the streaks tears have left on her cheeks.

"Maybe. If his heart isn't broken too badly."

Nadia snuggles up against me and wraps her arms around my middle. Despite the teenage attitude, she's still a little girl who smells of cookies and fresh bread and has childish ideas about how the world works.

"I bet I can fix him," she says.

She sits up and regards me steadily, wisps of hair escaping from the braids I put in last night. The style has the dual advantage of making her look like Wednesday Addams while also stopping her hair from getting tangled. I pick up one of the braids and run it through my fingers.

"Baby bear, it really doesn't work like that. I don't think you can just fix people."

"Mom, do you think you'll fall in love with my dad again?" Nadia's eyes scan my features carefully, as if she can find the answers on my face.

"I don't know, honey. Probably not. Ten years is a long time without seeing someone, and I didn't spend a long time with him in Russia."

"But you didn't say never. Isn't that what you usually say? Never say never?"

As I stand and bend down to press a kiss to her forehead,

footsteps head down the corridor. I pray to god they weren't Vadim's.

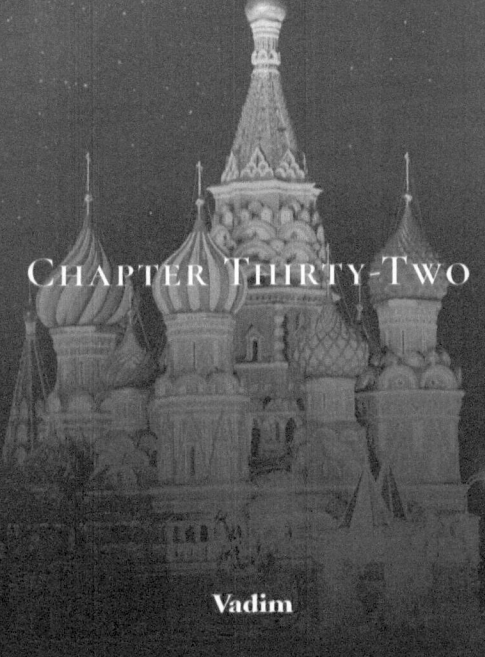

CHAPTER THIRTY-TWO

Vadim

The kitchen is a hum of activity. It's like a play where all the actors know their roles and I haven't learned my lines. I lean in the doorway and watch the morning tableau with a sharp stab of longing.

In another life, this could have been mine.

I shake my head to knock that string of thought loose. No good can come from it.

An older woman with wide hips and bobbed gray hair pours batter into a pan on the stove, making thin golden pancakes. I recognize Nona from Moscow. She flips the blini in the pan and browns the other side before sliding it onto a tall stack and walking the plate over to a small kitchen table. She sets it down before Dex, who grins and pulls it toward him.

"Nona, will you marry me? I'd ride off into the sunset with you for your pancakes alone." His eyes twinkle up at her.

"Stupid man. Blini." She points down at the stack of

crepes and shakes her head. "Not pancakes. Terrible American things. Don't taste good."

"I bet I could make you love them. With bacon and syrup." Dex licks his lips and blows her a kiss as she laughs at him.

My daughter sits between them. "Knock it off, Dex. Nona's not going to marry you until I'm grown up. She has to cook me all the good food until I'm big and strong." The words turn into a mumble as she talks around a mouthful of pancake.

"Close your mouth when you eat. And elbows off the table," Kesera says as she comes in behind me. "Sit, Vadim. You need breakfast. Is there sour cream, Nona? I'm not counting calories this morning."

"Shouldn't be counting calories ever." Nona brings sour cream, honey, and jam to the table. She gestures at an empty seat and I lower myself into it, trying to wrap my head around the scene in front of me and wondering what my lines should be in this play.

The presence of my daughter has thrown me for a loop. I know nothing about girls, let alone small girls.

Andrei stands at the back door with a smirk. "I'm going for a cigarette, boss. Enjoy your breakfast."

I'm about to flip him off when I remember my daughter is sitting opposite me. I look over at her as she watches me spear a forkful of blini and bring it to my mouth, choking it down at her next sentence.

"So, Dad, do I have any brothers and sisters?"

Dex snorts with laughter. "Way to go for the jugular, kid."

"What's a jugular?"

Dex grins at her and draws a line across his throat. "It's an artery right here," he says, pointing his fork at Nadia.

She smirks at him before turning back to me. "It would be

cool if I had a sister, but I'm not sure how I feel about brothers. Boys stink."

I smile at her and look over at her mother, who's standing by the table and watching me warily. I keep my eyes on hers as I reply. "You're my one and only."

"As far as you know." Dex chokes back another laugh, but stops when he sees my thunderous expression.

"This isn't something I would joke about. I wouldn't bring children into a world where I can't keep them safe. I'm quite sure." My gaze bounces between mother and daughter, taking in Kesera's tense posture and my daughter's carefree fixation on her breakfast.

"Is that why you didn't come and find us?" Nadia asks, tilting her head to the side as she picks up a bottle of honey and pours it all over her blini.

"Something like that. I thought it would be better for all of you if I stayed away."

Nadia raises her head and fixes me with her pale-blue eyes. It's like looking in a mirror. She looks so much like me. I meet her stare and wait to see if she'll look away, but I cast my gaze down first. Unlike when I'm staring down guys who work for me or men who owe me money, I'm the one who's most nervous in this staring contest.

"I'm glad you're here. I'd like to have a dad," she says, and then cuts her blini in half, jamming it into her mouth so that she's too full to say more.

Kesera scrubs at her eyes and then sits down at the table. I take a deep breath. My stomach might be in knots, but I promised I would try to be kind. There's no point being cruel for the sake of it.

I'm not sure if my next words are true, but what the hell?

"Pleased to meet you too," I say woodenly, not sure how to deal with a kid.

Her face lights up. "*Spasiba*," she says. "*Ochen' pryatnaya*."

Then in case I haven't understood, she smiles. "That's Russian. Nona taught me."

Kesera looks over at Dex and then back at me. "Can you two run through the threats we're facing and then brief me with a plan after breakfast?" She pushes the food around her plate and then rises abruptly, making the plates on the table clatter.

"You okay, Mom?"

"Didn't sleep too well. I'll go for a walk and clear my head," Kesera says. "Don't overload on screens while I'm gone. Draw a picture or pick up your guitar. The timer with your screen allowance will run out, and then you won't be able to watch a movie tonight."

"*Mom*," Nadia groans, drawing out the vowels. Then she looks at me with a sly grin. "I bet Dad would let me have screen time. I bet he'll let me use his phone."

"Sorry." I shrug. "I don't know about these things. You have to listen to your mother." I glance at Kesera, but she's looking out at the trees and avoiding my eyes. "Anyway, I don't think you'll like this phone."

I pull an old Nokia handset from my pocket and hand it to my daughter as I watch Kesera open the back door and step into the morning sunshine.

The kitchen is bigger than in our old place—and full of women and children—but it triggers old memories. My mind drifts back to a morning in the snow with Kesera on my lap in an empty house, lost to everything but the taste of her mouth and the roll of her hips.

This house is a mindfuck. What is she playing at, bringing me here?

"I'll check on your mother." I look at Nadia, who's now trying to get Dex to lend her his phone. She's nothing if not persistent, but she's not my problem. Right now, her mother is. I'm going to get answers.

Nodding at everyone, I step toward the back door and follow the path I saw her take into the trees.

Rows of spring plants poke through the dirt in a vegetable garden situated near the side of the house. I can see where the grass has been trodden black, so I follow the trail of footsteps into the trees, past a wooden shack that looks like the banya we had out in Moscow.

My lover has rebuilt my past with a Hollywood gloss, and it's making me feel dizzy. A daughter. A cottage in the woods. An angry Italian gangster who's probably got a bullet with my name on it, and a vengeful Night Governor.

It all whirls around my head as I crash down the woodland path winding through the trees. No answers immediately spring into my mind as the path opens into a sunny glade, where I find her sitting on a tree trunk and spinning a branch in her hand. I lean against the scraggy bark of a tree and watch her, my nostrils flaring as I struggle to keep my breathing even. I'm angry, but I don't know about what. Too many feelings and thoughts jostle for space, and I can't make sense of them.

When she spots me, she doesn't say anything, just regards me steadily.

"Is this some kind of joke?" I swing my arm around, pointing back at the house.

"Is what a joke?"

"You've rebuilt my life like some sort of Disney fantasy in the woods. And then you bring me out here? Are you trying to fuck with me?" I stalk toward her, my hands in fists at my sides as I glare down at her mess of bronze-and-gold curls. I want to thrust my hands into all that hair and use it to move her body.

Kesera's green eyes flash at me, and she springs from her seat, jabbing her finger into my chest. "My god, you're an arrogant asshole. I didn't bring you here. This is my life you've walked into. Our life. My family's life."

She's so tiny that her head barely reaches mid chest. I have a flashback of tangling in the sheets with her, her sucking and biting at my nipples. I can feel myself getting hard, even as I get angry.

"Then what the fuck am I doing here?" I ask.

She throws her arms up. "Why don't you tell me that? You're the one with the burner phones and the death threats and the demands to disappear." Her fingers thrust into her curls, pulling at them the way I've fantasized about doing myself. "Do you think I'm some sort of idiot? I've run a business and raised a child without any help from you for a decade. Now you're here with demands that we upend our lives." She bites down on her lip as if swallowing a rush of emotion.

Turning her back on me, she stalks to the edge of the trees, but I'm one step behind her, pushing her up against a birch trunk. Even this reminds me of Russia, though the leaves are green and I can hear birdsong. Last time I was in the woods with her, everything was silent and covered in snow.

"Tell me why the fuck you rebuilt this house in America." I push closer to her body, winding my fingers into her hair and using it to tilt back her head.

Her eyes burn with green fire, and unlike most of the men I've had in this position, she doesn't look scared of me. In fact, she looks furious. I step toward her, aligning my pelvis with the small of her back and caging her in with my arms.

"Why the hell should I tell you anything?" she says. "You said you don't want a relationship with either of us, so what does it matter to you?"

"A bit late for that now. Now that our daughter knows who I am."

"I didn't do it for you."

I step between her legs, circling her waist with one arm and pulling her body against me as I grasp her wrists with the other arm and pull them over her head. Sinking my nose into her hair, I inhale the scent of summer flowers. She smells just the same. Like every wet dream I've ever had.

"Are you sure about that, zolotaya?" I whisper against her neck.

"Don't." Her head leans forward, resting against the white trunk of the birch tree. "Don't do this."

"Don't do what?" I whisper, loosening my grip on her wrists so that she can wrench herself free. "Don't touch you the way I've dreamed about for years? Don't kiss you?"

She stays in the circle of my arms, her body trembling with fury, fear, or something else. I kiss the spot beneath her ear, and she shivers. She gasps as I keep kissing her neck, her collarbone, her earlobes. I revel in the way her breathing speeds up, and she arches against me.

"You can't tell me you didn't think about me the way I thought about you. Not now that I've seen this place." I let go of her wrist and reach down to cup her face, turning it toward me. My mouth ghosts across her lips and I whisper against them. "Please, baby. Kiss me back."

She sighs and opens her mouth, letting me sip at her lips, deepening the kiss until I'm drunk on the taste of her. She pushes back against me as I slide my hand down her body and undo the button on her jeans, toying with it and letting my finger stroke the lace against her skin but not moving closer. She sighs and bucks against me, and I sink into the kiss, my mouth burning against hers as she moans.

I pull back to look at her. Her pupils are blown wide within a ring of jade, and she gazes at me as if she can't believe I'm here. I slide my hand inside her jeans, touching the silk and lace resting against her heat, but I wait for her.

We look at each other, and she starts to buck against my fingertips until her desire soaks through to my skin.

"You want this, don't you? Tell me." I grind out the words as I dive beneath the lace and circle her clit. She's so ready, but she holds still.

Her breathing speeds up as I slide a finger inside her, rubbing her G-spot and leaning down to press a kiss under her ear.

"I'm going out of my head, and I know you feel it too." I slide a second finger into her tight, wet heat.

"Vadim, please."

"Please what, my golden girl? Please make you come all over my fingers? Do you need to come, baby?"

Her breath saws in and out of her, but she's trying hard not to react. "Don't toy with me. I want you. I want you so much."

The words shred the last of my restraint. I don't have a condom, and the last time we did this, we made a child, but I can't seem to stop. I pull my buttons open and push her jeans and panties lower until my cock slides against her hot, wet folds, bathing me in the evidence of how much she wants me.

She pushes back against me finally, bending at the waist so that I can move deeper between her legs. I grasp her hip, lean down to take her chin in my hand, and turn her lips to my mouth, kissing her deeply. With one last kiss, I move so that I can meet her eyes.

"Tell me you don't want this. I won't force you. Tell me you don't remember how it felt."

Her eyes glisten with emotion. "Vadim. You know how I feel." She closes her eyes and leans in to kiss me, as if looking at me is too much.

I won't pull more emotions from her, but I need to know I'm not stealing something that isn't mine. I'm not a good man, but I don't fuck women who don't want it.

"Tell me. Tell me no and I'll stop," I say softly against her pouting lips.

"Yes," she whispers. "Yes."

"Say it again. Tell me."

"You. God, yes. I want you to fuck me."

"Fuck, zolotaya. My girl. My girl."

I slide home and it's unreal. My bare cock against all that fiery heat. Nothing in the world has ever felt this good. I should have waited or shown more finesse, but I can't stop.

"Hold the tree and push back against me," I say as I bend her body and give her another inch. I want to slam into her, but she's such a tiny little thing and she's so tight. I don't want to hurt her. "Baby, I'll go slow until you can take all of my cock. Look at you being such a good girl for me."

I circle her clit again, and she moans softly.

"Show me, baby. Give me your hand and show me how you need it." I reach for her fingers and bring them between her legs to help me learn her rhythm. I want to make this everything for her. I want her to feel all the things I'm feeling. The way it was when we were together.

"Oh, Vadim. It hurts, but I don't want you to stop."

I edge in another inch. "Push back. Please take me. Take all of me."

I'm not sure what I'm asking for anymore, but she widens her legs and starts working my cock deeper inside her.

"Fuck," I moan as she slides back against me. I inch all the way home until my balls are snug against the warm skin of her body. "God, you're so beautiful. Nothing in the world makes me feel like I do when I'm inside you."

I move slowly, fucking her gently to allow her body time to adjust to my size. Moving in and out and remembering the feel of her makes me lose myself in time. I could be here in the woods on a spring morning or back in Moscow in the snow.

"Oh, god," she moans.

"You okay, baby? Are you with me?" My voice comes out sounding strangled with the effort of holding myself back.

"God, Vadim. Harder. I need you."

I can't form words, so I lean down and take her hand from between her legs and bring it to rest on the birch tree, twining our fingers together. Holding her hip with my other hand to anchor myself, I slam into her. Her body rocks beneath me, and I lose it. Rutting into her like an animal. Making her moan and cry out with every thrust.

Then I'm pouring my body, heart, and soul into her as the light behind my eyes flashes silver like the birch bark around us. With the walls of her pussy clenching down around me, I come.

She stills and tries to move away from me, but I bend over her back and turn her face toward me.

"Don't pull away from me now." I wrap her in my arms as we stand upright. Keeping my arm around her, I turn her to face me.

A tear slips over her crimson cheek. I lean in to kiss her, swallowing the trickle of salt water.

"Please don't cry, zolotaya," I whisper against her lips. I know I don't have the right to ask when I can't stay in her life, but it tears me up to see her so upset.

CHAPTER THIRTY-THREE

Kesera

"My god, we shouldn't have done that." I'm disgusted with myself as I frantically pull up my panties and jeans. Anyone could have seen me.

As I do up the button on my fly, the evidence of what we just did soaks through my panties. I cast my gaze around the trees, but there's only grass and branches and the soft rustles and chirps of a spring morning in my favorite part of New York.

The reality of Vadim and the life he lives has crashed into the fantasy cottage I've built in the woods. This was a place meant to shelter my family, not to break my daughter's heart. Or mine.

His arms are still around me, but I try to pull away. He lets me take a step before he stops me, tightening his arms and looking down at me.

"Please don't cry, baby. It's natural, what we did." He shrugs. "We want each other. We acted on it. It's not a crime."

He doesn't need to add "not like some of the things I've done," but I think it. The gun tucked into his waistband is all the evidence I need of the mess I'm in.

He pulls me into his arms and sits down on a log. It's been so long since a man held me, and I want to lean into it and make believe. I wish this was the fairy tale and he was back with us, but just two days ago he said he wished I hadn't found him. Whatever that was in the Brooklyn nightclub, it wasn't an advertisement for good partner material.

"What's happening here, Vadim? You blow so hot and cold I feel like I'm losing my mind."

"Well, that makes two of us." He chuckles, and a flare of anger flickers to life inside me. "We'll work it out. You can't say you didn't want me."

He looks so carefree that I want to punch him . . . if I didn't think I'd probably hurt my hand and leave him unaffected. He's still smiling like this is a great way to start the morning.

"How? How are we going to work it out? Are you going to move in with us? Be Nadia's dad? Are we going to be a family?" I blast the questions out like gunfire.

Looking discomfited, he runs his hands through his hair. "Christ. Give me a minute. You're going too fast for me."

"No, you are behaving like a child when we *have* a child. I won't play games with her life," I say, putting on my best mommy voice.

Another smirk. "That didn't feel childlike to me."

He thinks it's funny. He fucked me in the woods like an animal for anyone to see, and he thinks it's funny.

I'm so angry I'm vibrating with it, but underneath it all is a rolling tide of a bigger emotion. And all of a sudden, I'm doubled over. I've held it together for days, months, years. No one in the world has ever made me feel the way he does, and I've never wanted any other man that way.

"You think it's a joke." The words come out as a strangled cry, choked by tears I'm trying to swallow down, but my throat clogs, my shoulders shake, and I start to weep. Ten years of pent-up longing come spilling out. "You're here. But you'll never really be with me."

I push against him, but he pulls me closer. Then he's with me, just the way I've dreamed of. Wrapping me in his arms and crooning sweet nothings to me in Russian. Calling me golden and precious and his zolotaya.

"Baby, don't cry." His lips caress my cheeks, my eyebrows, my hair, before making their way back to my mouth as he rocks me back and forth. "My golden girl. Let me make it better."

That just makes me cry harder. I'm shaking and sobbing. Ten long years. He knew where we were all that time, and he never came. He never even got in touch.

"Oh, angel. Please don't cry. I can't bear to see you hurting like this."

I bury my head in his shirt. I remember everything. He smells the same. Pinewood and salt and something that's just him. And he only has to take one look around him, at the shrine I've built for our daughter, to know how I feel. How did I ever think I could keep my heart under wraps?

"My precious girl. Zolotaya. I'm here with you."

"Are you?"

He presses his lips to mine in answer.

I kiss him back, savoring his mouth on mine for a final moment, then search his ice-blue gaze and let my fingers run down the scar on his cheek. After kissing him one last time, I lean back, cup his cheek, and ask the question I know I have to ask.

"For how long?"

"I don't know," he whispers.

It doesn't matter what his reasons are. I won't play happy

families with a man who can't be a father to Nadia, no matter what I feel about him.

I inhale a deep breath and push myself off his lap, swiping at my eyes. He reaches for me, taking my hand in his, but I pull my fingers out of his grasp.

"Give me a minute to compose myself," I say.

He leans toward me, but I hold up a hand to stop him from coming closer.

"Please." With closed eyes, I brace myself against the fallen tree, then step back and regard him steadily. "I'm in love with you, Vadim."

He swallows hard. He's probably wondering if I'm waiting for him to say it back, but I plow on.

"Or the idea of you, at any rate. I'm not such a fool that I think I know you, but this house, the songs . . ." I spread my hands to him in a gesture of surrender. "There's no point in pretending I don't feel something very deep for you. But none of that matters. You knew we existed, and you never came to find me. To find us."

He looks at me quizzically.

"You've made it clear that you can't be in our lives," I say, "and I won't give my daughter half a father. I won't play games with her heart. Even if I was willing to gamble with mine, we're playing a different game now."

I pull my curls back into a twist and run my hands down my clothes, then sit next to him. His arm snakes around my shoulder and I allow him to pull me against him, soaking up the illusion of another adult on my side for a change.

Even if I know it can't last.

I look up at him. Even with that scar, he's still the most beautiful man I've ever seen. Perhaps it's because he's not manicured and buffed within an inch of his life like all the singers I work with. Stevie's not much to look at, but he magnetizes women with his bass playing. But Vadim? His masculinity is a dark magnet pulling every needle of my nerve endings to his polar north.

I stare past his shoulder, at the tree line. The woods are so quiet, just like every weekend we've spent up here. We moved to New York to get away from Jimmy in Nashville and find a city where I could snatch some shreds of anonymity and make a new start. I scoured the state until I found a plot of land that reminded me of the woods outside Moscow.

"Since you asked, I built this place for Nadia. I really wanted her to have a slice of her heritage." Reaching over, I take his hand and pull it into my lap. "I never had that. My mom was half-Japanese. My dad met her in Okinawa, and she died when I was young. I knew I was different, but I didn't know what it meant or who I was."

I tip my head into the crook of his shoulder and thread my fingers through his, tracing the outline of his long digits, which are surprisingly soft for a man in his line of work. A rabbit springs out of the bushes and bolts across the grass, its nose twitching. I turn my head to watch it bounce into the trees.

I look away from Vadim because I don't want him to see too much. "With her father out of the picture, I wanted to give Nadia all the things I never had. I wanted her to have a sense of where she came from. It wasn't about you."

That's half true. The other half of the meaning will be written in my eyes, which follow the rabbit's tail. Running and hiding are my heart's only defenses against Vadim.

Mercifully, he doesn't look at me. He just pulls me tighter against him and presses a kiss to my hairline. I feel him inhale, and then his words gust across my forehead on an out breath. "I couldn't have picked a better woman to be the mother of my child if I'd tried."

I bite my lip to keep from crying again. Enough with the

waterworks this morning. "Thank you," I manage to blurt out.

He pulls me to my feet and wraps me up in his arms, and we stand for a minute, listening to the sounds of the spring woodland. "Come on, zolotaya. I'd better go and do my job as a father and talk to Dex and make a plan."

We walk to the edge of the clearing before I pull him to a stop with a sigh. His idea of being a dad is talking to my bodyguard. "You're dealing with a ten-year-old, not just Dex."

His face scrunches into a frown, as if he can't compute what dealing with a ten-year-old involves, and I set off through the trees ahead of him, breaking into a run to get away from this man who sets my body alight.

I'll have to keep my hands off him moving forward. He's not family-man material, and that's never been more clear than right now.

CHAPTER THIRTY-FOUR

Vadim

Lighting another cigarette, I listen to the murmur of women's voices drifting from the window. A childish giggle rings out, then a deeper, throaty laugh that comes from Kesera. They sound so happy.

I let my head fall against the wooden slats with a *thunk* and watch the sun filtering through the green leaves as I listen to them like a creeper. I feel like I'm climbing out of my skin. I had to get out of that house.

Footsteps sound, and the window creaks open. Kesera appears like an angel above me, her head haloed by gold-and-bronze curls.

"Do you want to come in and hang out with us? We're going to play board games."

I look up at the hopeful expression on her face and watch it fall as I shake my head. "Too much to do," I say, the lie obvious since I'm leaning against the house, smoking and staring at the trees.

She waits for a moment before leaning down to touch me,

her hand stilling inches from my forehead. She shakes off the notion, her lips thinning as she nods and steps back from the window, closing it softly.

I just can't be around all those women. A little girl regarding me with eyes that look like mine as she chews on her braids. And Kesera, my fantasy made flesh. Her body under her clothes, the way she moves, makes me burn to get my hands beneath the fabric. I couldn't stop myself in the woods earlier, and I made her cry. Like the beast I am.

This place feels like a stage set recreated for me to listen to the echo of all my mistakes. My mistakes end with people I care about dying.

I won't start grilling shashlik in the backyard or drinking myself into oblivion, which is what I would have done back in Moscow. Without someone like Sasha to shoot the shit with, there hasn't been much to do other than walk circles in the woods. I've just been looking at my phone—which hasn't had a single message telling me what's going on back in Brooklyn —and avoiding my newly discovered family.

Sighing, I make my way around the front of the house to where we parked the cars.

Andrei stubs out a cigarette and throws it into the bushes as he leans against the hood of the SUV and watches the sinking sun slant through the trees. He looks at the barbed-wire-topped black walls. "What she build all this for? She expecting the zombie apocalypse?"

Footsteps crunch through the gravel as Dex emerges from the house to find us both aimlessly kicking at the dirt.

Idleness like this makes me crazy. I don't know what's happening in town, and I've got a gnawing sense that Sasha and I have missed something. Something important. But I can't think straight knowing that Kesera is so near and I can't touch her again.

"Zombies are the least of your worries when you're

famous," Dex drawls, kicking at our cigarette butts in the dust. "That's a disgusting habit."

"One of my many disgusting habits," I reply.

"This place is tricked out almost as well as the Night Governor's crib," Andrei says. I don't know why he insists on talking like he's walked out of a hip-hop video.

"Who's the Night Governor?" Dex asks.

Andrei grins. "Our boss. He's a psycho, but he likes his security. He'd love this place. He had an old dacha like this out in the woods in Moscow, but he was always alert for an attack. I don't know why you need all this security."

Dex folds his arms and looks at Andrei like he's a few ribs short of a barbeque. "Crazies."

"How many crazies are there in the woods?" Andrei sucks on his cigarette, the tip glowing red as the light begins to sink below the trees.

Dex speaks slowly, spelling out each word with exaggerated patience as if Andrei were a child. "They find you if they can. Every weirdo on the internet has access to Kesera's videos, or they can beat off to one of her songs, and I can promise you that there's more than one who thinks she's in love with him."

Bile rises in my throat at the imagery. "Do you have to talk about her like that?" I ask.

I know I brutalized her in the woods this morning, but the thought of other men imagining their hands on her body makes me feel like live ants are crawling all over my skin. It's why it was better to stay away. I can't remain logical when she's around.

"I'm not talking about her. I'm telling you what we're dealing with," Dex says. "There are some very persistent people out there, and every so often, one will get the idea in his head that he should be married to her. That's when they try to turn up at her doorstep or scale the walls or whatever. I don't think the fans know about this place, but we don't take chances. There's a panic room. Proper cameras."

"Why the blast walls?" I look past the trees at the high concrete barriers.

"Bomb threats last year from some fucker who wanted to blow her up. All the press around the court case didn't help. He said if they couldn't be together, then no one else would have her."

"And my daughter has grown up around this?"

Dex looks at the walls and then back at me. "She's an amazingly normal kid, considering. Kesera walks her to school. She's managed to carve out the semblance of a normal life in the midst of all this craziness," he muses. "I admire her."

I should have killed that slimy fucker Jimmy when I had the chance. I won't make that mistake a second time. But random lunatics who want to marry the woman I made a child with? Christ. The mafia sounds like a picnic in comparison. At least you know who you're dealing with.

As if he can read my mind, Dex turns to me. "And I hear you've got some less than salubrious friends who might want to pay us a visit."

"If they know where we are." I shrug. I wish I wasn't a catalyst for more chaos.

"She doesn't do press about this place. We could be okay. It depends on whether you were followed." He looks around as if an assassin might leap from behind a tree trunk or drop from the branches.

"There was no one on our tail, and I've ensured my electronics are untraceable." Given the enormous amounts of data on cell phones, that's a weak link when the police are so corrupt. I pull the old Nokia out of my pocket. "I've only got my burner phone with me. Four people have the number, and two of them are with us. If anyone followed us last night, they'd be here already."

"Um, boss." Andrei kicks at the dirt and looks at the gravel like it might hold the answer to an important question.

"What?"

Andrei pulls a smartphone out of his pocket. He shrugs. "I was texting Katya. She wanted to stay in touch, and I—"

"You stupid fuck." I snatch the phone from his hands and throw it to the ground, grinding it under my heel. I wind my arm back as if someone has coiled a spring so tight that its forceful snap back is inevitable. "Google." My fist hits his nose with a wet thud. "Apple." His neck snaps back as I pound him again, raining blows down on his pretty-boy face so hard that Katya or whichever slut he was texting won't be able to find his mouth to kiss it.

Dex approaches me from behind and holds my arms back without using much force, giving me time to catch my breath. Andrei doubles over, blood dripping from his nose to the gravel driveway.

"How could you be so fucking stupid?" I say.

"Sorry, boss," he burbles through bloody lips. "I didn't think."

I hold up a hand to stop him from saying another word as I shrug out of Dex's grasp. "Well, we'd all better start thinking. There's a long list of people who are pissed off with me right now. The Italians. My boss."

Dex nods. "This place is pretty easy to defend. We might be better staying put than trying to drive south when we don't know who's on our tail." He strides into the house, and I hear him say, "Nadia's not going to school tomorrow."

Jesus. School. It's like I've dropped through the looking glass into a different world.

On one hand, I've come here with a moron who couldn't survive two days without texting one of our hookers. On the other, the first order of business is whether or not my ten-year-old will miss school.

My head's spinning, but there's no time to think of how to balance the two worlds, because my ears ring with the sound of a blast, and flames shoot from the other side of the walls.

"Kesera!" I shout her name as I run toward the house, my only thought the woman I've never been able to forget.

CHAPTER THIRTY-FIVE

Kesera

At the sound of an explosion, Nadia drops the Monopoly money she was stacking. Paper rubles scatter across the board, and wide eyes search mine for answers.

I lean over to take her hand and pull her to her feet. "Let's go find Nona," I say, leading her away from windows and into the hallway.

Vadim bursts into the house, flinging the screen door open behind him. He's panting, rushing toward me with a frantic expression and grasping my shoulders with shaking hands.

My first—and most irrational—thought is to comfort him. I slide my hand up his scarred cheek as Nadia peeks out from behind me.

"It's okay," I whisper softly. "I know what to do."

He pulls both of us into the circle of his arms for a second, and I can feel his heartbeat and smell the pine and salt on his skin as he mumbles into my hair. "It's my fault."

I take his hand. His huge palm wraps around mine, and I squeeze a couple of times as I lead him toward a wall panel beneath a light switch. After sliding it away, I push my fingerprint against the glass screen. The door to the bunker under our little house opens, an eerie blue light shining up from the steel steps. I push Nadia ahead of me.

"Mom, can I—"

"No," I snap. "Just go. For once, don't argue with me."

I push her toward the steps and she stumbles, turning back with narrowed eyes to glare at me before obeying. Heavy footfalls ring on the steel as I look down the wooden corridor to see Nona bustling toward us, resolute and comforting as she follows Nadia through the narrow doorway. They disappear into the eerie light.

Wide hands knead my shoulders, and Vadim turns me toward him. He slides an enormous hand up my neck and into my hair to tilt my head toward him.

"Zolotaya, you need to go." His brow furrows as his wide eyes search mine.

"You're not coming with us?"

He pushes me through the doorway, and then his lips press into mine, hard and bruising, before he tears away. Biting his lower lip, he shakes his head. "Let me protect you. Please."

Gunfire erupts outside, and I'm stuck with the ghost of his stricken face as the door shuts, leaving me in the eerie, steel-lined silence.

I make my way down the steps on shaky legs. As Nona lays out a board game that looks similar to Monopoly, I sink to a soft couch and let my eyes roam over the boxes of bottled water and tins of food lit with blue LED lights.

"Mom, did we build this place because you knew my dad was a badass gangster?"

I spin to face Nadia, who's kneeling by the board game

and grinning the way only a ten-year-old can when they've got a captive audience. With a bowed head, she moves the pieces around the board, and thank the heavens she's still naïve enough to misunderstand the danger we're in. Vadim looked terrified.

"No, we didn't. You have to have these things when you're famous."

She starts stacking green cards with a sickle on the back and red cards with a star. "These ones are cool. They're secret police cards."

Nona catches my eye and tilts her head toward the sink, beckoning me to the other side of the room. She opens a huge fridge and calls over her shoulder to Nadia. "Finish setting up the board for me, then we will all come and play."

I reach her, grab a bottle of lemonade from the fridge, and press the drink against my forehead, taking a deep breath and letting the cool glass soothe my frazzled nerves. Unscrewing the bottle top, I glance back at Nadia. She's still laying out the board game as if this is a normal afternoon.

I turn back to the woman who has been like a mother to me for the last decade, and Nona strokes my arm and pulls me closer.

"I know him," she whispers, as if anyone can hear her through the steel walls.

"Who?" I already know the answer.

"Your man. Back in Moscow. He used to work for the Night Governor."

I lean against the sink, the walls closing in on me and the artificial light bathing everything in a blue glow. "He's not my man."

Nona just smiles at me like she knows I'm lying.

"The name sounds familiar, but who exactly is the Night Governor?"

"Nadia's father worked for the ruler of Moscow's darkness. The Kremlin runs the government, but the clubs, the drugs, the smuggling routes? The Night Governor controls all of those."

"How do you know all this?"

The woman bustling in front of me flicks a switch on the kettle and pulls out two mugs as if this is a normal afternoon. She leads me to a small table and pushes me to sit. "I worked for a billionaire called Antonov. He owned mines, trading companies, and a vodka distillery."

Nona looks over at my daughter as the jigsaw pieces slot together in my mind.

The nightclub gig in Moscow.

Vadim patrolling the club with his gun.

The threatening man with the gold tooth at the bar who knew Vadim and Sasha.

Nona settles opposite me. "The Night Governor killed my boss. Vadim works for him," she says in a low voice, glancing at Nadia to see if she can hear us.

I squeeze my eyes shut against the harsh truth. "So he's a gangster."

Nona takes my hands into hers, rubbing the tips of my icy fingers. "He's a good man, in a way. He saved me. Saved Antonov's children. Without Vadim, none of us would be alive and I wouldn't be working for you."

With that, she stands and strokes my hair before walking to the kettle and leaving me to run my fingers along the table's knotted wood as I try to figure out what I've done, who I've invited into my life, and how to untangle the mess of relationships around my daughter.

Aside from the clink of teacups, the room is quiet. We're so shielded from the outside world that Vadim could be murdering Dex or setting the house on fire, and I wouldn't know until it was too late.

CHAPTER THIRTY-SIX

Vadim

I charge into the kitchen and peer through the window. Three figures advance toward us through the trees. "Do we have enough to hold them off?"

Dex doesn't answer as he walks out of the storage closet in the kitchen, carrying two semi-automatic rifles and a grenade.

"Thank fuck. I thought we were outgunned as well as outmanned." I grab the guns from him.

"Give me a minute," he says, walking past me with the grenade in his hand. As he reaches the front door, he pulls out the pin with his teeth and hurls the grenade past the cars to the point where the gravel meets the tree line. A wall of fire knocks one of the gunmen off his feet and back into the woods where the dancing flames lick the trees.

My gaze bounces between the eerie red glow engulfing the birch forest and the three remaining gunmen advancing on the house. Gripping both guns, I rush to meet Dex in the doorway as he returns. He snatches a rifle from my hand and rushes toward the cars.

"Follow me," he says over his shoulder. "Draw them away from the house."

I don't need to be told twice.

Andrei walks at my heels, but one eye has swollen shut after the pounding I gave him.

I turn to him. "Stay here. Defend the doors to the basement. We don't want anyone getting to the women."

Andrei walks to the basement doors, wobbling on unsteady legs. I'm not sure how much use he'll be, but my options are limited.

After running to the SUV, I crouch behind Dex as the three men fan out across the yard. The man on his back still hasn't gotten up, so I think it's three against two-and-a-half men, given the beating Andrei has just had. I would feel bad, but the fucker brought this hellfire to my door.

Dex lines up his shot and releases a hail of gunfire on the nearest of the three men. I crouch behind the engine block, pointing my weapon at the doorway. I don't think anyone will come from the other side of the house, so my main goal is to make sure no one gets near my daughter.

"Wake up," Dex says. "Threat at six o'clock."

I swivel to fire over my right shoulder, but the man in black moves faster. I duck behind the car as a wave of bullets pings off the hood, but not before a lone projectile grazes my arm.

"Fuck," I say through gritted teeth.

"Can you still shoot?"

"Yeah, it's a surface wound."

At least, I think it is, but I don't have time to feel the pain as a mounting sense of horror engulfs me when Andrei emerges from the house. *What's he doing? He's supposed to be the last line of defense in case they get to us first.*

I'm tempted to shoot him myself, but a gunshot rings out and his legs crumple beneath him. I need to get to the house, but I can't do that without running across open ground.

"Dex. Can you cover me? If I run to the house, will I make it?"

"No," he snaps. "Stay the fuck put. If we can hold them off, help might be on its way." He fires another salvo across the driveway at the remaining two men, but they're out of range.

"I'm going to risk it." I can't take the chance that the family I've only just met dies because I wasn't there to defend them.

Keeping my head low, I crawl along the ground. The blood dripping from my shoulder leaves a red trail in my wake for anyone to follow. Another burst of gunfire erupts as I reach the doorway, praying I'm not too fucking late.

The kitchen is eerily quiet. A stack of pancakes under plastic film lies on the counter as the red light of sunset illuminates the empty room. Now it's silent outside as well. That could mean they've killed Dex and I'm waiting like a sitting duck for two gunmen to come through the front door.

Blood drips from my arm as I crawl along the corridor to guard the door where I last had Kesera in my arms. The scent of jasmine and roses lingers in the air where she's been, reminding me of the way she feels when I touch her.

Alive. Beautiful. Fragile. Breakable.

The sunlight breaking through the leaves dapples a dancing pattern on Andrei's leg, which lies at an unnatural angle just inside the front door. The sound of birdsong begins to filter through the silence, along with the scent of smoke. Are they gone?

I lie on my belly and crawl below the line of windows as I make my way toward the front door. Fuck whoever designed this house to have a glassed-in porch. I can't make it across the hall without being seen unless I slither like a snake, and if I lie across the panic-room doorway, I'll only draw attention to it.

The creak of a foot on wooden boards sounds as I crouch behind the door frame, keeping the door to the panic room in my sights.

The gunman must have seen me.

A shot rings out, and fire blazes through my arm. I look down to see my arm covered in blood.

Damn it. The footsteps are coming straight for the panic-room door. Wincing with each movement, I roll into the corridor and point the gun, pressing the trigger as I hear a voice shout in Russian.

Then the world fades to darkness.

CHAPTER THIRTY-SEVEN

Kesera

The door clicks open, and my heart thuds against my breastbone. I wait with bated breath as footsteps clang down the metal stairs.

"You okay there?" Dex's voice echoes in the steel-lined stairwell, and he beckons me toward him. "I've got good news and bad news."

"Bad news?" My eyes search the stairwell for Vadim's tall frame, for the hum of tension I feel when he's in a room with me, but I see only steel and blue florescent light. "Is he alive? Is he okay?"

Dex smiles at me as I follow him up the stairs, pulling the door shut before Nadia can charge after me. My heart is in my mouth as we step into the wood-paneled corridor and I see Vadim, his eyelashes casting shadows against his cheeks as he lies slumped against the wall.

Lowering myself to my knees, I touch his hair, his eyebrows. I feel the cool sheen of sweat on his skin, then lay my hand over his heart, reassuring myself with the steady beat.

"The good news is that we're all okay and Vadim took the last man out before he did any real damage," Dex says behind me.

I wrap my arms around Vadim, pressing a kiss to his pine-scented, sweat-soaked hair and tasting the salt on his skin. I shut my eyes and reassure myself I haven't lost him. "And the bad news?"

"This place is compromised. We need to get on the road as soon as possible, and you'll have to drive through the night if we want to get to a safe house. I'll get the girls and you grab your stuff."

Dex turns away, leaving me alone in the silent shadows of the corridor as I cradle Vadim's head against my chest. Shivers run from the base of my neck to the tail of my spine as Vadim mumbles something in Russian against my cleavage.

Cupping his face in my hands, I lift it toward me. His eyes search my face, as if he can't quite believe I'm here.

"We're all fine," I whisper. "I'm so glad you made it. For a minute there, when I saw you . . . God." I look away and laugh before pressing a kiss to his forehead, the relief of finding him alive bubbling up into a kind of giddy hysteria.

I pull back and smile at him as my hands drop to his shoulders. I wait for a hint of the tenderness from this morning when he called me angel and zolotaya, but his face is shuttered as he takes my hands off his shoulders and sets them back on my knees.

"I thought we'd lost you," I whisper.

He gets to his feet, wincing as he moves his arm, and looks down at me with a strangely blank expression. "It might be better for everyone if you had," he says, turning his back on me and giving me a view of his broad shoulders as he stalks away from me.

I lean against the wall, pressing my fingers to the wooden panels and feeling the grain beneath my fingertips. I let my heartbeat slow before I follow Vadim.

He's talking to Dex in a low voice outside the house. I can see the feet of a black-clad man poking out from underneath Dex's car.

"Is he dead?" I say, pointing at the man's boots. "Aren't we going to call the police?"

"Not a good idea." Vadim looks at Dex as he speaks, ignoring me like I'm not making the decisions, and despite myself, my eyes fall to the movement of his lips.

"And you didn't answer my other question. Is that man down there alive?" I point at the boots on the ground, my voice edging higher as panic bleeds into my words.

Dex gestures for Vadim to go on as he shakes his head at me, and I put my hands on my hips and glare at both of them.

Vadim sounds weary as he turns to me. "You are welcome to call the police if you want a bunch of fools crawling over your property and this story all over the press before we've even worked out who attacked us." He walks over to the figure on the ground and kicks gently at the man's boots so that his feet roll back and forth. "This one is still alive, and if we want to know what's going on, our best bet is to leave him for Sasha. He'll get the story out of him."

I turn to Dex and raise my brows in question.

He shrugs. "He's right about the press, but that's not a good enough reason not to call the police. It's the other stuff that worries me."

Vadim throws up his hands, muttering something in Russian before he turns to me. "Please, zolotaya, listen to me. I brought this mess to your door, and it's my responsibility to make sure you're safe. It looks like the Italians attacked us, and they own half the police. That's why I don't want to chance it."

He walks over to me, taking my shoulders in his huge hands. Heat from his fingers brands my skin as his eyes burn into me.

"Please, listen to me," he says. "We have to get out of here while there is still time."

TWO HOURS LATER, it's dark and I'm tired. The interstate flashes by in a blur of gas stations and rest stops.

My back is stiff, my eyes are gritty, and the strained silence has made my neck ache. I tilt my head, listening to the click of my vertebrae as I roll my left shoulder in a full circle. It sounds unnaturally loud in my ears. The only other sound is the even rhythm of Vadim's breathing as he slumps against the window.

Taking my attention off the road and the dark trees outside, I slant my eyes across to him. Even tired, with a bloodstained shirt and an injured arm, he's beautiful. Brave. Willing to put himself in the line of fire for me.

But he's been unreachable since we got in the car together.

I only offered to drive him because I wanted a chance to talk to him alone, but he shifted about his seat like a caged animal for an hour. When I asked him to tell me who those men were, he just snapped that I didn't need to know. I can find out more from Nona or get Dex to investigate, but I wanted *him* to tell me. To open up again. Instead, he remains shut down and distant.

The air between us felt so charged with static that I'm still humming like I've drunk a gallon of coffee. Even though he's passed out, a pulse of blood thumps between my legs as if my heart is thrumming in time with his because my whole body is aware of his next to me.

The gas light flickers red as Dex's taillights signal for the gas station turnoff ahead. Nadia's head pops into view as she waves from the back window. I lift my hand in reply, and her head bounces up and down.

The car jolts over a speed bump, and Vadim's head knocks against the window as I slow down to look at him properly.

"Polina. No. Wake up. Please. Polina," he mutters. His face twists in distress, and he keeps repeating the only two words that I understand: "no" and "please."

Putting the car into park, I grip his shoulder and shake him awake. He jerks upright and looks at me.

"Polina?" he says, eyes wide with fear.

I lay my hand over his shirt. Dried blood has stiffened the cotton. I let my hand drift inside his collar and find his skin clammy to the touch.

"It's me. Kesera," I say, and he screws his eyes shut, his face contorting in a grimace before he opens them and looks past me.

"I can drive," he says, going for the door handle as I open mine. The night air hits me with a whiff of gasoline and the scent of damp pine needles.

"Why don't you fill up the gas?" I reach under the seat to open the gas tank, gripping the keys tightly in my hand and sucking in a deep breath. I'm torn between wanting to scream at him to give me answers or beg him to give me another hit of tenderness. I settle for banality. "I'll buy you some painkillers," I call over my shoulder as I walk into the gas station.

Day-Glo plastic packets of salt, sugar, and hydrogenated fat blare at me as I edge my way along the aisles in search of painkillers. On stiff legs, I turn past the cooler and grab a couple of bottles of water as a pair of teenagers stumbles into me, giggling with their heads together.

The boy can't be more than eighteen, still too gangly for

his body and oblivious to the woman in the ball cap who watches him with tired eyes as he paws his girlfriend. The girl giggles and kisses him, knocking over a stand of candy. They laugh harder.

A sharp stab of longing pierces me, and I glance out the door at Vadim. He's leaning against the car and talking to Dex, and I can read the tension in his shoulders at this distance.

Sighing, I turn my back on the kissing teens and pay for the water and the painkillers with cash. I let the door swing behind me as I make my way back to the car, where Vadim has climbed into the driver's seat.

I sit down and snap my seatbelt without meeting his eyes. "Polina. That's Sasha's sister, isn't it?"

"How did you know that?" He stares at me, eyes heavy with questions when I look up.

I hold the keys between us like an offering, but he doesn't reach for them. He just watches me with wide blue eyes as the soft whoosh of cars passing in the night sounds in the darkness behind us.

"I remember everything," I say, annunciating every word.

He lowers his head and looks at my hands. I reach to clasp his fingers around mine, the keys gripped in a knot between us.

"So do I," he says gently.

We stay like that for a moment, the air between us filled with ten years of missed opportunities, sleepless nights, and awkward dates that didn't end in anything. I can hear the sound of his inhales and exhales and practically taste the mint of his kisses. He leans toward me, but a knock on the window stops him.

Vadim lowers the window, and Dex leans in. "Another forty minutes and we'll stop for the night. There's a place near here where we can break the journey." He glances at Vadim's stained shirt. "You good to drive?"

"I'm fine." Vadim raises the window and turns to me with his hand out for the keys. I reach down and pass him a pack of Tylenol, but he just shakes his head. "I said I was fine."

"Yeah, I'm sure you're just peachy. But you'll recover faster if you reduce the swelling." I tip two tablets into my hand and pass them over with the bottle of water.

He watches me for a moment and then comes to a decision before reluctantly plucking the tablets from my palm. His throat moves as he swallows them, and I wish he was mine to touch.

He reaches toward me. "Keys," he mutters.

"So, Polina?" I hold out the keys. "How did she die?"

He takes them from my hand, starting the car and looking more comfortable now that he has a task to accomplish. "I told you that?"

Laughing under my breath, I watch the dashboard. "I thought you remembered everything. You mentioned her."

"I remember you. The important stuff." He keeps his eyes on the road, switching on the wipers as a light rain dusts the windshield. "I don't talk about Polina much."

"I could tell it was painful. It's why I didn't ask more questions. So . . ." I let the unspoken question hang in the air between us.

"She overdosed. I found her body."

"God, I'm so sorry."

Dex's brake lights glow red in the darkness ahead of us. There's not much traffic on the road, and it's so quiet that I can hear Vadim thinking.

"I couldn't save her. She was the last person I ever loved."

My mouth screws up like I've bitten into something sour. The astringent taste of Vadim admitting he loved another woman when he's stayed out of my life is both acrid and sharp. I nod and wipe the condensation that has built on the window so I can look out into nothingness.

"I should have been able to do something. To pull her back. To make her feel again," he says to the night as I keep my eyes fixed on the dark road ahead of us.

"How old were you?"

"I was nineteen. She was sixteen." He sighs, like the memory hurts to speak.

"You were just a kid," I say.

"Old enough to go to jail."

"Not old enough to hold someone else's pain for them. I'm not sure if anyone is ever old enough to do that." I look over at Vadim, but he keeps his eyes fixed on the road, our headlights casting a narrow circle in front of us.

"How would you know? You've never lost anyone like that."

I throw his words right back at him. "How would *you* know who I've lost? Life doesn't stop when people die."

"You know nothing about my life," he bites out, blind to what I've been through. To my losses. To the pain of having grown up without my mother. To the way I picked myself up and kept going when my father and grandmother were killed in a car accident.

Why did I ever long for someone who is so shut down?

Turning my head back to the fogged glass, I draw a heart with my finger. I fill Nadia's initials into the point at the bottom and scrawl mine above them.

K.M.S.

+

N.S.

234

You know nothing about my life, I think so loudly I wonder if he can hear me over the hum of the engine.

Dex's SUV turns in at a motel ahead. The building has seen better days, and the M in the sign has blinked out. The OTEL proclaims its existence against the darkening sky. There are six trucks parked between the hotel and a bar next door, but it's quiet, and we sit in tense silence as Dex walks to my side of the car.

"Okay, lovebirds. I'm going to put you together in a family room," he says with a grin.

CHAPTER THIRTY-EIGHT

Vadim

Dex tips his chin at me. "Best you stay in the car. That way no one sees you and you can keep an eye out in case anything happens."

I watch his back as he walks toward the building, and Kesera walks beside him. He stops at the car ahead, and Nona gets out. Dex puts his arm around her and walks into the motel. Just a good old boy on the road with his grandma. Nothing to see here.

I pull out the burner phone and call Sasha.

"Mr. Wolf, at your service, *blatnoi*."

"You cleaned up?" Shutting my eyes, I let my head hit the headrest behind me.

"Yeah, it was a real mess. Two Italians and one Russian, by the looks of things." The world swims behind my eyelids when I close them and listen to Sasha's voice.

"Not Andrei." I think about the boy with the blond curls. Did he betray us, or was he really stupid enough to risk our lives for the sake of some pussy?

237

"He's messed up, but he'll live. That *muzhik* brought hell-fire down on our heads and left me one hell of a mess to clean up because he was texting a hooker." Sasha sounds exasperated.

I almost expect people to sell me out, but Andrei actually put our lives at risk for a woman. When he recovers, he'll carry injuries as a reminder of his mistake.

"You said there was a Russian among the dead bodies?" I dangle the car keys in my hand, feeling the reassuring press of the knife in my boot and the weight of a holster against my body.

"Looks that way from the tattoos." Sasha doesn't say what we're both thinking. The Night Governor probably knows about Kesera if there was a Russian with the men. "How soon can you get back to New York? I need you here. It's all moving too fast."

I look out at the blinking motel light and wonder if it's safe to leave the family behind. If we can be sure no one has followed us, then it will be better to leave them with Dex than to follow them to the safe house that Sasha has set up. Maybe they should head somewhere with Dex that has no link to me. The faster they cut ties with me, the safer they'll be.

"I'll see if I can get back tomorrow."

"Do that," Sasha says, and hangs up, leaving me to wonder how long I can afford to stay.

I'm so lost in thought I don't see a slight figure with a ball cap and dark glasses tapping on the window. I jump, pulling my gun out of its holster and pointing it before I realize I've just drawn a gun on the mother of my child. Christ, men like me don't deserve to father children.

I lower the window.

"Hey," Kesera says softly. "How are you holding up?

"Tired. I could sleep for a few days." My lips turn up at

the corners in the ghost of a smile. "The adrenaline has worn off."

"Then I'm glad we stopped for the night. It'd be pretty stupid to die on the run from the mafia because you were so tired you ran the car off the road." She smiles at me, but it doesn't meet her eyes. Her face mirrors the strain on my own.

"I don't think there's much danger of that."

"Well, better safe than sorry."

"No. I'm sorry. You'd have been safe if I wasn't here."

She reaches through the window and lays a cool palm against my forehead. Her touch feels comforting and restful, and I don't think anyone has touched me like that in years. I lean into her despite myself, and she brushes back my hair.

I open my eyes to see her watching me.

"Don't be sorry. And take some more painkillers in a few hours." She bites her lip, then turns and walks toward the other car as our daughter jumps out, braids bouncing.

The two of them laugh together, and I wonder what it would be like to be part of a family unit. I don't have to wait long for my first taste once Dex strides over with a key card.

"You're in with Kesera and Nadia. It's the family room. Number 243. We're right next door."

"Family room?"

"Yep. There are three beds. You can watch the girls. I'll bunk next door, and one of us will take a turn on watch. Got Nona a separate room." He turns toward the other car, throwing his next words over his shoulder. "Safer that way."

As if there is anything safe about me playing daddy in a family I've got no right to be part of.

CHAPTER THIRTY-NINE

Kesera

I shouldn't flee to the bathroom, but I need to wash off this day and compose myself before I spend the night in a room with Vadim. "I'm going to take a quick shower." I look over my shoulder, and Nadia quirks a grin at me.

"S'okay. I've brushed my teeth. Dad will read me a story."

Vadim looks like Nadia has pulled a gun on him; the expression of panic on his handsome face is so stark I choke back a laugh. The whole thing is surreal, and I can't catch up with all the ways my world has changed since this morning.

"Nadia, you can snuggle up and start reading to yourself. You're plenty big enough to read your own book," I say. "I'll be out in about five minutes."

"Don't rush," she says, walking over to her father, taking his hand, and pulling him toward the bed. I'm glad she had the good sense to grab his uninjured arm. She nervously fingers the dog-eared copy of *Winnie the Pooh*, but her smile is bright.

"We had Winnie the Pooh cartoons when I was a kid in Russia," Vadim says.

"Really?" she says as I pull the door to behind me and step toward the shower.

As the water pours down on my shoulders, I let the heat soften the fear and anxiety that cluster in knots along my vertebrae. I wash off the stress of the day, and my body loosens in the steam as I inhale the chemical scent of cheap soap. It reminds me of my childhood and a time when hopes and dreams came easier.

But Vadim is here with me, so a tendril of something bright and sweet unwinds in my chest as I step out of the shower and dry myself with the threadbare towel. He's distant. Difficult. But he's here with us, and that's enough for hope to bud inside me, despite my better judgement.

They're lying together on the pull-out child's bed when I step out of the bathroom, toweling my hair in the doorway. I stand and watch them for a minute with a sharp pang in my heart. Vadim's feet hang off the end of the narrow child's bed. He lies next to Nadia with his hands behind his head, smiling down at her as they compare notes on their favorite Pooh stories.

"I like the one where they have the balloons and they float into the sky." Vadim's deep voice rolls through the shabby room.

"My favorite is when he's a bear wedged in great tight-ness." Nadia's voice vibrates with excitement.

"What does it mean? To be wedged? How did you say it?"

Nadia snorts with laughter. "Pooh goes to Rabbit's house, and he eats too much honey, so he gets stuck in the door because he's too fat to move."

Vadim concentrates on his daughter, even though she's talking nonsense, and I wonder what it would have been like to have him in our lives. Would he have brought disaster with him like he said in the car? Or would there have been more nights like this?

"The shooting balloons out of the sky and the bees are my favorites." He leans toward his daughter and gently rests his hand on her shoulder, waiting to see what she'll do.

Nadia giggles. "Is that because you like guns?"

I perch on the end of the bed, next to Vadim's huge feet, and look over at the pained expression on his face. I take hold of his instep and grip his foot, and he looks over at me and nods. It's an innocuous enough gesture, but it makes me imagine what it would be like if his body was mine to touch. If we were a real family.

"You're off the hook. I can take it from here," I say.

Vadim shifts to get up, but Nadia pulls him down again. He collapses onto her pillow.

"It's okay. Daddy said he will stay till I fall asleep."

I raise my eyebrows in question but he doesn't get up, so I pad over to his head and put a hand on his shoulder as I reach to turn out the light. Each innocent touch cracks my wounded heart open a little wider.

Vadim lays his hand over mine and I smile at him. He looks so right lying next to his daughter as she curls against his side. The sharp yearning for more thrums through me like a heartbeat. I grip his fingers, letting my fingertips slide against the warmth of his skin as I pull away.

"Tell me the bear story, Mama." My little girl's voice threads through the darkness.

"Bears are the national animal of Russia," Vadim says. The depth of his voice and his slight accent make everything sound better. Sexier. More laden with meaning.

"Maybe that's why I like bears. Because I'm Russian," Nadia says, and he huffs out a laugh.

I begin the story. "Can't you sleep, little bear?"

"No, Mama."

"Well, the darkness is nothing to be scared of. It's where the woods keep the moon and the stars." I launch into the well-worn treads of a story I've told Nadia a hundred times about a bear who can't sleep because she's scared of the dark. I repeat the hypnotic words and familiar lines, ending on the closing stanza. "But the little bear didn't say anything because she was fast asleep."

A soft snore, barely loud enough to hear, drifts over from the pile of bedclothes.

"Does she always snore like that?" I can hear the smile in his voice.

"Baby snuffling snores like a cartoon character? Yep. It's the cutest thing, isn't it?"

He eases off the bed, letting her little body slide out of his arms, and comes to sit next to me. He takes my hand in his. This action is more intimate than the sex we had earlier.

"I can't believe I'm here," he rumbles, his Russian accent strong as he strokes his fingers across mine.

"Me neither," I whisper, holding back the questions about Nona, the Night Governor, the men who are chasing us. I drink in these quiet moments. There will be time for all of that later.

"I thought about you a lot over the years."

I lift my head from his shoulder and try to pick out his features in the darkness, but we're facing away from the window, so I'm left uncertain about his expression. How he really feels. I wish I wasn't such an open book for this man.

"Well, I think I revealed my hand with the house, if you hadn't already guessed from the songs." I can hear the embarrassment in my voice.

He presses a kiss to my head and then moves lower so our foreheads are pressed together. His breath mingles with mine. I can't see him look at me, but I feel the weight of his gaze. So close. After all these years, he's really here.

"Thank you," he says.

"For what?" My voice is a whisper against the column of his throat. He still smells of salt and pine woods. I remember the silence of the woods. The soft light of the snow. The way he touched me.

"For being a wonderful mother and allowing me a little slice of happiness with you tonight. I will treasure it." He makes it sound like a goodbye.

Pulling away from him, I lie down on the bed. He stretches out beside me, his head resting on his left arm. The light from the parking lot spears through thin drapes. Stripes of light and darkness paint our bodies and the space between them.

"Does your arm hurt?" I look over at his face, the sharp lines of his cheekbones and the square angles of his jaw. There is so much of him in our daughter. No wonder I couldn't forget him.

"Not too much. I've had worse."

"Do you need more painkillers? I've probably got some in my bag." I start to rise, but he stretches his wounded arm to push me back to the bed, wincing slightly.

"I'd rather stay sharp. I don't want to be foggy if something happens." He sighs, and the exhaustion is clear in every line of his body.

I roll over to face him, feeling the heat of his skin. "Rest. Please. We're in the middle of nowhere."

"Better to be careful. I thought we'd be okay at your place."

He turns to me, and I can see his face in the florescent light. Dappled moonlight casts gold and silver patterns across his skin.

"Nadia brought back memories," he says. I could listen to anything in that accent and it would sound better. "They used to replay these old Soviet-style cartoons when we were little.

I sometimes watched them in the orphanage with the younger kids. Reminded me of something happier."

"I didn't know you grew up in an orphanage."

"I didn't get there till I was ten. That's where I met Sasha and Polina. Their grandparents were still alive, but they couldn't handle him. I was a bit softer. Had a more normal life than he did before I got there. I'd never have survived if not for him. He's a natural gangster, but I was bigger."

"And Polina?"

He breathes out a long sigh. "She was a sweet kid. We grew up together and I always protected her. Until I couldn't."

I turn toward him, looking at the stripes of light across his prominent brow and the carved profile of his nose. He traces the line of my brow with his lips and then presses a kiss against my temple before he pulls me against his side.

"You're the only woman I've ever done this with since Polina."

"What? Bedtime stories?"

He laughs. "That too. But no. You are the only woman I've ever spent the night with." He tips his head down and drags his lips back and forth across mine, sending sparks of electricity through me.

"Let's make it count." I taste his lips as they curl into a smile against my mouth.

"What? With a kid in the room?" He sounds almost boyish with excitement.

"No. Get your mind out of the gutter." I gust out a laugh and kiss him again. "Put your arms around me and let me pretend."

"What do you want to pretend, zolotaya?"

"That we're a family who will live happily ever after. Just like in the fairy tales. Even the Russian stories have happy endings, right?"

"Okay." He draws out the second syllable, sounding dubious but also curiously hopeful. "So, what do I do?"

"You hold me," I say as he shifts closer and pulls me against his body. I feel so sheltered in his arms as he wraps them around me. I revel in the warmth of his skin and the steady beating of his heart against my ear.

"That's all?" His question rumbles through his chest and reverberates through my body.

"Yes. You hold me like it's easy and you do it every night, like there's nowhere you'd rather be."

He presses another soft kiss against my mouth. I open to him, the gentle touch of his tongue, and the taste of mint from his chewing gum. Swallowing the wonder of being so close after longing for it all this time. There's something achingly sweet about these chaste kisses as our daughter sleeps beside us.

"I never forgot you," he says. "I used to lie in bed and listen to that album and imagine something just like this."

"You did?"

"Sure I did. Well . . ." He chuckles. "My imagination was a bit more R-rated than what we're doing now. I used to imagine your mouth. You sucking me while I listened to that album. God, I remember how you felt in Moscow. Turned me on so much to think about it."

He kisses me again. Deeper this time. His tongue strokes mine, and his hips rock against me in a matching rhythm.

Then he stills and rubs his nose against mine. "I'm not pretending. There is nowhere I'd rather be, but I knew I'd be doing you a favor if I stayed away."

His words bring me back to the reality of our lives.

I pull back slightly to look at him. "How can you possibly think that?"

"How can you not, zolotaya? I brought death to your door. Our daughter could have seen her first dead bodies courtesy of my visit if we hadn't gotten them out of the way before she came out of the panic room. Is this what you want for her?"

"For tonight, you're just Nadia's dad. You're my man, and I'm just some woman no one has heard of in an anonymous motel."

I lie down in the crook of his shoulder and let the questions about who he is and what he does settle softly, tucking them away for another day. I edge closer to him, soaking up the comfort of his arms around me and the gentle rise and fall of his chest as sleep takes me.

Tonight we can be all the things I've dreamed of. Even if it's only for a night.

CHAPTER FORTY

Vadim

The sound of a backfiring car has me jumping out of my skin. In seconds, I'm off the bed and at the window. The parking lot is quiet in the gray dawn, and the lights of a nearby diner flicker on and off, advertising all-day breakfast.

Turning back to the bed, I look at Kesera's blond curls, and Nadia's tiny body huddled on the pull-out bed. They both look so fragile. So easily damaged.

I'm standing with my back to the window when I hear a knock. Dex stands on the landing outside. Opening the door a crack, he gestures with his thumb at the pull-out bed.

"Better wake the kiddo. We'll head out to get pancakes and bring some back to you in an hour. The two of you stay inside and keep a low profile." He walks past me to the rumpled bedding that covers my daughter and tickles a foot that's sticking from beneath the sheets. "Rise and shine, sleepyhead. Pancakes with sausages and syrup wait for no man."

There's a groan, and then a little voice pipes up. "I'm not a man."

"Sausages and pancakes wait for no kid either. Come on. You've got five minutes." Dex strides over to Kesera, who is curled on the bed. "Breakfast order for me to bring back?"

She opens one eye. "Whatever you pick is fine. Can I sleep a bit longer?"

"We leave in ninety minutes at oh-seven-thirty."

"Kay." She sits up when Nadia squeals as Dex tickles her. He swings the little girl over his shoulders before setting her on her feet and handing a sweatshirt to her. Nadia stares up at him sleepily.

"Pull that on and brush your teeth, and then we can get going. If we're on the road by seven-thirty, we'll be there before nightfall and you can all relax."

"Is there a TV?" Nadia asks.

"Sure, kiddo. I bet there's a TV, but only for little girls who brush their teeth and eat their breakfast," Dex says, taking Nadia by the hand and pushing her into the bathroom before heading to the door. "I'll wait outside. Send her my way."

The door slams behind him, and we're alone in the room for a moment.

Kesera sits up, brushes the hair out of her face, and rubs her eyes. Mornings with a woman are a foreign country. I don't know what the rules are.

But if we have an hour . . .

My eyes follow Nadia as she skips out of the bathroom and bounces toward the door. "Do you want me to bring back pancakes, Daddy?"

I walk toward her and put my hand gently on her head. "Sure. Whatever you like, you can get for me."

She beams up at me like me being happy with the same

breakfast order holds the secrets to world peace. "That's great. I'll get you the best stuff."

Upon seeing her smile, a tight knot in my chest unfurls and I breathe more easily.

I let the door swing closed and walk back to the bed as Kesera emerges from the covers, somehow even more beautiful when she's untouched by the day. Instead of meeting my eyes, she crosses the room to a black duffle bag and begins to rifle through it. I walk behind her to put my hands on her shoulders. Freezing, she stops and then stands, her back against me. Her body quivers.

Pulling her closer, I whisper into her hair. "You smell of jasmine and roses. I remember thinking it strange that you smelled of spring flowers when we were surrounded by snow."

I lift her hair and breathe in the scent of her neck, pressing a line of kisses up to her ear. She sighs and leans her neck against me and looks up. I fall into the green water of her eyes. She stares for a moment, and then her dark lashes lower and she sighs.

"Zolotaya." I don't have the right words. "What can I say to make you feel better?"

"You can say that you'll stay forever and we'll all live happily ever after." She chuckles as if she knows it's a joke.

I pause and wrap my arms around her waist, pulling her body into the shelter of mine. "There's no one else in the world I would rather be with. But this is bigger than us."

I want to swing her into my arms and carry her to the bed like a bride, but one arm is still bandaged up. Instead, I lead her gently to the mattress and lie down beside her, watching the soft morning light glinting off the gold of her curls.

"I'm afraid." She smiles sadly. "Not of what you'll bring to my door. Of how I'll feel once you're gone."

"I'm here now."

She puts her hand on my shoulder and stills.

I can't tell if she's pulling me closer or pushing me away, so I lay my hand over hers and ask, "Is an hour long enough to show you?"

"Show me what?"

"All the things I don't have the words for."

A strand of bronze-and-gold hair lies across her mouth, catching the sunlight. I brush it away and trace the shape of her pout with my fingers before I lean down, pressing my lips to the side of her mouth, her chin, the fragile skin of her eyelids. I have never kissed anyone so slowly. I bury my fingers in her hair, just breathing her in before I move my mouth against hers, sliding my tongue between her lips. She wraps her arms around me, tracing my muscles through the soft cotton of my shirt.

Her lips are so soft. Her hair is a cloud of sunshine. I'm inhaling her as if she's as necessary as air.

She pulls back, her hand cupping my cheek as she smiles at me. Her eyes look like spring leaves in this light. They change color like the woods.

"It's real, you know," I say, turning my face into her hand and pressing a kiss to her palm. "Everything you remembered is real."

"I know," she breathes, her fingers tracing the line of my cheekbones and feathering across my brow.

There's more to say, but I don't have the words for it. The feelings are bigger than anything I can form into speech in English or in Russian, so I just stare at her, trying to memorize every line of her face, the creases around her eyes from her smile, the fullness of her mouth.

She looks at me with as much wonder as I feel.

I kiss her and she slides her hands under my shirt and against my skin, scoring my pecs with sharp fingernails until her hands dive beneath my waistband and cup me softly. She watches me silently as she slides her hands around me. We stare at one another for a moment before she slips lower under the covers, her mouth level with my cock as she gently sucks the tip between her lips.

"Fuck. Jesus fuck." My eyes roll back in my head as her mouth envelops me and her hands beat a rhythm at the base of my cock. It's such bliss that I want to lie back and soak it up, but the minutes are slipping away from us like sand in an hourglass.

"No, baby," I grit out, and she pulls up the sheet, her eyes wide.

God, the sight of her looking up at me, her curls tumbling around my hips and her mouth full of my cock. I can see the smile in her eyes, and I laugh and shake my head.

"No. Not like this. I've waited so long for you." I pull her up, kissing her deeply and rolling her onto her back. "I want . . ."

She widens her legs, nothing on under her long t-shirt, and wraps me in the cradle of her hips. "I'm ready," she whispers.

I reach down and thread my fingers through hers, pressing her into the mattress as I hold my body above her and feel the heat between her legs.

"Fuck," I say. "Sucking me made you so wet."

"Wanting you made me this wet." She smiles up at me.

"Yesterday morning in the woods. I'm sorry I didn't use protection. I wouldn't put you in danger like that." My smile is wry. I don't need to spell out all the other ways that just knowing me will ruin her life. "Zolotaya. I promise. I've never taken chances like this with anyone else."

I look down at her, searching her eyes for the answer to a question I didn't quite ask, but she bites her lip and nods. I slide into her so gently, so slowly, feeling every cell where we join as I look in her eyes. We're so close it's almost painful, so

I tear my eyes away and bury my face in her neck as I groan against her skin.

"Only you, zolotaya. It's only ever been you." Feeling her heat against my bare cock, I repeat the words like a prayer as I rock into her body. "Only you. Only you. Only you."

She gives a breathy sigh each time I bottom out inside her, her legs wrapping tighter around me, arms wound around my neck, her hair a golden cloud against my face, fingers twined around mine.

"Vadim," she whispers, "I need to see you."

Leaning back, I look down. She's gazing up at me, her eyes glimmering with unshed tears.

"Did I hurt you?" I hold still, wanting to tear into her body but too terrified to hurt her more than I already have.

"I promise I'm happy."

I wish this could go on forever. That the door wouldn't open in minutes.

I shut my eyes and lean down to kiss her, joining with her everywhere. My skin slides against hers, our bodies slick with sweat as I press her hands into the mattress. I grasp her fingers and with each kiss and movement of my lips on hers, with each rocking motion of our bodies, I tell her about the tides of emotion I don't have the words for.

She pulses around me as I let go of all the things that can't be and the things I wish I could have had. I pour them into the heat of her body and her wide-open heart. She's everything I want. Everything I can't afford to keep.

CHAPTER FORTY-ONE

Kesera

I want to lie in bed all morning and map every inch of Vadim's skin with my hands, my mouth, my heart. But the door will open any minute, so I press a last chaste kiss to his mouth and start to move away.

He pulls me toward him again, branding my mouth with his kiss and holding me tight against the heat of his skin. He leans back and we look at each other, smiling like idiots.

I feel so alive.

After we release each other, every muscle in my body continues to vibrate with his touch as I fumble through my bag for panties and a phone.

Vadim's footsteps sound on the carpet behind me, and he pulls me against him, banding his arm around my waist as he reaches into his bag and pulls out an old phone.

"Use this," he whispers, pressing his mouth against the crook of my neck and tasting the salt on my skin.

I dial the number I know by heart. "Hey, Stevie."

My best friend's voice sounds strained as he picks up on

the first ring. "Sera. Thank Christ. I've been out of my head with worry. I've been trying to get hold of you for days. Where have you guys been? I called your PA, and she didn't know anything. Aren't you supposed to be preparing your deposition today?"

Vadim lets his hand drift up my arm and across my shoulders as he walks past me to stand in front of the sink. He produces a toothbrush and begins his morning routine.

I grin at Vadim, only half my mind on the conversation with my bandmate. "Some things came up and we had to get out of town."

"Out of town where?"

"I can't tell you. We're keeping everything on the DL."

Vadim nods at me in the mirror, his mouth full of toothpaste and a smile in his eyes.

"For crying out loud, what are you playing at, Sera? Does this have something to do with that Russian bastard?"

Turning away from the bathroom, I frown at the way my friend still talks to me like a wayward child rather than the person who pays his salary. And this petty jealousy has to stop. "Watch it, Stevie. He's Nadia's dad. You might not like him, but he's part of her life."

"Since when?"

"Since now. Since forever. She only has one father, and you can't talk about him like that." The sound of a toothbrush clattering against the sink distracts me as I turn back to see Vadim staring at me, the smile wiped from his face.

"Sure I can," Stevie says. "I can talk about the bastard who abandoned you any way I like. I've been more of a father to Nadia than he's ever been. What are you doing?"

Stevie carries on ranting at me, but I'm only half listening as I watch Vadim stride past me. Picking up the bag next to me, he begins sifting through the evidence of his presence in this room, in my life, and starts packing it away.

"Stevie. You are my best friend. Please don't be like this."

"Can't you see the mess you're making of your life?"

I look out of the window, at the parking lot and the bright sunlight. I bite down on my lip. "That might be true. But it's my life and it's my mess, and I'm the only one who gets to decide what is best for my daughter. Do I make myself clear?"

There's a long pause, and then Stevie grudgingly cedes some ground. "I'm not questioning your parenting."

"That's exactly what you're doing," I bite out. "We're out of town for a few days, and then we'll be back with increased security. But from now on, I really need you to watch how you speak about Vadim. He's her father, okay?"

I look over at Vadim, but he's got his back to me. His head bends over his duffel bag in a posture of defeat.

"Are you two together, then?"

"No, Stevie . . . but I don't want you badmouthing a man who might be part of Nadia's life." I put every ounce of hope and conviction I can into my tone, even though the lines of Vadim's body are spelling out a message I don't want to read.

"So what, you're drawing up shared custody arrangements?" I can almost hear the sneer on his face.

"Don't get on my case like this. I'm firefighting on so many fronts right now. A court case. A media battle. A new album."

There's a pause. "I hope you know what you're doing," he says.

This time, I pause. I don't say that I don't have a clue. I didn't get to where I am today by admitting that to any of the men in my life. Give them an inch . . .

"Yes. I know exactly what I'm doing. I'm doing what's right for my daughter, and I'm writing the lyrics to the next album." My voice sounds confident to my own ears as I hang up and toss the phone on the bed. It's a lie, because I'm standing in my underwear, watching the man who holds my heart avoid my eyes as he pulls on his clothes.

Each sound is unnaturally loud. The ticking of the clock, a slam of a car door, and the roar of a motorbike as some racer goes speeding by. I pull jeans on, fumbling with the buttons as my fingers shake.

Vadim walks over and kneels in front of me. Taking my hands in his, he presses his lips against the lace of my panties, kissing every inch of skin before carefully doing up each button of my jeans. He leans his head against my stomach as I rake my hands through his hair. The strands brush gently against the exposed skin of my navel. I want to burn each touch into me like one of his tattoos, permanently branding my body with the way I feel about him.

But I hear what he doesn't say. It wouldn't change the fact that he has to leave.

He pulls tighter against me and presses a last kiss against my skin before reaching for the white shirt I've left on the bed. It's a strange thing, the way I'm letting him dress me like a child. He slowly does up each button, wrapping the lines of my body in a cover for the day.

His hands reach the last button, and then his fingertips tap against my collarbone, tracing the line from my shoulder to the point where the gold necklace with Nadia's name hangs. Picking up the pendant, he rubs the Cyrillic script between his thumb and forefinger as if it might release a genie who will grant us three wishes.

We're still standing in silence, me watching his fingers and him trying to melt the pendant with his stare, when the door crashes open and Nadia bounces in.

"I ate seven pancakes and I feel a bit sick." She throws a Styrofoam takeout box on the desk and bounces onto the pull-out bed. Her pajamas are strewn across the sheets. She ignores them as she reaches for her school computer. The need to switch into mama-bear mode saves me from myself.

"Ah ah ah, no you don't. Pick up your clothes and put them away." I glance up at the clock. "We've got ten minutes before we have to go."

"Aww, I wanted to watch cartoons. Can't I relax?"

I'm relieved to see Dex's shadow appear in the doorway before he steps into the room. "No way, kid. We leave at zero-seven-thirty. Get a shuffle on."

I pick up Nadia's overnight bag and throw it on the bed. It's an excuse. Something to do with my hands and my eyes so that I don't look over at Vadim and beg him to stay. The way he just made love to me . . . Now I know it was a goodbye.

Stepping away from me, he looks over at Dex, his back to me as he says, "Were we followed?"

Dex shakes his head. "It's all clear. And I've sent for backup, so we'll have an escort to the safe house. I've set up our own location, so there's no need for us to stop at the place you've recommended. Cleaner that way, and easier for our team to secure."

Part of me is glad that Dex is so professional, but I wait for the man who made love to me to offer me some tenderness, some sweetness to take the edge off the goodbye.

But Vadim doesn't look back at me. Instead, he walks over to Nadia and crouches in front of her.

"*Devuchka*. This is for you." He holds out his phone.

"It doesn't even have any games on it."

"No, that's the idea. It's a phone that's a bit harder to trace. Will you keep it with you?" He looks up at her face.

"Sure, Dad."

"And you'll call me if you are ever in danger? If you need anything?"

She nods at him.

He doesn't say another word. Just stands and puts a hand

on her head, then turns and walks toward the door. I stand and wait to see what he'll say to me, but he walks to Dex and hands a phone to him. Now I realize why I couldn't find the phone he gave me at the club. He's taken it back and given it to Dex instead.

"I've only got two of these. If you're in charge of her security, perhaps you'll need to reach me too," he says.

Dex takes the phone and thrusts it into his back pocket, and I wait. For Vadim to turn. To tell me how to reach him. For him to say something, anything. But he doesn't. He walks to the door, opens it, and steps into the bright sunshine.

The sunlight casts his face into shadow and outlines a halo of light around him as he stands in the doorway. He opens his mouth to speak but drops his head and looks at the ground for a moment, as if searching for the right words.

Then he looks up again and says, "Goodbye, zolotaya."

His steps reverberate off the metal walkway, each beat striking me as he descends into the parking lot. The sunshine outside feels like a rebuke.

CHAPTER FORTY-TWO

Vadim

When I told my daughter to text me if she needed anything, I opened a can of worms. The first thing she does is send me a text flagging their location. This might be a burner phone, but how do you tell a ten-year-old she shouldn't let anyone know where she is so they don't track her down and kidnap her or worse?

> Sunnyvale is boring. Can you get me out of here?

> I want to live with you in New York.

I look down at the phone. It feels like I'm handling an unexploded bomb. But I reply.

> Listen to your mother

I stuff the phone back in my pocket.

It's a clusterfuck, but I can't think about it as I pull

up to the docks. It's dark and silent at this time of night. A nest of yellow-and-black striped barriers lies in shadow away from the streetlights. Sasha put shipments on hold until we know who's planning to move against us. A couple of red shipping containers perch on the concrete over the foul water of the Hudson, and a light shines in two rectangles around the edges of one of their doors.

That must be where Sasha is keeping the man we picked up in the attack upstate. If the light is still on, then he's probably still alive. Good news for me. Less so for him.

I've seen shipping containers used for a lot of things, but they're surprisingly effective as torture chambers. Rinse them off with a power hose, stick them on the back of a truck, and drive the evidence away. Stick it on a ship back to China and no one will be the wiser.

I walk toward the two rectangles of light around the container doors. Opening them, I see Sasha standing over a man slumped in a chair. The man's feet have been bound to the chair's legs with duct tape, his hands cuffed behind him. He's passed out. He'll wish he stayed that way by the time we've finished with him.

"What are you waiting for?" I point at the bucket of cold water in the corner next to a table of saws, drills, and pliers that Sasha has laid out for effect.

Sasha gets off on the fear men feel when they see the hardware store he's laid out for them, but it's not usually my bag. I doubt anyone would survive long enough to tell you anything if you used the entire toolbox. I like my kills quick and clean.

This time, though, I'm almost shaking with rage. I want to tear this fucker limb from limb and then slice what's left into little pieces. He threatened my kid and my woman. Even if I can't be with them, they're still mine.

"Let's wake him up." I pick up the bucket of cold water and the power hose lying next to it.

"Hang on a minute." Sasha eyes the door.

"For what? You've gotten what you need, haven't you?"

"No. Kai and Dima are on their way. They're almost here." He sits in a folding chair opposite the slumped man.

"Why do we need them?"

"If we want to take over the Bratva and sideline the Night Governor, we need to know who else is coming for us." Sasha kicks his feet against the metal floor, and they make a clanging noise, but the fucker slumped in the chair doesn't stir. "Was it a kidnap attempt? A hit? Who did the Italians want to piss off? Us? The Chinese? There's a whole spiderweb to unravel here, and this guy is the only fly we've caught."

"He's mine." I run my fingers over a saw and then pick up the power drill before putting it down.

"You can kill him, but we aren't wasting our chance to see what we've gotten into here. We can't give back the girl you snatched and smooth things over now that they've lashed out at you. The only way out of this is to escalate." Sasha ignores the toolbox he's laid out on the table in favor of the curved blade he always carries. He pulls it from his boot.

"Where's the Italian girl now?" I look over at Sasha.

"The *principessa*? With Kai. He's done us a favor, but he doesn't want to keep her unless we can figure out what's going on," he says.

"And if we can't? What then?"

"That scene at the New York dacha in the woods wasn't pretty. I haven't had to dispose of two dead bodies in one weekend for a long time." Sasha looks pensive. He's twirling the carved scimitar blade that matches the one he gave me. It's a nervous tic we both share when things are bad.

"I'm still shocked Andrei survived. I thought he was done for."

"He's pretty banged up. Serves him right for disobeying orders and bringing trouble to your door. He won't be back in action for a couple of months." Sasha smirks at me. "I suppose you'll want to bang him up again once he recovers."

I shrug, looking at the miserable fucker slumped in the chair in front of us. "I might. We've got our hands full for now."

Sasha cups the back of his neck and closes his eyes. "I was trying to get us out of this mess. I want to make millions and attend political fundraisers, not hang around in a shipping container on the docks, beating some fucker to a pulp on a Tuesday night." He sighs and casts his eyes toward the ceiling as I listen to tires crunch on the gravel outside. "I thought we were over that shit, but it follows us everywhere we go."

"It's my fault."

"It is." Sasha glares at me, but then his face softens. "But I don't know if I would have done it differently. It's like years of work we've laid out are about to come crashing down. My dead sister's look-alike appears in a brothel when you go to pick up protection money, and how were you to know she was related to Spataro, daughter of the craziest fucker in New York?"

"And then to top it all off, my long-lost daughter turns up." I laugh. "I feel like we're living in a Mexican telenovela." I look over at the red and pulpy face of the man slumped in the chair. "Why did you call Dima over? I thought he was in London."

Sasha looks toward the door. "I asked him to fly back. The tectonic plates are shifting, and we're in for earthquakes. We could end up controlling a lot more money or losing everything."

Dima's black curls appear in the doorway, and he steps in. "Good evening, gentlemen. Let's get this party started."

"Ever the optimist." Sasha grins at him.

Kai follows Dima through the open doors and closes them behind him.

"Well, sometimes it all works out for the best. I was ready for a trip to New York. London is dismal and gray at this time of year." Dima cracks a grin. I don't see the joke, but who knows.

I walk over to Dima and grab him in a one-armed hug. "How's London?"

"Easier pickings than New York. We've bought half the government. Those fuckers would sell their grandmothers for a donation to their political machines. Getting access is a piece of cake." Dima smiles, but it doesn't quite reach his eyes.

I turn back to Sasha. "Dima's always glass half-full. But why are you hopeful that my fuck-up in picking up the girl could work in our favor?"

Sasha looks over at all of us. "Because someone lashed out by sending men against us. Why not just call me in for a meeting? Why send the cavalry over to carry out a hit?"

"Doesn't make sense," I say. "It's not something I would have done. It's the act of a panicked man."

"Have you been working closely with the Italians?" Kai says from the doorway, where he's leaning against the side of the shipping container.

"We're better with money, if you ask me, but they have stronger ties with America, which used to work well for everyone. We rub along well enough with them." Sasha looks over at the other two men. "This kind of drama is out of character."

Dima looks pensive. "Yeah, Sasha's right. They've never ordered a hit without a conversation. Something must be going on inside their ranks to have triggered it."

Sasha stares at me. "It might be worse. It could be something going on in *our* ranks. One of the bodies had

Russian gang tattoos." He glances over at Kai. "How's the girl?"

"First she was scared. Now she's just furious. I've left her alone to cool off. She's entertaining some fantasy that I'm going to let her go." He shrugs. "But at least the food bill's not big. She says she's going on a hunger strike."

"Sorry I brought trouble to your door, man. I'm glad you were able to step up." I nod at him.

What if that happened to my daughter? This is not a world to bring a kid into, and if I need any more proof, I only need to look around me.

"Let's get this show started." Sasha picks up the bucket and dumps it over the guy's head. "Rise and shine, fuckhead."

The man slumped in the chair groans. One eye is swollen shut and the left side of his face is already a puffy mess, but he opens his right eye enough to take in the four of us standing around him. "I didn't do anything. I was just following orders."

From behind me, Kai's deep voice echoes off the container's metal walls. "And those orders were?"

"Pick up the pop star and her daughter and get out of there as fast as possible."

"So you were supposed to keep them alive?" Kai adds.

"I guess . . ."

His words fade as Sasha takes a knife and slices through the man's pants in a couple of sharp swipes. He gouges deep enough to draw blood and show he means business, but not enough to do much damage.

The man bites his lips until they're white, but he doesn't scream. "Fuck. I don't know anything. You can hack me to pieces, but I won't be able to tell you much." He levels Sasha with a direct stare.

"Well, we can do this clean or we can do this messy," Sasha says with a grin. "It's entirely up to you."

"We were supposed to pick up the woman and the kid and the tall guy with the scar. But we didn't know there would be three tall guys. It was a mess."

"There now." Sasha pulls out the pliers and walks over to him with a big smile. "That's something that we can agree on." He grabs the man's hand and rips out a fingernail.

I'll give the fucker credit. He doesn't scream then, just bites his lips and pants heavily.

"We wasn't gonna kill them. We was supposed to hold 'em and exchange them for the girl."

"Which girl?" I ask to be sure. As if it isn't obvious.

"Spataro's daughter. She was supposed to marry who she's told to." He looks at me through his swollen eye and tilts his bloody face to the light. "You shouldn't have touched Alessandra," the man bites out. "Spataro had been holding that girl until he found the right use for her, and now you've fucked up his plans with the Russians."

Sasha goes still. Then he turns to me, and we share a look. "We haven't just pissed off the Italians. The Night Governor has his hands in this," he grits out.

The man in the chair is a bit older—a slight paunch hangs above his waistband, and his muscles have turned to fat—but he can control his emotions. Sasha picks up the drill and starts the bit whirling, but the man in the chair just closes his eyes and takes a deep breath. No drama.

"What did Spataro want to do with the Night Governor? Why did he need a marriage?" Sasha asks.

"I dunno, man. It's above my pay grade," the man says. "I was just supposed to pick up the women and bring them back. I think the boss was gonna swap them for his daughter."

I look over at Sasha. "Do we give the girl back?"

Sasha picks up the drill again. "Too late for that, I think. He's already struck us. We back down now, we look weak."

"Where were you going to take the singer and her kid?" I ask the man.

"Back to the boss's penthouse. He said it would be safer that way. We wasn't gonna hurt them."

"That's good." I can hear the smile in Dima's voice. "You've got a little girl, don't you? Isabella, was it? And Chiara? Such a pretty name for a wife," Dima adds, walking toward him. He doesn't need to brandish a weapon. The names of this guy's family members are sharper than any blade on the table.

The man begins to shake. "Don't touch them. Don't fucking touch them. Women and children should be off limits." His voice wavers, but I cut him off before he can say anything else.

"Like my family? Or did the limits not extend to them?" I say. "We could have handled this in a civilized manner."

The man in the chair lifts his head. "What are you going to do to my daughter? Where is Isabella?"

"Your daughter went to school today, and she came home to your lovely wife," Dima says. "They were wondering where you'd been when I went to the house and asked for you."

The man raises his head and glares at Dima, but he appears to come to a conclusion. He has to give us something.

"Spataro is weak. He needs this marriage. If you don't return Alessandra to her father and she doesn't marry the Night Governor, then the Italians will start fighting over the businesses in the US. The garbage and recycling will be first. Then the drugs and the girls. It'll be carnage, and for no good reason." The man pleads with us as if we can stop Spataro and the Night Governor from picking fights.

Dima picks up the gun and aims it between the man's eyes. "Tell us everything or it'll be your wife and kid next."

"Spataro is getting old. He's losing his grip, but the Night

Governor is a psychopath. It won't be great to have him in control. We respected the don, but people fear the Night Governor because he's unpredictable."

"We know what we need to know." Dima lifts the gun again, but Kai's voice stills his hand.

"Keep him alive. He could come in handy."

Dima lowers the gun, and Sasha glances over at the power drill.

"Christ, Sasha. I thought you were trying to move in more elevated circles," I say. "Playing with the contents of a hardware store in a shipping container isn't exactly going to help you win friends and influence."

Sasha cracks a grin. "It might. Depends on the people."

As if to highlight the mess my life has become, the burner phone buzzes in my pocket.

> When we come back home will you come over?

> Can I come and stay at your house?

I look at the slumped man in the chair. The man whose wife and daughter we just threatened.

I cock my head at Sasha. "He's mine."

I walk to the chair, send a fist into his stomach, and then rain a series of blows down on his face. His cheekbone cracks against my knuckles.

"That was my kid you threatened. That was my woman!" My fists fly faster now, and his face is a bloody mess. His blood coats my knuckles before Sasha grasps my arms and pulls me back.

"If we want to leave him alive, then you'd better give it a rest," he says.

His steady voice anchors me back to the grubby steel

walls and the swinging overhead bulb. I pull out my phone to reply to my daughter's text, getting blood all over the keys of the old Nokia.

CHAPTER FORTY-THREE

Kesera

The kitchen door bangs as loud as a gunshot, and Dex jumps as Nadia's voice screams from the corridor of the safe house we've stopped in.

"I hate you! I want to live with my dad!" Her voice echoes from behind the closed door, and her footsteps stomp away from us.

I let my eyes fall closed and my head drop back against the wall. I can't win. The usual questions assail me before I can stop myself.

Why did he leave?

Why wasn't I enough to make him stay?

Needing to release the tension somehow, I lash at the cupboard, kicking it until it bangs like the door. The top hinge comes loose and rolls to the floor with a *clink*, leaving the door sagging at an angle.

Dex's snickering makes me look up and glare at him.

"What's so funny?" I snap.

"Nadia reminds me of you at that age," Dex leans against

the sink, smiling wryly at me. He steps toward me, clamping his big hands over my shoulders, and I try to shrug him off. "So much spirit," he adds.

"There's one big difference. When I was Nadia's age, I had a dad who loved me." I try to pull away from him, but Dex grips me tighter and gives me a gentle shake until I look up into the twinkling eyes of my father's best friend.

"It's not that different. Your dad was deployed for long stretches. Vadim is probably doing the best he can, given the circumstances."

I pinch the bridge of my nose and stare at the toes of my boots. "I can't put my life on hold for another man who doesn't care. I've got to get back and fight this court case."

Dex pulls me over to a chair, pours a cup of coffee, and slides it to me across the table. I take a sip. It's bitter and acrid. It tastes how I feel.

"Kesera," Dex says softly. "What makes you think he doesn't care?"

I run my finger across the top of the cup rather than look at him. "He never came to find us."

"Hey." I look up at the sharpness in Dex's voice. "If I were him, I would have done the same."

I can't help my mouth pulling into a sneer. "What? Avoided your family?"

"No. I'd have tried to protect them by staying away. I think that's what he's doing." He stands and points a thumb at the closed door to the bedroom where Nadia is hiding. "Come on. Go and get Nadia. We're going riding."

"What?" I step back. "I thought you said it wasn't safe to leave."

He grins at me, white teeth gleaming against his tan. "I said it wasn't safe for Nadia to go to a mall, but I've got a military buddy with stables near here, and I think we all need horses and sunshine."

"You sure?" I look out the window at the anonymous street.

"Yeah, no one is going to spot you on the back of a horse. Go get ready."

"Okay." I pad down the corridor and press my ear against Nadia's door. Hiccupping sobs filter through the wood, and my heart sinks.

I go to my room and pull on some jeans. I'm pondering the mess we're in as my phone rings. Maxine's name flashes across the screen, and I swipe my thumb over it as my heart thuds against my ribs like a drum.

"I've got good news and bad news," she says. Her nasal accent comes down the line, reminding me that my battles are still being fought in my absence.

"Give me something good. Please." I twirl a curl of hair around my finger.

"You aren't alone. There are at least three more artists who've been harassed and have confirmed that Jimmy is an equal-opportunity monster." I can hear the smirk in her voice as she adds, "He spreads the love around."

"But?"

"Well, the bad news is that no one will go on the record if you've disappeared. You'll need to meet with these women. You have to be ready to lead the charge, not hiding from life in bumfuck nowheresville."

"I'll get back as fast as I can," I say. I can't let victory slip away when we're so damn close.

BY THE TIME we get to the stables, I'm determined to find a way back to my life. I've left Nadia at the car so she can fiddle with her riding boots and I can speak with Dex. I enter the barn, the scent of hay and horses doing nothing to calm me down.

"We can't stay here, Dex. I've waited years to go after the monster who made me a star, and I need to win this lawsuit. I can't do it from the middle of nowhere."

Dex walks over to me and lets his hands drop to my shoulders, giving me a gentle shake. "You can't do it at all if you're dead."

I tense under his fingers, and he rubs my shoulders with a wry smile.

"Give me another day. We'll be out of here soon." He spins me to face the horses. "Here you go. That's Whiskey. She's pretty gentle. Why don't you brush her down?" he says, pointing to a bay mare. "We'll put Nadia on Snort. That horse is so old he just wants to eat grass, so Nadia will have her work cut out to keep him moving."

"I feel like a failure," I say, dipping my head against the horse's nose and breathing in her soft, grassy breath.

"Don't beat yourself up, kiddo. I think you're doing pretty well." Dex moves around the front of the horse, places a brush in my hand, and lifts the brush to the top of Whiskey's flank, helping me drag my hand lower in repeated motions. "Brush her. It'll soothe the horse, and it'll soothe you too."

"How am I doing well?"

"You're protecting your kid. You're planning your court case, and you've handled this situation with Nadia's father with dignity and grace."

"You don't think I'm an idiot? Stevie thinks I shouldn't talk to him."

Dex snorts as he bites back a laugh. "Stevie's carried a torch for you for years."

My head jerks up. "He hasn't. He said—"

"I know what Stevie said, but he didn't mean it. Anyone

with eyes can see he's lovesick. He just knows you're out of his league."

"That's what Vadim said."

"Smart man." Dex nods, taking his own brush and going to the black horse in the stall next to Whiskey's.

"You don't think I shouldn't be talking to him?" I run the brush down the horse's flank. "Not that I have a way of reaching him. He gave the phones to you and Nadia." I bite down on my lip, the churning uncertainty rising up my throat.

"Nadia's your daughter, and I work for you. He only had two phones with him. I think he's putting your safety first." Dex looks over, his brush pausing halfway down the horse's side. "You can reach him if you need to. Honestly, I think he's firefighting at the moment. That scene at your house was a shitshow."

"I just wish . . ." My sentence hangs in mid-air, the scent of straw and the grassy perfume of horses mingling with my unspoken desires.

"Kiddo, I've known you for years, and you've built this business with very little help from the men around you. You didn't ask for Nadia's father to come blazing back into your life, and now you're handling it with the same grace and sense as everything else."

"Then why won't life cut me a break?" I say, watching Nadia walking toward us from the car.

"You know what your dad would have said?"

"What?" I wave Nadia over with a falsely bright smile before looking back at Dex.

"It's always darkest before the dawn. Hang tight, kiddo."

I lean against the horse, wondering just how much darker it will get before the sun comes out again.

CHAPTER FORTY-FOUR

Vadim

Dad. I want to come and live with you

You'd better stay put.

Why? Don't you have a bedroom? How long will it take you to get one? Mama is driving me crazy.

A bedroom?

Yeah, all my friends who've got divorced parents have their own rooms.

We're not divorced.

Ok, so you can come and stay with us? Mama won't let me do anything. I need help.

I'll think about it.

CHAPTER FORTY-FIVE

Kesera

We've been back for two days, but New York has never felt less like home. Even though Dex has a huge team in place, I'm on edge. My so-called best friend isn't helping either.

Stevie paces our living room, circling a coffee table stacked with books that an interior designer thought would look good, but which none of us have ever looked at. He picks up one of the guitars lying on a stand in the corner and puts it back. I guess he's not here to work on a song with me today.

We've spent many hours sitting here, working out songs together and viewing Central Park as the light floods through the windows. He's always been the person I bounce lyrics and melodies off, but if we aren't working, I don't need him here.

I pick up my phone and run through the latest encrypted message from Dex outlining our security arrangements for the day. So much sits on my shoulders, and the stakes have never been higher.

"Will you sit down, Stevie? You're going to wear tracks in the carpet."

He stops, spins the leather bands that circle his wrists, and pulls on his hair. "You don't have to fight this in the courts, you know. Maybe you can make another album with Jimmy and get this over with. You won't have to go into the studio alone. You know I've got your back."

I sink into the white cushions, pulling at my cashmere wrap. "I do know that, but it just turns my stomach that I have to deal with Jimmy at all. I was so young when I signed to his label, and I didn't know better." I shake my hands out as if I can rip away the crawling feeling talking about Jimmy gives me. "Nothing about this is fair. Him saying he doesn't have a public profile so he needs a lower burden of proof for defamation, and then dragging my name through the mud." I bang my hand against the stack of books on the table. "I'm fighting back."

"Are you sure you want to do this? We both know you'll be the one on trial."

Stevie plops onto the couch opposite me. His skinny legs spread in a power pose in his drainpipe jeans. I can't help comparing him to Vadim in my mind. He looks like half the man.

"Have you heard from Nadia's dad?" Stevie asks, reading my thoughts with uncanny accuracy.

"No. Dex let him know we were back in town, but the scene at the Gingerbread House was ugly. I think he's keeping a low profile." I shrug as if I'm not bothered. As if I'm not replaying the way he touched me when we were together. He makes me feel alive, even when I know he's bad for me.

"You don't want to be arranging shared custody if there's going to be a shoot-out." Stevie chuckles as if it's all a big joke.

"I agree the timing is bad, but it would be good if Nadia

could form some sort of relationship with him. She's been talking about going to live with him."

Stevie's eyes widen, and he looks at me, aghast. "You can't be serious."

"Well, I'm not serious about it, but it's hard to stop her from fantasizing about him." I don't add that she's not the only one. "He's Nadia's father."

"He's a thug."

"You don't know what's between us," I bite out.

"And what is between you? Nothing. This guy turns up, you go on the run for a week, and now you can't even walk Nadia to school. How is anything about this good?"

I think back to the morning in the motel. Vadim kneeling before me, his lips on my stomach. Gazing into his eyes as he moved inside me.

"My god, Sera. Please tell me you didn't let that man anywhere near you."

"What business is it of yours?" I snap. I stand and walk to the window, looking down at the trees below. I don't want to confront questions I don't have the answers to.

"It's every bit of my business. I'm your best friend."

"Then you should be happy I've found him." I spin to face him. He might think he's questioning Vadim, but really, he's doubting me. My judgement. My choices.

"My god, how naïve are you?"

Anger flares like a bright flame. Something about those moments with Vadim—being cherished as a woman and respected as a parent—has made me feel braver. "I'm a grown woman with a kid. I've survived in this business for a decade while surrounded by wolves and predators like Jimmy. Don't talk down to me."

"Is that why you won't settle the case out of court? Because this Russian criminal is back in your life?" His lips curl into a sneer. "Why aren't you just dropping this lawsuit?

You got enough material from the last album to do another tour. I don't see what the big deal is."

I rear back as if he's slapped me. "You don't?"

My voice sounds unnaturally loud to my own ears, but Stevie just glares at me like nothing is amiss. His once boyish face is lined and gray from the hundreds of lines of coke he's stuck up his nose, and the petulant set of his mouth makes me wonder where the sweet kid I met at open mic night all those years ago has gone.

My eyes narrow into slits. "I had to walk back into the studio and work with a man who raped me because I have a family to support. I haven't been wasting my earnings on models and blow."

"Oh, and you're saying I have?" My friend jabs his finger at me, his mouth curling into a snarl.

"Well, what are you doing with your life, Stevie?"

Stevie jumps up and throws his hands in the air. "Waiting for you to see how I feel. To see that I love you."

I look at him and think back to times he's used my fame to hook up with younger women. How can he possibly call what he's been doing *waiting* for me? And now, he's pressuring me to work with a man I hate.

The silence stretches between us before he sinks to the sofa, resting his forearms on his knees and burying his head in his hands. Walking over to him, I rest a hand on his trembling shoulder as he stares at the floor.

"You were supposed to be with me," he mumbles. "You were supposed to love me back."

I look down at him. At this guy who's helped me write my songs, who I've played video games with on a tour bus, who has walked beside me for the last ten years, but who still relies on me to earn his money. A wave of sadness washes over me.

I love Stevie, but he will never be my equal. He's never once made me feel cherished the way Vadim did.

"I'm sorry, Stevie. But I'm going back to court." I pause, and he looks up at me through his fingers. "And I'm going to find another bassist for the next album."

Stevie jumps to his feet. "You're making a mistake, Sera. That man will never make you happy."

I watch his retreating back as he stamps out of the room like a little boy having a tantrum, but I won't chase him or change my mind. This time, I'm fighting to win.

Chapter Forty-Six

Vadim

We're back. When can I see you?

This is not a good time.

I'm back at school, but mama's busy with the lawyers or she's in the studio. I should have at least one parent around.

And you think that parent should be me?

When can I come to your house to stay?

Soon kiddo. When it's safe.

CHAPTER FORTY-SEVEN

Kesera

I sit on my bed and pick up the burner phone, looking at it like it's a burning coal in my hands. Hold on to it too long and it's going to hurt me. Gingerly, I dial the only saved number, and Vadim's deep voice echoes down the line.

"Dex. Is something wrong?"

"It's not Dex. It's Kesera."

"Zolotaya. How did you get this phone?"

My stomach hollows out at his response. "Dex has set up our security plans, and we're back. I borrowed his phone so that I could check in and see what your plans are for seeing Nadia."

I can almost taste all the unsaid words crowding on my tongue as I bite them back to stop myself from begging to see him.

"I don't have any plans to see her, zolotaya." A door slams in the background. "Give me a minute and I'll find somewhere where I can hear you." His footsteps echo, then stop. "That's better. I've been thinking about you, but . . ."

Men's voices come through the phone as distant mumbles, and there's a long pause as unspoken words hang in the air.

"Are you okay?" I ask.

"I've been better." He sighs deeply, and I'm filled with the sharp urge to comfort him, but I push it down. "It's not a good time. I care about you both, but I can't see her. Or you."

I swallow down a surge of frustration. Why does every man in my life say that he cares about me, then fail to back his words with actions? Part of me wants to scream at him to step up for me now that he's found us. But the rational side wins.

I sink against the cushions in the wide, empty bed, feeling so damn lonely as I tell myself it's for the best. "It's okay, Vadim. I understand."

"You do?" He sounds surprised, and his voice is lighter.

"Honestly?" I laugh, despite myself. "I don't feel like I understand anything. This is all moving too fast for me, but I'm trying my best to do what's right for Nadia."

I don't say there was a little part of me that called him just for myself.

There's a silence, and then his voice sounds softer as he adds, "Me too. I know she wants to see me. She's been texting me."

His admission gives me a jolt, and I suck in a breath. What's she been saying? How can I stop her? I'm torn between jealousy that she's in touch with him and fear for her safety. My daughter's growing up and away from me, and the stakes have never been higher.

I get up and walk to the door, padding down the corridor toward her empty bedroom.

"Zolotaya, you still there?" Vadim's voice sounds strained.

"Yeah," I breathe, standing in the door to my little girl's room as I look at the stuffed toys and dolls she's about to grow out of. How will I keep her safe?

"It's pretty natural," he says. "I used to fantasize about my dad coming to the orphanage to pick me up and take me away to a better life. I don't want to make promises I can't keep."

"She misses you." I lean against the door frame and wish this was the kind of relationship where I could tell him I miss him too.

"I know. She's welcome to call and text, and I'll answer when I can." There's a pause, and the men's voices grow louder.

"Let me know through Dex if it's possible for her to see you. It would mean a lot to her. I'll leave the phone with him while he's in the city with us. If that's what you'd prefer."

Instead of answering my unasked question, he changes tack abruptly. "What's happening with that slimy fucker you're suing? When are you back in court?"

"The hearing is set for July. I have more hope of a victory now, but Jimmy's pretty vindictive. I'll be dragged through the press. I don't want Nadia involved, but it's hard to see how I'll keep her out of the story when the whole case revolves around whether I'm a good person, not whether he attacked me."

"My god, you don't deserve this, and he—"

"Well, you saw it all in Moscow."

"How many times do I have to warn him to back off? Why can't he just take a hint? Men like him really piss me off."

"What?" I spit the word out in shock. A dizzying wave rushes through my legs. How long has Vadim been hovering at the edges of my life? And how much does he know about Jimmy?

His chuckle breaks up my circling thoughts. "That's why he walks with a limp now, but apparently, he didn't get the message. Why is he so fixated on you?"

I'm silent for a moment as the implication slowly sinks in. Vadim never forgot me. But if he can fight for me, why can't he love me? I don't ask the question, though. I just answer him.

"Money, control. The chance to do this to more young women. I don't know. I'm not the only one, but other stars see what's happened to me and they don't want to stick their heads over the parapet. He's vindictive."

"Zolotaya?"

"Yes?" I cradle the phone close to my ear, listening to his deep voice and missing him as I walk out of Nadia's room and back to my own.

"You're not alone."

"I am. It's always just been me and Stevie, and now it's just me. We've had a falling out. He wanted me to settle."

"That little fucker. He wants you and he's just jealous."

"I know."

"You do?" Surprise tinges his voice.

"I do now," I admit softly. "He told me over the weekend that he thought we should be together."

"Zolotaya. You are the only one without eyes to see how beautiful you are. Of course he wishes for you. Anyone would."

I listen to his voice, wondering if this means he longs for me the way I've been longing for him.

Someone shouts in the background, followed by the sound of a door banging shut. "I've got to go, golden girl. I . . . just look after Nadia for me."

And then he's gone and I'm sitting alone in my bedroom on my king-size bed, looking at the space next to me that's always been empty. Is Vadim protecting us or just protecting himself?

CHAPTER FORTY-EIGHT

Vadim

Sasha and Kai are sitting at a round table with open bottles of champagne when I walk into the private dining room at Forbidden City. The walls are a symphony of gold dragons flying across a black lacquer background. Gold-studded black leather tops the gilt chairs. Understatement isn't a Chinese look.

I smile. Reminds me of Russia. It's a welcome change from the twenty-seven shades of gray and beige that dominate so many of the rooms in New York. You'd think Americans were allergic to color.

With a sharp stab of longing, I think of Kesera's house in the woods and how familiar it felt.

"Do you have any beer?" I look at the open bottles of Dom Pérignon, and my mouth curls in disgust. "I have peasant tastes."

Sasha pushes a red button, and a waiter appears with two enormous plates of lobsters set on piles of steaming, crispy noodles. Kai nods at him and points to something on the menu.

"Tsingtao coming up. Lobster too highbrow for you?" Kai raises his eyebrows at me, and I nod absentmindedly.

Only half of me is here to discuss the consequences of one of my bad decisions. The rest of my thoughts are with Kesera, wishing I could check on her and protect her from the sharks that are circling her.

The men in her life aren't fit to call themselves men, and part of me wants to stake a claim on her and get every slimy fucker in the music business to back the hell away. And I would if I didn't worry that getting involved with her would draw out even worse men from the darkness that I live in.

Kai laughs and pours a glass of champagne for Sasha. "Well, not everyone likes lobster and champagne. I can barely get the Spataro chick to eat."

Sasha slants a look at him, and his shoulders tense. "You need to give her back to us?"

"No, man. I'm just grumbling. She's just a royal pain in my ass. Such a fucking princess. God knows how long she'd have lasted in one of the Night Governor's brothels." He picks up a lobster claw with his chopsticks. "You think she'd be grateful, but no. Nothing is good enough for the *principessa*."

"I think we need to get the Spataro girl out of town," Sasha says.

Kai ponders for a moment. "I can take her to Hong Kong. I have to see some associates over there."

"So, if we get the girl out of the way, what do we do about the rest of the Italians?" Sasha looks over at me as he picks up a mouthful of noodles. They dangle from his chopsticks. "That attack was an escalation. We can't just hand the Spataro girl back and hope it will all evaporate. And one of the dead men was definitely Russian."

"Someone thought it was important enough to attack my woman," I say.

"Attack your woman? I think the plan was to snatch her and trade her for the Spataro girl," Sasha says, his eyes widening a fraction as he turns to me. He's picked up on the way I'm talking about Kesera.

I glare at him, avoiding the question he's asked. "Well, nothing went as planned, thank god, but it was a shitshow. We're lucky that no one called the police and created more drama."

The waitresses come in with more plates of seafood and beer, but Kai waves them out and goes to the door.

I take a sip of my beer and look over at Kai and Sasha. "There's something else going on. Something we're not seeing."

"I think it's pretty clear," Sasha says. "The Night Governor thinks we've gotten too big for our boots, and he's losing his grip."

I turn to him with a frown. "But they wanted to pick up Kesera and the kid for ransom."

"Or did they just want to kill you?" Sasha says. "That whole attack was messy. Badly planned. Involving civilians. Whoever ordered it was desperate and panicking. It's not a clever move."

Kai sits back in his chair and picks up a pair of nutcrackers to attack the lobster he's piled on his plate. "Not the Night Governor's style?"

"No," Sasha and I say in unison.

"The Night Governor finds out your secrets, and then he pulls your strings like a puppet. He's not an all-guns-blazing kind of guy," Sasha adds.

I look over at the two men. "You know what else is weird? That Spataro wanted to marry his daughter to an outsider. The Italians stick to their own."

"I don't suppose you're up for marrying an Italian?" Sasha says to Kai.

Kai grimaces. "It wouldn't be a hardship to fuck the Italian girl, but I'm not marrying a psycho."

"You'd probably be a little psychotic after the month she's had." I pull out a cigarette, my lips twisting in distaste. Thinking about bringing my daughter into this world has soured my appetite. I picture Kesera whispering to me in the dark about being a family as I wrapped my arms around her.

"The Night Governor wants the girl back," Sasha says, "but see if we can buy some time until we work out what's behind that attack. You'll take the girl out of the country?"

Kai nods, pushing away his plate and lighting a cigarette.

I lean back and shut my eyes as I think about the string of text messages from Nadia. I have to keep her out of this world.

Standing, my eyes dart to Sasha. "Are you coming back to Brooklyn tonight?"

"Yeah, I want to go home and pretend I'm in Russia." He rises and claps his hand on Kai's shoulder. "Thanks, man. Whichever way the chips fall, I'm going to make this worth your while."

Sasha and Kai share a look that speaks to some shared history I wasn't part of.

Kai unfolds himself from his chair and moves to shake my hand. Sasha trusts him, but the situation is moving so fast I can't get my feet under me. And that's before I've even thought about Kesera or my daughter.

We all walk out of the restaurant, and Sasha calls his driver.

"Do you want to ride back to Brighton Beach with me?" he asks.

"Sure. I need to ask you a favor anyway."

Sasha slings an arm around my shoulders. "Ask away, old friend. What fresh hell are you bringing me?"

"It's not Bratva business, but I need you to help me kill someone. Do you remember that slimy little shit that was managing my woman in Moscow?"

Sasha raises an eyebrow and pulls out a cigarette. He lights it and blows the smoke into my face without answering my question. "So, she's your woman now, is she?"

The car pulls around with Alexei, Sasha's heavyset driver, in the front seat. With his bald head and his bull neck, he looks like we pulled him straight from central casting.

"Once they attacked her, it changed everything." I drop the cigarette butt on the pavement and grind it under my heel.

Sasha takes another drag and regards me thoughtfully. "I see." He blows out the smoke and looks toward the ranks of parked luxury cars. "I do remember the little shit you're talking about, actually. He blew up my phone for a summer, asking for gigs on yachts in Cyprus or Italy. I wasn't sure if he was more interested in making money or a summer holiday. Idiot. I don't like to see you so loved up, but I didn't like that fucker."

"I'm not loved up." I shake my head.

"Oh yeah? Your daughter's nanny is someone we just happened to have run across in Moscow, and you're telling me that had nothing to do with you? And now it's all 'my woman' this and 'my woman' that." His gaze slides to me under raised brows. He drops the cigarette and grinds the butt underfoot. "Drop the act."

He pulls open the car door and slides into the back seat, and I follow him in and pull the door closed behind me.

"So why are we killing that slimy little shit now? You could just threaten him. Blow out a kneecap or something. Less final. Less messy."

"I already did that. Years ago. I paid him a visit before she left Nashville, but the message didn't stick."

Sasha starts laughing. He's bent over, tears in his eyes and arms clutching his sides. When he sits back up, he looks over at me. "And you tell me you don't love her? This is a mess."

I glare at him. "Will you help me or not?"

"You didn't need to ask. I've always got your back." He grins at me. "Even if I give you a hard time." Once he's stopped laughing, the smile slides from his face and he looks out of the window, avoiding my eyes as he shrugs. "Love is a weakness I don't need, but if there's a kid involved, then you're vulnerable anyway."

I lean my head against the back seat and breathe out a sigh. "I don't want to leave a trail. If I stand a chance with Kesera, I can't have a lot of talk about this guy Jimmy going missing just as I appear back in her life."

Sasha taps on the divider between us and the driver. "Don't worry about it. No body. No crime."

CHAPTER FORTY-NINE

Vadim

My old burner phone buzzes, and I pick it up with a smile tugging at my lips. It might be my daily pancake update. My daughter has taken to giving me regular status reports on her breakfast and sleeping habits.

But my heart thuds against my breastbone when I see that the message is from Dex.

> Nadia has gone missing. Meet us at the penthouse as soon as you can.

By the time I fly into their lobby, my stomach is in knots. I don't believe this is a coincidence. Spataro's men know who I am, and they know about my connection to Kesera.

The doorman must have orders to let me straight upstairs because he waves me toward the dedicated penthouse elevator. When the doors open, Kesera stands in front of me, red-rimmed eyes puffy from crying and her arms wrapped around herself.

"Zolotaya. Come here." I step toward her and wrap her in

a bear hug, squeezing her tight against my chest. She feels so right in my arms and I pull her tighter, relishing the chance to shelter her. "What can I do?"

She pads into the kitchen on leaden feet, pulling me to join Dex at the table. Nona stands at the sink and continues rinsing dishes as if this is a perfectly normal workday. Kesera sinks into a chair, staring dead-eyed at some printouts of two girls walking out of the gates of Blessed Heart International Elementary School.

"We pulled this from the school's security footage," Dex says. "This is Nadia and her best friend Daniella leaving the school at lunchtime. They didn't return to school, and they didn't come back to our place for a sleepover as planned."

"What did you say her best friend's name was?" I ask.

"Daniella Greco. Why?" Dex looks up at me.

"Is she Italian? How long have they been friends?"

Kesera must pick up on the agitated tone of my voice because she jerks upright in her chair and watches me intently.

"Danni joined the school when her family moved from Italy last year, and the two girls just hit it off," Kesera says. "They've spent a lot of the last year at each other's houses, making dance videos, putting on plays, baking cookies."

"You say that she only moved here last year? And she's Italian. It could be a coincidence, but I don't like it." I look over at Dex, who nods as he pulls out a computer.

"It's an international school. There are a lot of diplomats' families and people from the UN, as well as the usual banker and hedge-fund kids. It's not unusual for people to move from overseas." Kesera's voice sounds reedy, as if she's trying to convince herself.

I take Kesera's hands in mine. "I could be panicking over nothing, but her going missing with an Italian friend when the Italian Mafia are baying for my blood gives me a bad feeling."

Dex looks up at me. "We ran checks on Daniella when we got back. There were no immediate red flags, but I agree. I don't like it. Nadia's been going back and forth to school, and Danni's been meeting her here, so we minimized the risk."

"It might be nothing, zolotaya," I say, ignoring the churning in my gut which tells me this couldn't possibly be nothing. I pull her chair toward mine and put my arm around her shaking shoulder.

"Or it might not," Dex mutters, keeping the drama to a minimum but backing me up.

I pick up my phone. "Sasha. Are you in town?"

"Yes, I was heading to the banya."

"Well, can you head over to Central Park West? I need you to meet me at an address I'll text you. Something has come up."

Kesera looks up, confused, and I shake my head.

"That's not your usual part of town. Sounds serious," Sasha says.

I hear the question in his voice, but I don't want to go into details on the phone. He's already met Kesera, and he was such a raging asshole that I didn't see her again for years. This has the potential to go badly, but I need my best friend.

"Serious enough," I say, and he grunts an affirmative before I hang up.

Laying my phone on the table, I say, "Do you have any faraday bags?"

And to my relief, Dex walks over to his backpack and pulls out a lightweight silver bag that blocks phone signals and tosses it over to me. I slide all of our phones into the bag and seal it shut.

"There," I say. "Now no one can turn our phones into microphones. The Italians own plenty of corrupt cops."

So do we, but who knows who's listening in?

I turn to Dex. "My business partner Sasha is on his way. Can you send someone down to meet him once we find out where Danni lives? Then we can take it from there." I force my voice lower and project as much calm and certainty as I can as Kesera's shoulders start shaking again.

She chokes back a sob, and I haul her onto my lap, pulling her into my chest and putting a finger under her chin so that I can look into her jade eyes. They're still beautiful, even after hours of crying.

"Don't worry. We'll get Nadia back," I say. "It's probably just kids being kids, but even if this is linked to the Italians, the girl I picked up is safe with us. We haven't harmed her, so there's no reason for the Italians to hurt our daughter."

Kesera bites down on her lip, and then she looks up at me. "Two dead bodies at my place in upstate New York say otherwise." Her eyes swim with tears.

I rock her back and forth on my lap. "They were foot soldiers, zolotaya. Pawns. Nadia is a queen in a chess game. She'll be safe until the players work out how to put the other side in check. You don't waste pieces like that."

"You can't be sure." She looks away from me, but I pull her tighter into my arms.

"If you put a trace on her burner phone," I say, "we can narrow the area down, but it's not precise."

"I don't think she carries it," Kesera says.

I shake my head. "I think she does. I've been getting daily updates on what she's had for breakfast, and why she's angry you won't let her organize a spa party."

"My god, how often is she messaging you?" Kesera looks upset.

"Daily. She has strong opinions about spa parties. I'm sure we can track her down and everything will be fine," I say with more assurance than I feel.

I almost think I can make her believe me, but the elevator doors open and Sasha strides into the kitchen with a face like thunder.

"What the hell is going on?" he says, throwing his tall frame into one of the kitchen chairs with enough force to break it. "I've just had a message from Dante Spataro asking for a meeting in Westbury."

Who the fuck is Dante Spataro? I look over at Sasha. "I thought the don's name was Vincenzo."

"It is," Sasha says, nodding briefly at Kesera. "But apparently, Dante is his son, and he says he's holding your daughter."

Kesera slides off my lap and I nod at Sasha, picking up my phone and checking my gun is securely tucked in my waistband. I'm moving into work mode.

"Let's go," I say to him, but Kesera puts a hand on my chest and pushes me backward.

"No one is going anywhere to look for my daughter until you've explained what the hell is going on." She pushes me into the chair and spins to face Sasha, who's smirking at her like this is a joke. The animosity between my best friend and the woman I'm falling for hums through the air like pressure before a storm.

CHAPTER FIFTY

Kesera

I remember the first time I met Sasha. He cast a shadow over the golden moment Vadim and I had created in the Russian woods.

Time has not improved his personality.

His moods are a like a weather front, and I can feel the pressure change when he enters a room. He walks across the kitchen, talking to himself under his breath in Russian loud enough for Nona to hear and start glaring at him. Vadim stands at the table and watches him, looking warily between us like an umpire.

"Vadim, are you coming? I haven't got all day," Sasha calls over his shoulder as if I'm not in the room. The final thread of my patience snaps, and a bright, energizing fury takes its place.

Jimmy, Stevie, and now Sasha.

I turn to Vadim with a harsh whisper. "Don't even think about it."

To my surprise, Vadim just smiles as if he's party to a joke

I'm not in on. He pulls me against his side, but I'm too rigid with anger to take comfort from his solid presence.

"No one is going anywhere to find my daughter without talking it through with me," I say, lowering my voice and striving for calm as I place both palms on the kitchen table and look between Vadim and his best friend.

Vadim smiles down at me like I've done something he's proud of, while Sasha just rolls his eyes.

"Come on, Vadim. We don't have all day," Sasha bites out, his hand on the door frame.

Vadim comes to stand behind me, then strokes his huge palm up and down my back in a steady rhythm.

"She's my daughter too," he says softly, leaning his body against me as if he's trying to shelter me.

Sasha's eyes narrow, and he steps back into the room, watching me and Vadim and looking over at Dex, who has been sitting silently and letting the drama unfold. Sasha paces slowly to the table facing me, but he looks over my head.

"What are you waiting for?" He continues talking to Vadim as if I'm not here.

Vadim eases into a chair and tugs on my hand, but I remain standing, sucking in a breath as fear for Nadia wars with anger at my powerlessness in this situation.

"I'm waiting for Kesera to tell us what she wants," Vadim says firmly, pulling me into the seat beside him and throwing his arm around my shoulder.

"Spare me the happy families role play and let's just get on with it. We need to find out what the younger Spataro wants, and we aren't getting any of it done in this kitchen."

Vadim says something to Sasha in Russian, which I don't catch, but Nona nods approvingly as Sasha walks back to the table and glares at me.

"I don't need this shit. My friend asked for help, and I'm here." He plunks into a chair opposite us and presses his hands to the table, fingers gripping the wood like he could burn through it.

Vadim's low voice washes over me. "Let's all take a breath and calm down." He looks over at Dex, who nods.

"If you need backup, we have a security team on site," Dex says, forearms on the table as he watches me for a cue. I smile at him, glad I can count on someone to have my back.

Sasha taps a rhythm on the tabletop with his fingers as he and Vadim have an unspoken conversation. Sasha bites his lip and breaks eye contact, looking down at his hands. For a moment, I glimpse the little boy behind the man, uncertain and ill at ease in a room full of strangers who don't like him, his one ally slipping away.

"Sasha," I say, and his head snaps up as if he didn't expect me to talk to him. Then he remembers to glare at me. "Thank you for showing up to help."

He doesn't speak, but his fingers slacken their grip on the table, and he looks over at Vadim as he blows out a breath. Vadim's hand tightens on my shoulder, and his lips briefly brush my temple to signal that I did the right thing.

"When Spataro called, did they ask you to come alone? Money? Other conditions?" Vadim asks, looking over at Dex.

Sasha sighs and pulls out a packet of cigarettes, but Vadim shakes his head, and he jams them back into his pocket with a huff.

"Look, the Spataro boy sounded young," Sasha says. "He said he'd picked up your daughter and we should be glad he had. He gave me the address and told me to come and get her. No conditions. No demands. Didn't sound like a stake-out." He shrugs like it's no big deal to him, and I feel the fibers of our fragile truce snap one by one.

"You should take Dex as back up," I say, making the effort to keep my voice steady.

He leans over the table and jabs his finger toward me like

a weapon. "Listen, lady, I was driving over here to do your man a favor when I got the call. You don't want me to get your daughter? It's no skin off my nose."

Vadim places his large hands over mine on the tabletop and speaks very slowly, each word landing with a thud. He's like a mountain behind me, towering over my small frame and sheltering me. "She's my daughter too."

Sasha stares at him, and I see the emotions play across his face. A flash of anger before he tamps it down and nods, tightly compressing his lips.

Vadim bands his arms around my waist and steps closer to my body, and Sasha flinches as he looks at us. Something about Vadim having a family hurts him. If there was more time, I'd try to handle him more carefully, but we're talking about a ten-year-old girl who's gone missing.

"I'm coming with you," I say firmly, but Vadim shakes his head, his fingers tightening over mine.

His Russian accent sounds stronger when he says, "There is no way." My frustration increases when Sasha smirks, but I watch the smirk fall off his face when Vadim adds, "I can't risk losing you."

He pulls me to my feet, nodding at Sasha as he draws me out of the room. He leads me along the corridor into the light-filled sitting room and shuts the door behind us. Pushing me against the door, he cages me in his arms and touches his forehead to mine, his pale eyes creased with worry.

"Tell me you understand, zolotaya," he whispers, and I can taste the mint and cigarettes on his breath as he leans into me. "Tell me I can protect you. *Pozhaluysta*." He shuts his eyes and pulls me into him, lips landing softly on mine like a question.

He's so soft for such a hard man as he presses his mouth against my top and then my bottom lip. These featherlight kisses ask for something he's not willing to put into words. I open to him, and his tongue dances with mine. The low groan he makes reverberates through my chest as he pulls me against him, fisting my hair to pull me closer. He drags his hot mouth away from mine, arms tugging me against him as his lips paint a trail of fire up my neck.

"I can't risk you, zolotaya. I can't lose you when I've only just found you again." His voice wavers against the column of my neck, sending shivers down each of my vertebrae.

Pulling back, I look at the desperate expression on Vadim's face and nod. He sags with relief, closing his eyes on a sigh and pressing his lips against my forehead.

"I know Sasha is a raging asshole." His laughter shakes his body as it surrounds me, as if the tension between me and his friend is a joke. "But no one else has my back the way he does. Let him help me find Nadia. I trust him in this."

Stepping back, he holds my shoulders and searches my face, worry lining his forehead and creasing his eyes. I can't resist sliding my palm against his cheek to reassure him. He squeezes his eyes shut, pressing his lips against my palm before he looks back at me, eyes burning with pale fire.

I nod, not asking him to confirm which other ways he doesn't trust Sasha. Pressing a quick kiss to his mouth, I bite back the observation that Sasha will never support Vadim being with me. Instead, I focus on what is really important.

"I need you to take Dex with you if I can't be there."

He pulls my hand against his chest, letting me feel his heartbeat against my palm. If there's any hope of getting our daughter back, I'll have to trust him, but something holds me back.

Vadim hasn't committed to us, and concern for Nadia doesn't mean he's ready to love us.

I turn my head away, trying to slip from his arms, but he hauls me against his body and whispers against my mouth.

"Believe in me, zolotaya. Wait for me."

My heart says yes, but years of disappointments and wrong turns tell me to hold myself back. He cups my face in his hands, searching my eyes before he nods. I see something I'm not yet willing to put into words.

CHAPTER FIFTY-ONE

Vadim

Whatever I expected when I arrived at the Spataro mansion out in Long Island, it wasn't this. I've got Dex as back up outside like we are preparing for war, but the man standing in front of me and Sasha is barely worthy of the term. He's dwarfed by the desk in front of him, and his suit hangs off his shoulders like a shopping bag. He's a boy playing dress-up.

He stands as we enter the room, then reaches over to shake my hand. His grip is surprisingly firm, and he holds eye contact like this is a regular business meeting. "Dante Spataro. I believe you know who my father is, but I'd like to assure you both it has no connection with Nadia's presence in this house."

He waves the two of us to a pair of leather armchairs in front of the desk, which sits on a raised plinth to give the man behind it the advantage of height. I've heard that Vincenzo Spataro is short, but his son probably won't need a raised desk to tower over his guests once he grows into his suit.

Looking around the room, I wonder if the Spataro family knew Nadia was my daughter before I did and planted their kid in Nadia's school.

My eyes slide over to Sasha, who nods, compressing his lips in an effort to keep a straight face. The rush of amusement we're feeling is dangerous when we don't really know what's going on in this room. This boy may not be a threat to us, but his father is, and he's still got a hold of Nadia.

Standing in front of the desk, I nod at him and study his body language. "So, you're the man who has kidnapped my daughter."

He looks surprisingly at ease, but there's a sprinkling of acne on his face and although his hair is dark, there's no five o'clock shadow on his jaw. If he's shaving, he doesn't have much of a beard.

"She hasn't been kidnapped." He waves to a pair of mahogany chairs that stand in front of the huge desk. "Please. Take a seat. Let's discuss this in a civilized manner."

Sasha looks over at me, and I can see he's biting back a smile. We both sit down and neither of us speak.

"Can I offer either of you a drink?" The boy points to a tumbler of cognac—something both the Italians and the Russians like to drink. "It's a little early in the day for me, but if the two of you would like a drink, I'll join you."

"Thank you. But no." I give him a cold smile. "I'd like to see Nadia before we talk about anything else. Proof of life, as they say."

"Of course. How inconsiderate of me." He picks up his phone and puts it to his ear. "Danni, can the two of you come downstairs? Nadia's dad is here."

I hear giggling, followed by the sound of footsteps overhead.

"They'll be right down. I overheard Nadia saying she was planning to go missing to worry you. She and Danni concocted a plan to vanish on the streets of New York for a couple of days." He looks over at the door as if he's waiting for them to emerge. "I hope you'll forgive me. I took the liberty of both keeping them safe and arranging a meeting with you. I didn't fancy the idea of two ten-year-olds roaming Manhattan, and I thought this might be a more effective way of giving you a scare."

He gives me a sly grin, but he's saved from an angry retort by the arrival of the two girls in question.

Nadia, sporting a pair of long braids wound around her head and a long, flowing black dress that makes her look like a nineteenth-century Russian peasant, follows behind a girl dressed head to toe in bubblegum pink.

"Did it work, Dante?" Danni says. "Was he scared? Is he moving back home?" She rubs her hands together gleefully. Behind her, my daughter looks sheepish and a little frightened.

"Sorry, Dad," she says in a small voice. "I only wanted to see you."

Next to me, Sasha bites back a snort of laughter.

"Girls, I'm sure that Nadia's father will be happy to take her back to her mother when we've finished our discussions," Dante says. "Work on your video or finish whatever you're doing, and we'll call you when it's time to go."

"Aww," Danni groans. "Can't Nadia stay for a sleepover?"

"Not tonight, Danni. I think you'll have to clear it with her mom, and after this stunt, she might not be too favorably disposed toward you. Imagine if you'd really gone missing in Manhattan and I hadn't overheard your crackpot scheme. You'd likely be in trouble with more than Nadia's parents."

"But Dante," she whines.

The older boy holds up a hand and stops her next

sentence. "Don't 'but Dante' me. If you pulled a stunt like this and our father found out, your life wouldn't be worth living."

Danni's shoulders hunch when her brother mentions the don, and she nods, edging toward the door.

"Go upstairs, Nadia," I say. "We'll see you soon." I don't want her in this room until I know what's going on.

She swallows whatever she was about to say, spinning on her heel to follow her friend. All of us listen to the footsteps pounding up the spiral staircase in the hallway as Dante pours three tumblers of cognac and slides two across the table.

"Nadia is free to leave when you do, but I wanted to discuss an alliance." He looks between Sasha and me as he tries to work out which one of us makes the decisions.

Sasha picks up his cognac and swirls it around the glass, regarding the young Italian over the rim. "And what exactly would this alliance involve?"

Dante puts his glass on the leather-covered desk without taking a sip. "I want you to help me kill my father." He stares at both of us, leaning back in the chair and clasping his hands over his midriff. He's trying to look relaxed, but his knuckles are white.

"Patricide. That's a bold move." Sasha takes a sip of his cognac and mirrors Dante's posture.

"I know you've got my sister. Alessandra. My father sent her to that brothel because he wanted her to think there are worse fates than marrying the Night Governor." He taps a pen against the desk and looks from me to Sasha, the question written clearly in his dark eyes. "But I'm not so sure. Yevgeny Guelman makes my skin crawl."

Sasha leans forward. "The Night Governor breaks women. My sister . . ." He looks up at the bookshelves, no doubt thinking of the Night Governor's study. "She didn't survive Moscow. How much of that was Guelman's doing, I'll never know, but if I were you, then I'd be glad we picked her up."

312

"What are you planning to do with my sister? I understand that neither my older sister Alessandra nor I were ever going to choose our own partners, but a man like the Night Governor is a bad match. She'd never be a partner, just a plaything."

He stands and starts to pace around the desk, finally taking a sip of his drink, so I take a sip of mine and watch him as he runs his hands along the books before pulling out a copy of Machiavelli's *The Prince*.

"My older sister is clever. If it was played right, she would be an asset. A queen. Not just a pawn." He pauses, fingering the pages. "It's a sign that he's losing his edge, and it's an opportunity for me."

He's a boy. But I've got to admire his nerve.

Sasha looks over at me and we share an unspoken understanding. This is an opening for us too.

"What are you proposing?" Sasha takes a slow sip of his cognac.

"Alessandra marries into the Russian Mafia, which will strengthen my hand," Dante says. "We work together on the recycling business and beef up our legitimate operations. And most importantly, we get rid of my father."

"Why are you so keen to get rid of your father?" I ask. "Surely you're next in line to succeed him, so you would do better to wait until you're a bit older." I can't imagine this boy could control New York's Italian Mafia, even with our help.

Dante sinks into the chair, putting the half-drunk glass of cognac down beside him. "There won't be much left of our operation if I wait. The old man is losing his grip. He was never loved, but in the last few years, he's become volatile, vindictive. He commands very little loyalty among the men. This deal with the Night Governor speaks of desperation. It will strengthen my father in the short-term but weaken us.

The Night Governor never had alliances before. He won't start now."

Sasha and I exchange a brief look and then turn back to look at the Italian boy. The Night Governor has always worked alone, and this kid has read Guelman better than his father, which is impressive, but working with him will be a gamble. He's pacing behind the desk and talking as if he's thinking through the problem out loud.

"You get rid of my father, and I owe you. We work together, and I come out of this stronger. We'd be in a position to control New York." He places his palms on the desk and leans over, looking at Sasha and me as if he expects an immediate answer.

He's clever and bold, but he's got a lot to learn. He grins at me like faking a kidnap attempt is a big joke, but his smile drops as I pull out a gun and point it at him.

"I'm not going to shoot you now," I say. "Not with my daughter and her friend in the house, but you and I are going to have words about this. You can't threaten people's children and think there won't be consequences."

Dante pulls himself up to his full height, throws his shoulders back, and glares at me. "Let me make myself very clear," he bites out. "I didn't threaten anyone. You should be thanking me."

I raise the gun and shoot at the bookcase past his shoulder. He keeps entirely still, and his eyes don't move from my face. Despite myself, I'm impressed that he's unruffled.

"And what the fuck should I be thanking you for?" I ask.

"Uncovering Danni and Nadia's crazy plan to go missing, make you worry, and get you to come running to find her. It could have gotten them both killed or worse. There are a lot of sick men in this city who would love to get their hands on those two. They didn't even know how to behave, because

314

Nadia doesn't understand that she's the daughter of a mafioso."

"Oh really? And your sister didn't have a part to play in this?" I say.

He swallows, and I watch his Adam's apple bob as he looks away from me for the first time. "My father did an equally poor job. It's something I can remedy once he's out of the picture." He sits down slowly, clasps his hands in front of him, and regards me and Sasha with an unwavering stare. "These girls can be assets, but they're liabilities if they're blind to the consequences of their actions. That happens when they don't know what's at stake. When they make a misstep." He looks toward the door. "Like the two little girls upstairs."

"And your sister. Alessandra? Wasn't defying your father a misstep?" Sasha throws the questions out with a sneer. "She shouldn't have been in that brothel. It's complicated all of our lives."

"Alessandra had nothing to lose. She was desperate, and he forced her into a corner. I would never make that mistake." He looks over at me. "I won't tell you how to bring up your daughter, but I can see the errors my father made, and I'm not about to repeat them with my younger sister once he's out of the picture."

He picks up the phone and sends a text, and then footsteps pound on the stairs. Nadia appears in the doorway, looking scared. She twists her fingers together when she's nervous, just like her mother does.

I stand and open my arms to her, and she steps into them. She smells of hot baked bread, sunshine, and hope. I wrap my arms around her and breathe her in. My heart is in my mouth as her narrow shoulders tremble against me.

"You, little girl, are in trouble."

"Really? How much trouble?" Her eyes search mine, and I pick her up and crush her in a hug.

"A lot of trouble," I say. "You now have two parents to get in trouble with. And I'm going to have to answer to your mother for this mess."

I might have gotten our daughter back, but will that be enough for Kesera to accept me as well? If the tables were turned, I wouldn't want anything to do with a man who brings so much chaos and darkness with him.

CHAPTER FIFTY-TWO

Kesera

The elevator opens and Nadia steps in front of Vadim, jutting her chin at me defiantly. I hold back the impulse to scream at her when I meet Vadim's crystal-blue gaze behind her. He smiles at me as he puts a hand on her shoulder.

"What on earth were you thinking, Nadia?" I step toward her and her chin wobbles before she hurls herself into my arms. Her voice is muffled by fabric as she buries her head in my chest.

"I just wanted Daddy to come home." She wraps her arms tighter around my midriff.

"It worked." Vadim moves toward me and pulls us both into the circle of his arms, and I finally let myself sink against him. I can feel my shoulders shaking as he wraps one arm around me and another around Nadia. He leads us both across the hardwood floors to the couch.

He pushes Nadia into the cushions, and her eyes widen as

he removes his gun from its holster and places it on top of a stack of books on the coffee table.

"Nadia, do you realize that a stunt like that could have gotten you killed?" He sits on the coffee table, facing her as I look down at the two of them.

"It wasn't real. Danni and I thought that if we pretended to get kidnapped, then you would come and find us." She looks up at her father through long lashes. She and Danni were obviously experimenting with mascara while pretending to get abducted.

"And what did you plan to do on the streets of New York?" Vadim leans his forearms on his knees, forehead creasing with worry.

"Well, Danni said that her dad owns some bars and we could go and hang out in the back room for a night."

Vadim blows out a whistle through his teeth and looks at the ceiling. "My god, this keeps getting worse. Why did she think you could go there?"

"One of her dad's security guys likes her. He said he could look after us if we needed somewhere to hide, but Danni's brother found out, and he said he was going to kill him. But that was just a joke, wasn't it, Dad?" Nadia looks at the gun and back at me, her lip twisting. "He wouldn't really do it, would he?"

Vadim looks over at me and reaches for my hand, twining his fingers around mine and squeezing. "Your mother and I think this is really serious. If Dante hadn't overheard you and called me, I can't imagine what could have happened. Those kinds of bars and clubs are not a place I ever want you or Danni to hang around. The kind of men that go there . . ."

He closes his eyes and swallows, shaking his head, and I rest my hand on his shoulder.

"Kesera." He looks up at me, eyes pleading. "What do I do now?"

"Why don't we all sleep on it, and we'll talk about it in the morning. In the meantime, Nadia, you are grounded and there's no screen time for a month."

I expect a tantrum, but she just smiles at both of us. "Daddy came and found me, though," she says, getting up and skipping down the corridor to her bedroom.

As the sun dips lower between the skyscrapers and the shadows lengthen across Central Park, I sink down to rest on the cushions. Vadim drops next to me and slings a heavy arm across my shoulders.

"I've never been so terrified in my life." His deep voice shakes. "Come here, zolotaya." He pulls me toward him, and I rest my head against his chest, breathing in the pine-and-salt scent of his skin and listening to the comforting thud of his heart.

"Do you have to leave?" I whisper.

"I'd prefer to be near you. I'll sleep easier knowing you're both close." He looks down at me, the ring of icy blue around his pupils narrowing.

"I'm going to jump in the shower. Why don't you go and sit with Nadia for a bit?" I smile at him. "Seems like she went to a lot of trouble to get you here."

"I've never felt so wanted." He huffs out a laugh, and I reach up to press my lips against his, taking his full bottom lip between my teeth and biting it. He groans and opens his mouth to deepen the kiss, pulling me onto his lap.

"You *are* wanted," I whisper into his ear as he pulls my leg across his waist so I'm straddling him. The hard heat of his cock presses against me. I lean back and look at him, hands on his shoulders, and shake my head. "Not here. I need to be able to touch you properly. Go and say goodnight to Nadia."

I walk to my bedroom and sit on the bed. I'm nervous. The jagged edges of my emotions smash against each other in my gut—fear, lust, relief, anger. The cocktail of feelings swirls around, making me nauseous. I don't even realize Vadim has entered the room until I see him standing against the door frame, regarding me steadily.

"Does she always fall asleep so quickly?" His pastel stare is like blue fire.

"No. Not usually. It was probably the adrenaline. She must be wiped out."

He stalks toward the bed and cages me in his arms so that I can smell the salt on his skin. "I feel like I've gone ten rounds in a boxing ring. Today was exhausting." He rests his forehead on mine, the tenderness of the touch at odds with the next words. "Zolotaya, I need to fuck. I need to be back in control."

I close my eyes and hear the click of a belt buckle and the slide of leather against fabric. I open my eyes with a question as he holds the belt in one hand and steps out of his trousers.

"Strip. Quickly," he says.

I pull my shirt overhead, ripping a button on the cuff as I tear it off my arms. I'm reaching for my bra when Vadim leans down. Grasping both arms, which are already behind my back, he slides the leather over my wrists.

"Zolotaya?"

"Yes."

The word comes out in a hiss, and he pulls the leather taught against my arms, belting them together behind me and thrusting my chest forward. He pulls the cups of my bra down and bites my breast, pulling it between his teeth and squeezing the other one roughly. Two twisting ribbons of pain and lust shoot down to the pulsing nub between my legs.

His eyes meet mine as he sucks away the pain, tonguing my sore nipples and drawing a low moan from my throat. Hearing the almost animal sound tear out of me brings me back to myself, and I look down at him in a panic.

"Vadim. The door . . ."

He stands up with a wolfish smile. "Let me see you struggle out of the rest of your clothes without the use of your arms, baby. Show me how you work for my cock."

I watch him walk toward the door and hear the click of the lock as I rock back and forth against the edge of the bed, pushing the pants and panties I'm wearing lower by humping against the covers.

"That's right. Show me how much you want me," he says, standing at the door and watching me kick the clothes away.

I'm wearing nothing but his belt and my bra, my tits thrust upward. Embarrassed, I go to close my legs, but he shakes his head.

"Ah-ah, no." He shakes his finger at me. "Spread your legs and show me what's mine." He pads across the carpet, sinking down between my spread legs and looking at me. "Wider, zolotaya. As wide as you can."

Drawing on all the years of dance rehearsals, I pull one leg onto the bed and stretch it out, bearing myself to his flaming face. Heat races up to his cheeks, and I wonder if it's matched by the fire that's racing across my body.

He stretches out a finger and draws it through my center, pinching my clit before he sucks it into his mouth and closes his eyes as if he's savoring the taste.

"Delicious. Just putting yourself on display for me makes you this wet." He splays his hand against my stomach and gently pushes me against the sheets, the care of his movement at odds with the two fingers he jams inside me.

I cry out.

"Quiet, my little songbird."

He leans down and takes a nipple into his mouth, sucking it hard as his two fingers curl upward against the walls of my pussy. He strokes in a circle and makes me whimper.

"My good girl. Being so quiet for me. You're being so careful. Let me hear you whimper as you come on my fingers."

He fucks me with his hand as he licks and bites my tits, a stream of Russian ghosting across my skin as I arch against him. With my heels against the mattress, I start to pant as I ride his hand.

Leaning back, he watches me. He adds a third finger, his gaze glued to the sawing motion of his fingers. The only sounds in the room are our harsh breathing and the wet noise of his hand moving inside me.

He leans down and sucks my clit into his mouth, and I go off like a firework. Sparks explode behind my eyes as he sucks and licks me like I'm an ice cream on a summer day.

My voice sounds like it comes from someone else as I beg. "Stop, baby. I can't. It's too sensitive."

"You can. I love that I make you sensitive." He looks up at me, one hand deep inside me and the other pressing my stomach into the bed. My arousal glistens on his lips. "I fucking want another one. I want to drink you down." He lowers his head and mumbles between my legs. "I can't get enough. Can't fucking get enough."

He punishes me with the flat of his tongue. I don't have the leverage to get up. My arms are bound behind me, and I'm riding Vadim's face to another explosion that has me shaking and trembling.

He gets to his feet and strips off his clothes. His cock stands out, red and angry against the geometry of scars and muscles across his torso, and he lifts me gently, rubbing up and down against my arms.

"You okay, my sweet zolotaya?" he says as my gaze bounces between the tender smile crinkling his eyes and the throbbing vein and red crown of his cock that's level with my face. He presses his thumb against my bottom lip as he cups my chin and tilts my face upward. "My beautiful girl. Open for me."

And I do, falling on him, licking and sucking him as if my lips can bathe him in every bit of devotion I feel. I sink my head as low as I can, taking him to the back of my throat and closing my eyes against the gagging sensation.

He leans back, watching me as I suck on the tip. I swirl my tongue around the crown.

"Fuck, fuck yeah. Don't stop." Meeting my eyes, he cups my face and threads his fingers through my hair as he inches forward. "My sweet little songbird. Look at you. Working so hard to love me."

He feeds me half of him and stops, allowing me to breathe as he tenderly strokes his fingers across my forehead, along my eyebrows, until he cups my chin.

"Breathe in, zolotaya," he says.

His hand remains around my chin as he watches my tits thrust forward with the in breath. Then he slides to the back of my throat, fucking me gently and bringing tears to my eyes.

"Fuck. You're so good. So good the way you cry for me."

He pulls back as I breathe out and take another breath in, and then he closes his eyes as he pumps back and forth. A series of grunts and Russian words fall from his lips as his face twists as if he's in pain.

Pulling out, he sinks to his knees in front of me, thrusting his tongue into my mouth and kissing me deeply. He unties the belt and pulls off my bra before pushing my back onto the bed and climbing on top of me.

His fingers slide through mine as he pulls my arms over my head. "I need to touch you everywhere. Hold you everywhere," he says as I spread my legs, twist my ankles behind his back, and draw him against me.

He stops and pulls back, watching me. He eyes the place where our bodies join as he slowly sinks inside me. My mouth falls open in a moan, and I lose myself to the kiss of his hip bones against my pelvis as I take all of him.

"Fuck, baby. I can't be gentle. I need to fuck you hard." And then he's slamming into me, making the bed thump against the wall. The mattress slides against the headboard with a shudder, and he hits me with the full weight of his body.

I cry out, and he stops.

Letting go of my hand, he sinks his fingers into my mouth. "Suck on me, baby. Taste yourself so you don't make a noise."

My thoughts warp into incoherence, and I whimper as I tilt my pelvis toward him, sucking hard on his fingers as I push against him. Our eyes meet as he pulls his fingers away. He drops to his elbows and pistons into me, and my teeth sink into his bicep as I claw at his back, my pussy pulsing around him. He throws back his head with an almost animal groan.

Our bodies are slick with sweat as he sinks against me and rolls to pull me on top of him. I tuck my head into the crook of his neck and listen to the thud of his heart against my ear, the beats slowing as the sweat cools on my skin. The moment of space allows unease to creep in.

What we just did was animalistic, an explosion after the tension of the recent hours. It made me feel alive, but now I'm humming with nerves, bracing myself for another goodbye.

Vadim must sense the change because he pulls me tighter against him. "What is it?"

I don't answer.

He rolls to his side, facing me as he strokes my hair away from my face. "Zolotaya, talk to me."

"Are you leaving again?" I whisper as I listen to his heartbeat slow.

"I'm not going anywhere, zolotaya. I'm staying right here as long as you'll have me." But even as he looks at me, I have a gnawing sense there's still something he's not telling me.

CHAPTER FIFTY-THREE

Vadim

The back room of Bolshoi has the fetid smell of yesterday's alcohol, stale cigar smoke, and other men's cum. I don't like to look at the black sofas, and I make a point of not resting my hand on the leather as I sit down and lean back.

The door creaks open and Oksana, my old lover from Moscow, walks in. She manages the strippers and the dancers and the girls behind the bar with an iron hand. Never one for subtlety, her hair is dyed fire-engine red this week.

"What have the girls been up to?" I ask.

"The usual." She smiles at me, holding the eye contact a beat too long. "The same round of rivalries, catfights, and drug problems." She shrugs. "Nothing I can't handle."

"Did you find an aspiring singer to lure Jimmy in?" I pull a cigarette from the pack and slide it between my lips as I search my pocket for a lighter, but she moves faster, leaning across with a lit flame. Finding an excuse to touch me.

I wave the packet at her, and she shakes her head. "I'm

going to need fillers to deal with my pout if I keep it up," she says.

She sits down next to me and lays her hand on my thigh, but I give her a squeeze and return her hand to her lap.

"So, it's like that, then? It's serious?" She gives me a pensive smile.

"Yeah. Serious as a heart attack. Or a kidnapping. Or disposing of a body." I slant my eyes across to her.

"I found someone, but you're not going to like it. I had a look at the girls, but he wants someone fresh and talented and young. *Really* young, but not desperate. I think he likes to break them."

"Okay." I'm curious. "Who did you pick?"

"Julia." She gives me a hard stare.

"Christ, Oksana. Your own daughter?"

"Well, you're serious about getting rid of him, aren't you?" Oksana shakes her head. "After all the damn money I spent on her education, Julia wants to follow in my footsteps and try to be a singer. We all know how that ended up." She gives a harsh bark of laughter. "I want the girl to be a surgeon or a dermatologist. Make a mint. Be respectable. She's got the grades. I don't want her in this world, and this will be a lesson to her."

"Sasha and I will be taking him for a little walk." I nod at her.

"Off a long pier, I hope."

"The less you know, my dear," I say, grinning at her as I bump her shoulder.

She smiles at me with a hint of her old warmth. She's been a good friend. "I want that fucker out of here. He's been wining and dining Julia. Telling her she can make it. I want her to understand what's at stake in this world, and I want him to pay. I don't know what your woman went through, but I can imagine."

I nod but say nothing else. As I said, the less she knows.

BY THE TIME Sasha arrives in the evening, I have a headache. The back rooms of Bolshoi echo with the sound of groaning men, and the *thud-thud-thud* of an Usher song comes over the speakers from the room next door.

God, the sound of other men getting off turns my stomach.

Sasha and I watch the cameras in room seven. Julia is there, giggling as Jimmy pushes her long blond hair behind her ear. He looks even sleazier than he did a decade earlier—the chin a little weaker and softer, the waistband of his jeans a little snugger.

We'll pull the footage later and replace it with footage of Sasha getting a lap dance from Oksana. The alibi will be watertight once Marat, our tech guy, splices the video.

Jimmy moves a little closer and shoves his hand up her shirt. Here it is. The moment he lives for. The power move where a woman gets scared.

Julia shakes her head and puts her hand on his arm, as if to reassure him and push him away at the same time.

"Do we go in now?" Sasha asks.

I see the moment I met Kesera. Him on top of her. Her eyes begging me for help in the back room of a seedy club in Moscow.

"Get him," I say, walking to the door. "Don't give that slimy little shit a moment longer."

We walk from the control room at the same time as Oksana.

"No, please don't," a girlish voice says as we push open the door.

"Mama," Julia says when she sees Oksana.

329

Jimmy leaps back. "It's not what it looks like." He stands, wiping his palms on his jeans as he looks at Oksana bristling like a lion going in for the kill. Behind her, Sasha looks threatening.

But he can't see me.

"We were just having a little fun," he says, as I step into the room.

"Is that what the kids are calling it these days?" I say with a tight smile. "I believe I warned you what would happen if you didn't leave my woman alone."

When he sees me, he pales.

"You!" he exclaims, stepping back toward the wall and shaking his head. "What are you doing here?"

"Dealing with unfinished business. I told you not to touch her again."

He puffs out his chest. "I didn't fucking touch her. I'm suing her."

"You aren't fit to look at her, to breathe the same air, whether it's in a courtroom or anywhere else. I warned you."

He turns on me, going on the attack as if that will help. "She had a contract. You can't just ignore contracts. Business would fall apart. She owes me."

I sit down across from him. I think he knows that judges don't rule my world, but it's worth reminding him. "I'm not sure how you got the impression I'm a man who cares about the law. You didn't take the hint last time I paid you a visit, so now I'm going to have to deal with you the hard way."

"You can't do anything about the lawsuit," he says through a sneer.

"I beg to differ." I shrug as if it's a shame. I'm enjoying toying with him. "Dead men can't sue people."

Sasha walks over to him and pushes a rag against his mouth. Jimmy struggles against him, arms flailing, muffled screams blunted by the rag, before slumping as the chloroform works its magic. Julia is crying now. Soft sobs shake her shoulders.

"Next time, you'll listen to your mother," I tell her. I lift Jimmy's limp body and throw it over my shoulder.

"Where to?" Sasha says. "Do you need help?"

"It's a one-man job. I'll take him down to the docks," I say.

Sasha fishes in the man's pocket for a phone. Finding one, he unlocks it with a press of Jimmy's limp thumb. "I'll deal with the phone. Marat can make it look like he hasn't been here. He'll keep the text messages for a day or two. That guy can hack anything." Sasha walks to the door. "You timed it just right. We've got a shipment heading to China. Just stick the body in an empty crate, and we'll push it off the ship once we get out to sea."

I grin at him. "That's right, my friend. No body. No crime."

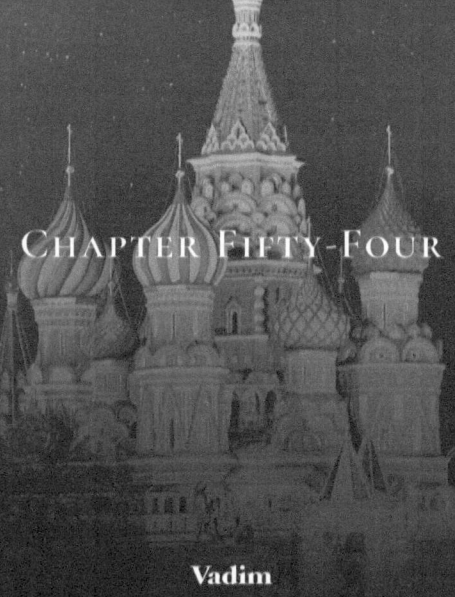

Chapter Fifty-Four

Vadim

Morning light floods the family kitchen as I stand at the counter. I still feel like an interloper as Nona brews coffee and Kesera sips at her disgusting green juice.

"I don't know how you can drink that muck." I shake my head at her.

"Yeah, Mom. You should be eating blini with us." Nadia grins.

Kesera shakes her head and runs her hand across her flat stomach, meeting my eyes for a beat too long. Last night, I lay my head on the same place after making her come so hard that she almost blacked out.

"I'm watching my figure," she says.

"I'd love you if you were the size of a house. Feel free to eat as many blinis as you want," I say, sitting down with my black coffee and looking out at the view of the trees below.

Kesera comes over and lays a hand on my shoulder. I want to pull her into my lap, but I settle for wrapping my arm around her neck and drawing her down to kiss me.

333

Nadia's voice breaks the moment and reminds me that I've still got a lot of work to do before I'm really part of this family. "God, you two are so gross." She snorts a laugh.

I smile sheepishly at our daughter, throwing my arms wide. "You wanted me here. I'm happy to give you a hug too."

"No. Lame." She shakes her head and stalks out, and I grin at Nadia's back.

The smile slides away as I look up at Kesera's face, which is framed by the halo of golden curls. "Am I doing okay? Was that not the right thing to say?" I ask.

She leans down to kiss me. Her lips are cool and taste of fruit as I let myself sink into the warmth of her mouth, losing myself for a moment.

"You're delicious, even when you taste of green juice." I smile at her, but it must not reach my eyes because she circles the chair and sits on my lap, cupping the side of my face and rubbing her thumb back and forth along my scar.

"You're going to get it wrong. And sometimes, there won't be a right thing to say." She leans back, watching me. "Are you sure you're really up for this? Nadia's going to blame you for being absent, and she'll blow hot and cold sometimes."

She stands and walks back to the counter, leaning against it as she pours a cup of coffee. I stand and walk over to cage her within my arms, resting my forehead against hers.

"I only stayed away because I thought it would be safer. It was never that I didn't care."

Kesera tilts back her head, her green eyes promising springtime. "It's going to be difficult."

I laugh against her curls, leaning down to whisper in her ear. "My life has never been easy. This will be worth it."

On the counter, Kesera's phone vibrates. She reaches over and breaks into a smile that lights her face as she bounces on her feet.

"I can't believe it. He dropped the lawsuit. I never

thought he'd let it go, even with other women coming forward." She steps toward me, and I pick her up, spinning her around in my arms as she laughs.

Gently setting her on her feet, I smile down at her.

She reaches for my hand, almost shyly. "What are you doing today? I'm suddenly free. I was supposed to meet my lawyers. I can't believe it."

"You deserve it," I say, hoping I sound surprised and not like a man who put a bullet in Jimmy's head and then boxed him up in a half-full shipping container with instructions to dump everything into the Pacific.

"I still feel worried, but I don't know why." She goes to pick up the phone, and I walk behind her and circle her tiny waist with my arms.

Leaning down, I whisper, "I have a few ideas to keep you occupied." I pull her against my body as the front door slams when Nadia leaves for school. "Let's go back to bed. I'm free today too."

EPILOGUE
FOUR MONTHS LATER

Vadim

I'm standing at the altar, waiting for Kesera, with Sasha at my side. I look over at Nona, who stands next to my old Moscow friends Dima and Marat. My heart feels like it's going to beat out of my chest.

"Have you got the rings?" I whisper to Sasha, who stands glowering next to me.

"I have. But it's not too late to back out. Are you sure about this?" he says under his breath in Russian.

Nona gives him a dark look. He's not particularly subtle, and she probably heard him.

"God, you're an asshole," I say. "Why wouldn't I be sure?"

"Well, it's a big commitment." He shuffles from foot to foot, his discomfort visible.

"What? And two children aren't?" This family is everything I've ever dreamed of.

"Well, you ignored the first one for a decade. I don't see what's changed now that you're expecting another kid." There's a strange edge of desperation in his voice.

337

"You're a hopeless case, Sasha. Don't try to drag us all down with you."

He looks at me seriously for a moment and then reaches into his pocket for the rings, holding them out to me in his palm. "It'll make you vulnerable," he adds.

"I'm already vulnerable. The minute everyone knew I had a daughter, the pretense was over. My family makes life worth living."

He throws out a last-ditch idea. "You could make an alliance. Marry Alessandra Spataro instead."

I shake my head at him. He's scared he's losing me, but he wouldn't dream of saying it. "I'll always be your brother, but I won't marry a teenager to widen our smuggling routes. Kai shouldn't be contemplating it."

Sasha gives me a wolfish grin. "I don't think he'll be complaining. Nineteen. Well connected. I can see the attraction."

I shudder. "If you're so in favor of arranged marriages, why don't you marry her?"

"Because I've got bigger fish to fry. I'm moving beyond the mafia. When I get married, I'll control the real levers of power."

I stare at my friend. "Have you gone mad?"

"No. Stalin was a gangster, and he controlled the state. Why shouldn't I get someone at the top of society to wield like a weapon?"

"You're going to wield your wife like a weapon?" My face must betray my incredulity. I can imagine him using his wife, but I didn't think he'd ever want to tie his fate to someone else's since he seems so dead set against me doing so.

"Maybe." He grins. "Everyone has a price. It's not just mafia dons who sell their daughters. When I get married, I'll sell my soul for something bigger. That senator's daughter.

The one whose fiancé was banging some film star. She's ripe for the picking."

"And why would she marry you if she's nursing a broken heart?"

"Because I'll ruin her father or hurt someone she loves. Everyone has a price. Love makes you vulnerable, Vadim. You would do well to remember that."

At that moment, everything Sasha says fades into the background as the doors of the little church open.

My bride stands against the light. Her hair is a bright halo, and she's dressed head to toe in gold, not white.

My breath catches as I stare at her walking slowly toward me, the candlelight glinting off the Japanese print on her full skirt. The glittering bodice pushes up her full tits, which have grown rounder since she told me we're going to have another child. A thin gold veil obscures her face, but her golden curls halo her head like a Russian icon.

She looks otherworldly, like something from a fairy tale.

Behind her, Nadia carries her full skirt, holding it off the floor. I catch my daughter's eye and blow her a kiss, and she grins at me as they walk closer and closer, bringing my very own happy ending toward me, step by step.

When Kesera stands before me, I reach out to lift the veil and pull it over her curls, looking down into her smiling green eyes.

"My love. You are the most beautiful thing I've ever seen," I say.

She doesn't say a word. Just reaches to clasp my hands and squeeze them, all while smiling at me. And before I've said a vow or made a single promise, I know that wherever she is, I'm home.

THE END

Dear Reader

Thanks so much for coming to Moscow with me to read Vadim and Kesera's story. I hope you'll consider leaving a review so that other readers can see what you thought of *Brutal Secrets*. Even if it's only a sentence, reviews help indie authors find new readers and help readers discover new books.

Ready for Sasha's story? Turn the page for the blurb, or get *Vicious Longings* here: https://books2read.com/u/mlMdnW

Please use this QR code to access Raven's link tree, where you can subscribe to her newsletter, get sneak peeks of upcoming projects, and so much more:

VICIOUS LONGINGS
AN ENEMIES-TO-LOVERS DARK MAFIA ROMANCE

Sasha Sorokin is a vicious, calculating killer. He's the last man on earth I'd want to marry, if I had a choice . . .

Kennedy

Ever since he appeared in my life like a dark angel, punching my deadbeat fiancé and making me go up in flames with his touch, I've been unable to forget Sasha Sorokin. Now he's blackmailing my father and forcing me into a loveless marriage. Yet every day, I'm falling deeper for a man who is playing a game where I don't know the rules. Vicious Longings can only get you hurt.

Sasha

Kennedy Kiernan is a passport to power, a weapon to wield for revenge and a body to warm my bed. Nothing more. So why am I losing control of the plan to break her spirit? Why does this marriage feel more real every day? And how will she ever forgive me when she finds out what I've done?

Acknowledgments

Writing a book is a solitary pursuit, but getting this book from my mind to your hands was a team effort.

Heartfelt thanks to Brooke Hazelip, my brilliant editor—you sharpen my words until they glitter. Vadim and Kesera came into focus through your eyes as well as mine.

Hannah, PA, newsletter ninja, tech support, cheerleader, and above all, good friend—which buttons would I press without you?

The brilliant folks at Deranged Doctor for design inspiration.

Mr. Carlyle and baby JC—thanks for letting me bang on about Vadim and Sasha as if they are real people.

My first fans, Lyric and Claudia, for cheering me on before you even read the book.

And to Japan, thank you for making me see the beauty in everything and giving me the space to reimagine my life.

ABOUT THE AUTHOR

Raven Carlyle is a mafia romance author who writes about tortured bad boys and the women who are strong enough to crack their hearts wide open.

She's the author of the Night Governor Bratva series, which is set in Moscow, New York, London, and Hong Kong. Raven dreams up scarily gorgeous mafia heroes faster than she can write about them.

When she's not writing, she's exploring the world and finding delicious things to eat in far-flung locations. Her travels inspire many scenes in her books. She's lived in Moscow, Tokyo, London, and Kabul, and is about to move house again with her husband and daughter.

www.ingramcontent.com/pod-product-compliance
Lightning Source LLC
Chambersburg PA
CBHW032136190626
46814CB00005BA/1719